TOUCHEd

ALSO BY CYN BALOG

✦

FAIRY TALE

SLEEPLESS

STARSTRUCK

DEAD RIVER

TOUCHED

Cyn Balog

EMBER

Text copyright © 2012 by Cyn Balog
Cover art copyright © 2012 by Cliff Nielsen

All rights reserved. Published in the United States by Ember, an imprint of Random House Children's Books, a division of Random House, Inc., New York. Originally published in hardcover in the United States by Delacorte Press, an imprint of Random House Children's Books, New York, in 2012.

Ember and the E colophon are registered trademarks of Random House, Inc.

randomhouse.com/teens

Educators and librarians, for a variety of teaching tools,
visit us at RHTeachersLibrarians.com

The Library of Congress has cataloged the hardcover edition of this work as follows:
Balog, Cyn.
Touched / Cyn Balog. — 1st ed.
p. cm.
Summary: Nick is tormented by visions of "future memories," and although he can risk changing these events if he goes "off script," the results are often worse than what he has seen, but when he meets Taryn one summer at the Jersey shore he begins to understand where this hated power comes from and what it means.
ISBN 978-0-385-74032-6 (hc) — ISBN 978-0-385-90834-4 (glb) —
ISBN 978-0-375-89906-5 (ebook)
[1. Magic—Fiction. 2. Blessing and cursing—Fiction. 3. Love—Fiction.
4. Mothers—Fiction. 5. Beaches—Fiction. 6. New Jersey—Fiction.] I. Title.
PZ7.B2138 To 2012
[Fic]—dc23
2011022114

ISBN 978-0-385-74033-3 (tr. pbk.)

RL: 5.5

Printed in the United States of America

10 9 8 7 6 5 4 3 2 1

First Ember Edition 2013

Random House Children's Books supports the First Amendment
and celebrates the right to read.

FOR MOM AND DAD

ACKNOWLEDGMENTS

This novel has not had an easy time of it. The poor thing was seriously neglected for years, had many starts and stops, and, like Nick, spent much time in chaos and had its life fully revised multiple times. Nick and I owe a big debt of gratitude to those who have helped us make sense of it all along the way. Thank you to readers Brooke Taylor, Teri Brown, Maggie Stiefvater, Mandy Hubbard, Cheryl Mansfield, Heather Dearly, Karen Kincy, and Jennifer Murgia. Thank you to my agent, Jim McCarthy, for having unwavering faith in this book from the first few chapters. Thank you to the editorial team at Delacorte Press, including Stephanie Elliott, Wendy Loggia, and Krista Vitola, as well as everyone at Random House Children's Books, for being so lovely to work with every time. To my readers, and to book bloggers and book lovers everywhere who have spread the word about my novels, thank you just isn't enough. And once again, thank you to my wonderful family, because it's your love—the one constant, unshakeable thing in my otherwise chaotic life—that made this possible.

"That's the effect of living backwards," the Queen said kindly: "it always makes one a little giddy at first—"

"Living backwards!" Alice repeated in great astonishment. "I never heard of such a thing!"

"—but there's one great advantage in it, that one's memory works both ways."

"I'm sure mine only works one way," Alice remarked. "I can't remember things before they happen."

"It's a poor sort of memory that only works backwards," the Queen remarked.

– Lewis Carroll, *Through the Looking Glass*

Chapter 1

It had taken years, but finally, I had everything down. Perfect. For three months, everything had been perfect.

But of course I went and screwed it up.

You will pedal three blocks. Slowly. You won't be out of breath. You'll see the cat lady on her front porch and she will wave at you, ask you how that mother of yours is doing. She will be wearing her red housecoat and fuzzy orange slippers, and she will be petting either Sloopy or Joe, one of the calicos, though you won't know which. You will answer, "Fine, thanks."

"How is that mother of yours doing, Nick?"

I glanced up at the decaying home, just enough to see the orange and red on the old lady's skeletal figure, and a furry creature in her pockmarked arms. "Fine, thanks."

That morning I'd awakened with the prickling sensation I always got when something big was on the horizon. Every turn of the wheels on my rusty old bike seemed to shriek "Something's coming, something's coming, something's coming. . . ." I knew I would save a little girl on the beach one day, or at least, that was what the jumbled flashes of memory in my head seemed to say. Since summer began, I'd relived the experience over and over in my mind, my mouth against her cold, salty lips, the moment her eyes flickered open and I knew I'd done it, saved her. Was today that day?

You will notice how the sun sparkles on the blacktop, as if it's covered in crystals. Steam will rise from it. You will see a little boy on the boardwalk, eating a rocket pop and carrying a green bucket. He will have a cherry mustache.

I turned to the pavement. Noted that. Looked up on the boardwalk. Smiled at the kid, but wasn't sure if I was supposed to. Wondered if that smile would come back to haunt me. The smallest mistakes were the ones that kept me up at night.

You will bike across Ocean Avenue, right in front of a green pickup, and the driver will beep at you and yell something that sounds like "Dumbass!" You will not turn around.

I veered to the right. Held my breath. Wasn't sure I was supposed to. Cringed. The sound of the horn wasn't what I expected. It was a blaring honk instead of a cheerful beep, and it rattled me. I had to straighten out the bike to keep from swerving into a pile of sand, and suddenly found myself in the middle of the next memory.

—straight up the ramp to the boardwalk, climb from your bike and lean it against the fence, under the Dogs Prohibited sign. You will twirl your whistle cord around your fingers and ask Jocelyn how it's going.

I jumped off the bike and carefully propped it against the fence. It started to slide, so I reached over and grabbed it, realizing this was going to make me late. "—going?" I huffed out, a good portion of my words getting lost in my struggle to breathe. Jocelyn, the badge checker at the entrance to the Seventh Avenue beach, gave me a confused look, confirming my suspicion.

You will not stop to say anything more and will arrive at the lifeguard stand as the noon siren sounds.

Great. Wasn't I supposed to twirl my whistle or something? Was it too late for that? I reached into my pocket and pulled it out, gave it a few rolls around my wrist for good measure. I could sense that the noon siren was about to go off, and there I was, a good football-field's length from the stand. If I didn't hurry, I'd be toast. I started to break into a jog, and that was when I heard a kid's voice. Had I been farther down the beach, where I was supposed to be, it's likely the fragile voice would have been drowned out by the crash of the surf or the sound of kids playing hide-and-seek in the dunes. But there I was, a step away from the boardwalk, turning to see the little boy with the cherry mustache screaming at something on the street below the boardwalk, out of my view. I couldn't be sure why he was frantic, but what he was saying was perfectly clear:

"Watch it!"

There are certain phrases that are impossible to ignore. I knew I should have hurried off to the stand, head down, completely oblivious. But in my past three months as a Seaside Park lifeguard, I'd gotten cocky, I guess. For a split second, I thought, Maybe it will be okay if I let my guard slip for just a moment. And by the time I realized it probably wouldn't be, the damage was done.

You will climb to the top of the lifeguard stand and Pedro will be asleep, snoring.

Just great. I knew I shouldn't have left him alone. I started to pick up the pace but then stopped short when I heard a whistle blowing behind me.

You will nudge him awake. He will sit up, blink, and point, saying, "Pink bikini at two o'clock."

Of course Pedro would be pointing out the hottest pieces of ass on the beach instead of doing his job. I found myself wondering why, of all the lifeguards in Seaside, I had to be paired with the biggest horndog in Jersey, when another memory broke through.

You will follow his pointing finger down the beach.

My pulse quickened. It was getting way ahead of me. I knew I looked like a total jerkwad to everyone nearby, pretending I didn't hear that boy on the boardwalk as I continued onto the beach, but they didn't understand. My whole life was on the line.

Like a mole, Jocelyn quietly poked her head up from her three-foot-by-three-foot box. She was so unremarkable, like a streetlight or a piece of litter, that people often walked onto the beach without seeing her. Even her "May I see your badge, please?" was feeble and spiritless and rarely turned heads. She always had this look on her face like she'd smelled something bad. Her eyes fell on me. "Can't you do something, lifeguard?"

She had to have known my name. Ten years ago, Jocelyn

had been part of a long line of sitters Nan had used for me when she'd gone off to play bridge, before it became obvious that babysitters shouldn't do the Cross house. We scared them all away. Unlike Jocelyn, we Crosses were unforgettable. I'd liked Jocelyn, though. She'd tried to play games with me, unlike all the others, who spent the time ignoring me and blabbing away on the phone.

Maybe that was why, when she asked, I stopped. Forcing a new memory down, I backtracked toward the boardwalk, kicking up scalding sand as I ran. I took all three steps at once and followed the little boy's line of vision into the street.

You will . . .

A girl about my age was crouched down, tying her running shoe. She was wearing nylon shorts, a tank, and earphones, which accounted for her nodding along to the music, completely oblivious to the fact that a furniture delivery truck was slowly backing into her. Okay, yeah, in terms of distance, I was pretty close to her, maybe only twenty yards away. But though it was a hot August day and the place was swarming with people, everyone else was just staring, like invalids, or like they wanted to see the girl get flattened. Some of them looked at me expectantly, like it was the duty of the guy in the red shorts to break into action à la *Baywatch* and save the day.

I strained to see the lifeguard stand in the bright noon sun. I could see only the top of Pedro's head. He was slumped down, still, unmoving. Asleep. That morning when I'd arrived at the stand, he'd smelled like a brewery. He'd said he had the hangover from hell, but I thought he was still drunk. He kept pointing out hot girls and whistling at them, as if he was at some bar in the Heights. I probably shouldn't have left him alone for lunch, but it was in the script. And I never went against the script.

Until now. I turned back toward the girl. Crap. I knew that even just standing there, frozen with indecision, was probably going to throw everything off. Sure enough, the first pangs of pain rapped at my temple.

You will . . .

My grandmother always said that God puts signs everywhere. Maybe if the girl in danger hadn't looked like my best description of an angel—a lion's mane of curly platinum hair pushed back with a headband—I wouldn't have destroyed that perfect future I'd found for myself. In that split second that she flipped her angelic white hair back to reveal skin so perfect it practically glowed in the sun, I realized it was a sign. God wanted—no, demanded that I step in.

You will . . .

It was almost like I was outside my body, watching myself break away from the script. I took a few flying steps and launched myself off the boardwalk and onto Ocean Avenue, my fall cushioned by a pile of sand. Something in my head began to whir, softly at first. Yet somehow, in that moment, I held on to the naïve hope that everything wouldn't change.

It might still be okay, I thought as I grabbed the girl's arm and guided her out of the way. She was limp as a rag doll and didn't fight, as if she was used to being pulled in different directions by complete strangers. As I positioned her safely on a plank near the boardwalk, I could hear the bass thumping from her earphones.

It wasn't a very heroic scene. The rather large audience that had gathered didn't applaud; they just quietly turned back to what they'd been doing, almost as if they'd wanted to see a tragedy. By that time, though, I wasn't looking for applause. My hopes of getting back everything I'd had dwindled as my brain began to pound, flip-flip-flipping as new memories shuffled like cards.

I grimaced and blinked hard to stop the throbbing, the commotion in my head so loud that it drowned out the noon siren.

Chapter 2

I'd grown used to the cycling of my future "memories." Before that summer, it had happened every day, just a little. When I was a kid, before I'd learned to deal with them, my mind would shuffle constantly, weaving in new futures in place of the old ones, leaving others in the dust, like dreams. Maybe I'd forgotten, but back then, the cycling hadn't seemed to hurt this much.

Of course, I'd never been able to go so long without any major cycling. Somehow I'd managed to make it almost three months without veering away from the future I saw in my head. It was a good future. A future I wanted desperately to keep. And now it was gone.

I collapsed on the pavement, breathing hard. Lifted my arms over my shoulders and squeezed my head between my elbows like a vise. Senseless images of people I'd never met, things I'd never done, shattered fragments of my future, sputtered through my head.

You will . . . can . . . . be . . . . not . . .

"Hey, are you okay?"

It was a girl's voice. The angel. In my blurry vision I could see two silvery pink running shoes, toes pointed at me.

"Yeah, yeah, yeah," I blurted out, trying to look up at her, when a surge of agony pulled my head down again. "Sun glare."

She didn't speak. I tried to raise my head, but it was a no-go, as if a fifty-pound dumbbell was dangling from my neck and someone was playing the drums on my cerebral cortex.

"Well, thanks. I didn't see. I, um . . . ," she babbled, all the while forcing me to the sad recognition that this girl was intensely sweet and shy and everything I would look for if I didn't know I was destined to marry a redheaded nurse named Sue from Philly in ten years. Except, I realized as my memories shuffled at a maddening speed, that outcome was gone forever. Sue existed somewhere, still, but she'd probably never be with me. And now my crash-and-burn with this girl was inevitable. I'd lost two hot girls in one morning.

Without warning, I smelled apples laced with cinnamon, like someone was baking pies nearby. I could almost taste them. My salivary glands kicked into overdrive and my mouth began to water. Then, suddenly, the memory disappeared. Whoosh. Gone.

The girl was trying to tell me about how she was new in town. It was where any normal guy would say something like "Where are you from?" or "Can I show you around?", but instead, my eyes bulged, heavy, and I couldn't bring myself to raise them higher than her perfectly shaped ankles. To top it all off, I felt drool bubbling over my bottom lip. Awesome.

Just my luck. Why couldn't she just leave? Leave now, but come back later so we could continue this conversation at a time when I wasn't cycling, when I felt more normal? But for me, abnormal *was* normal. I'd been fooling myself, thinking I could change who I was.

Suddenly I saw craft paper and a paperback romance novel and water dripping on hardwood. Fear curdled in my body. A scream bloomed in my throat but came out as a muffled moan. A jolt of pressure rocketed through my eyeballs, seeming to slice them in half. I pushed my palms hard against my eye sockets. "No. No. No!"

Most girls ran screaming from me, but this girl wouldn't leave. Perfect. She put her hands on her knees, and though I couldn't see her face, I knew she was squinting at me like I was some experiment gone horrifically wrong. "Are you having an aneurysm?"

"No, I'll be . . ." Another jab in my eye, and then a picture

Me, screaming flashed in front of my eyes. My next word was a muffled groan—"Fine"—because another memory was fighting against the rage of others, floating to the surface kissing soft lips, blond curls in my eyes and giving me a warm, tense feeling between my legs. What? I get to kiss her? Seriously? I was drooling in front of her, for God's sake. I hadn't completely ruined things with her with this moronic display? Just as I inwardly started to celebrate I caught another . . . it is unexpected tragedy that brings us together today the unexpected is often the most difficult to deal with and clenched my fists. Sure, in the future I'd perfected, there were funerals. But nothing horrible. My mother wouldn't go until she was in her sixties. And my last official memory was digging for sand crabs in the surf with my grandson—I could even feel the ache of my bones with that memory, so I had to have been old. My poor grandson. That little blond kid. He was gone now, cast into dreamland with the others. God, I'd loved him. When I was young, I'd always hoped that when I cycled away from an outcome, all the progeny I remembered wouldn't just disappear forever, that they'd have a chance to exist somewhere, with other families, like Sue. The more kids and grandkids I recycled, though, the less I believed that was true. Every time the experiences started to shuffle, I felt like I was murdering them.

Murderer! You killed her!

The words sliced through my head. I smelled something sour and felt a hot breath on my neck. The voice was so vicious and the memory so vivid, I thought it was real; I looked around and saw a small crowd of a dozen or so people in bathing suits, carrying their beach chairs and towels, staring at me. But no one was standing close by accusing me of being a killer. I would have wondered where the hell that came from if I hadn't already known. The weirdest and most unimaginable things only came from one place: the land of the yet-to-be.

I shuddered and gripped my head tightly in my hands. "Green elephant," I muttered under my breath.

She leaned forward. Apples again. Her hair smelled like apples. I inhaled deeply, feasting on the smell, since it was the only nice thing I could find about the moment. "Excuse me?"

I clenched my teeth. "Green elephant, green elephant. Green elephant."

I figured that if anything could send her away, me muttering nonsensical phrases would be it. The phrase "green elephant" didn't mean anything to her, but I'd invented it when I was nine or ten, and it meant everything to me.

"Do you want some water or something?"

Why did she have to be so damn nice? I pulled my head up and stared into her eyes, blue and endless, and

Blood on the staircase

I knew right then I was going to be sick. "Look." I tried to keep my voice even, but it came out as more of a growl. "I don't want anything from you, so just get the hell away from me."

I was surprised by two things. First, at how I could bring myself to sound like a total jerkwad, which was what I probably was, but I'd always been too absorbed in my future to dwell on it. And second, at how she just nodded, as if it all made sense. She hurried up the ramp and jogged off, fastening the headphones over her ears as if we'd been chatting about the weather.

I sat alone for a moment, eyes closed, green-elephanting until the pain subsided and my mind slowed to a peaceful lull. A thousand new memories of the future bubbled under the surface of my eyes. On the bad side, there was something about blood on the staircase, and I had this strange ache in my chest. On the good side, there was kissing that girl. The rest I would have to sort out later. I felt like I'd gone ten rounds of a heavyweight title match. I couldn't tell if it was because of the cycling or because the new memories would prove too horrifying to bear. I could change them. I could change the bad things, sometimes, by going off script.

The problem was, changing the bad things usually took away the good things, too. And there always seemed to be more bad things to replace the ones I managed to escape. The future I'd given up was a one-in-a-thousand future. I went to college, married Sue, who understood me as well as anyone could, had children and grandchildren. It wasn't anything awesome, but it was normal, and that was all I wanted. The other hundreds of futures were like episodes of some bad television show. High drama, all the time. Once, I'd choked to death in my teens. Once, I'd accidentally caused a fire while making bacon in the kitchen and ended up homeless. Once, I'd wound up addicted to crack, in a loveless marriage to a Vegas stripper, and murdered in a drug deal in my early twenties. I'd done it all. In my head, at least.

And sometimes . . . sometimes, try as I might, I couldn't change things. It was like certain past events sealed that certain future events would occur, and they couldn't be changed, or it wasn't clear how to change them. Once, when I was ten, I was trying so hard to follow the script that I tripped and broke my wrist. After that, I had this strong feeling I was going to get a huge bump on my head, but I couldn't tell how. I tried not following the script, hoping to avoid that bump. But it didn't work, because I didn't know what in the script to change. Turned out that I had to give up skateboarding until my wrist healed, so I put my skateboard on the top shelf of my closet. I opened it one day and the skateboard fell out and whacked me on the head. So sometimes bad things were just impossible to avoid.

You will climb up to the boardwalk and smile at Jocelyn. She will eye you up and down, and a couple of children and a man with a Boogie board will step aside to let you pass.

Crazy Cross. That was what they called me at school, and as I felt the eyes of all the beachgoers on me, I knew it wouldn't be too long until they thought the same. I knew they'd run home and tell their friends what they'd seen, and I'd be the talk of the town again, and not in a good way. As I climbed up the ramp, quickly, trying my best to ignore the stares, that same sinking feeling resurfaced. For three months, I'd shed it, but now, it wrapped around me, heavy, like a winter coat.

You will bury your feet in the sand and hurry down the beach.

I groaned and stepped off the boardwalk, sinking ankle-deep into the hot sand.

You will hear the radio crackle with "Ambulance . . . Seventh Avenue." You will see the crowd gathered at the waterline. Chaos. Shouts. Pedro will narrow his eyes at you when you break through, and scream, "Where the hell were you?"

They will tell you there's no hope of saving the girl in the pink bikini. And you will know it is because of you.

Chapter 3

I was usually too busy getting tripped up by my future to think about the past. But that afternoon, I couldn't stop thinking about the past. I couldn't get that little girl's dead blue lips out of my mind. Those long eyelashes, coated in salt water and sand. She wasn't one of my dreamland kids; she'd been living and breathing and growing on this earth. And now she was dead.

The girl had been playing in ankle-high water. We'd had a storm the night before, and she'd been dragged out by the strong undertow. In my memory, I'd shaken Pedro awake in time for him to point out the little girl. At the time I'd thought he was pointing out a piece of ass, but eventually I would have realized it was a drowning and I would have saved her. I *did* save her, dammit. I had the sore neck muscles to prove it, where her mother had hugged me so tightly, shrieking an endless supply of thank-yous into my ear.

In reality, though, Pedro slept through the noon siren, only to be awakened by the little girl's mother screaming. Yeah, outwardly, it was Pedro's fault. But my lunch break was up at noon, and I'd been late. I'd also known Pedro wasn't in any condition to man the stand himself. I could easily have prevented it. But I didn't.

It would take days or weeks or months to sort out what lay ahead in this new future, but I already knew some things. I knew that Bill Runyon, our captain, had summoned me to headquarters to can me. I knew he would give me that pity look, the one teachers reserve for students who "had so much potential" but still manage to become total screwups anyway. I knew he would use phrases like "good kid" and "take a breather" and that he would shift uncomfortably behind his desk while fingering the cords on the hood of his SPBP sweatshirt. He could single-handedly carry a four-man rowboat down the beach, but he was piss-poor at confrontation. I guess I could have left my whistle and ID on the bench outside headquarters, then biked away and considered my three-month tenure as Seaside Park lifeguard finito. That was what Pedro did; he'd wandered off quietly somewhere in the middle of the chaos, and I found his things lying on the bench. But I went in for the torture anyway. I had nothing better to do.

Besides, if I listened to Bill, chances were I wouldn't have time to think about anything else. It was the thinking that killed me.

You will sit on the chair at Bill's desk and start to fidget. He will pretend to be going through papers, but you will know he is just avoiding this.

I sat down and laced my fingers in front of me. I fidgeted

even when I wasn't nervous, though I couldn't actually remember a time I wasn't nervous about something. Bill riffled through papers, and I wondered if he was thinking about my mom. Supposedly, they'd gone to high school together, which was why he always asked me how she was doing. Usually with the same kind of face you'd have if you were inquiring about a puppy that got run over by an eighteen-wheeler.

No, I wasn't the first Crazy Cross he'd had to deal with. But I knew that if he—if anyone—had the chance to see things the way my mom and I did, he'd be just like us. I'd been the only one who'd seen the happy ending—the one where I'd carried the kid to the sand and performed CPR until she regained consciousness, coughing up seawater, in my arms. Now that outcome existed only in broken fragments, bits of sensation—the relief when she finally began to stir, the feeling of her sandy cheek against mine as she hugged me—somewhere in a corner of my mind. The rest of the world—the real world—had seen me arrive on the scene minutes too late and try to get her going, screaming "Breathe!" and pressing on her tiny little corpse chest over and over again, way past the time any normal dude would have given up. People in the crowd turned away, disgusted, but did I care? No. Instead, the EMTs who arrived with the ambulance five minutes later had to tear me away from the dead body.

You will hear the faraway screams of glee from the children on the Tilt-a-Whirl at Funtown Pier and you will think of the little girl in the pink bikini. Bill will turn at that moment and see the anguish in your face. "Tough day," he will say.

The children's shouts made me cringe. The dead girl was probably in kindergarten, at an age when kids love school. Her friends would probably wonder where she was on that first day in September and then they would learn the awful truth. It would be their first taste of death, of mortality. It would likely scar them for years, maybe forever. Way to make your mark on the world, Cross, I thought. A dozen kindergartners will wet their beds for years to come because of you.

Once, Nan had sat me down to watch her favorite movie, *It's a Wonderful Life.* I hated that movie, maybe because I envied the Jimmy Stewart character. He had such a positive impact on the world. Everything I did always turned to crap. I mean, lifeguarding? What was I thinking? Of course I couldn't be a lifeguard, not when I could so easily go off script and have thousands of futures competing in my mind, destroying my concentration. It was like Betty Crocker running a weight-loss clinic.

"Tough day."

You will nod but say nothing.

I pushed away the thought of five bright-eyed tots being reduced to tears in the back of the school bus when another kid let the news spill that the little girl was dead. That wasn't real. After all, I assured myself, I couldn't be on the school bus with them. Sometimes it was hard to distinguish my thoughts of the future from the spirals of my imagination.

Still, I could clearly see that snot-nosed kid sputtering "—is dead."

Hell, I didn't even know the little girl's name.

You will—

Sometimes I could think something so hard, I couldn't see the script. I did that now, picturing instead my old standby, the green elephant. "What was her name?"

My mind began to shuffle before I could finish the sentence. But it wasn't like the cycling had gone on a rampage, like before. It was only a small pang-pang-pang against my temple. I rested my elbow on the padded armrest and dug my fist into the side of my head to steady the throbbing.

Bill's eyes were always soft. He was the good-natured, back-slapping, even type whose voice never rose beyond a whisper. He'd been readying the Good Kid speech, but his eyes narrowed. "Come on, Nick, let's not go into—"

More shuffling. "Tell me." But the truth was, I really didn't need him. All the answers were already there in my head. I just needed to commit in my mind to travel far enough down a path to retrieve them. I could do it, if the answer could be found somewhere in the immediate future. I could find out anything if I wanted it badly enough. I just had to contend with the pain. I sat for a moment, imagining myself tracking down the answer, the pain escalating all the while. If I stopped right now and went back on course, followed the script like a good boy, the cycling would stop. But I couldn't. I needed to know. Once I followed the path far enough in my head, the one where I lunged over the side of the desk and ripped the paper from Bill's hands, receiving a punch from him that would make my lips bloody and swollen like raw sausages for weeks, I squeezed myself back in my chair, digging my fingers into the armrest to keep my body from actually doing it. Then I pressed my eyes closed and silently green-elephanted until only two words appeared in my mind.

Emma Reese

I opened my eyes. My mouth still smarted from the punch I'd never receive. "Emma? Emma Reese? Is that her name?"

Bill's eyes flashed surprise for only a second before melting into acceptance, and I knew he was thinking of my mother. I really didn't know what strange things he'd seen my mother do that summer before she confined herself to her bedroom, but it was clear he'd seen something. I was afraid to know what. "Yes, it is."

Finally, peace. That lasted about one-tenth of a second. Somehow, knowing her name made the burden heavier.

He put his hands up gently, as if motioning a car to a stop in a tight parking spot. "Listen. This isn't your fault. You couldn't have done any more than you did. Jocelyn said you were helping her with a situation on the boardwalk."

I'd been so busy concentrating on what I needed, the mention of Jocelyn surprised me. "She said that?"

He nodded. "Pedro, well . . . I'll deal with him separately."

I cringed at the mention of Pedro. Maybe he thought his mirrored sunglasses could disguise a little catnap, but in my vision, he'd been out like a light, snoring. I could have done something. I could have told headquarters that he was hungover. I could have stayed at my post instead of getting lunch. I could have ignored everything else and arrived at my post five minutes earlier, like I was supposed to. Bill went on about how "these things happen," but he didn't see what I saw. It was my fault.

He closed a thin manila file. On the tab, I saw CROSS, NICK in black block letters. "I'm sure a bunch of us will attend the funeral, and you're more than welcome to—"

"Let me ask you a question." I leaned forward, took a breath. "If 'these things happen,' like you say, and it's not my fault, then why am I being fired?"

He sighed. "Aw, kid. Look. It's politics. And you don't want to be caught in the middle of an invest—"

"I killed her." I spit out the words. "It is my fault. You can tell them whatever you want, but I could have saved her."

I wanted to see what else he had written in the file. Maybe Terminated. Crazy as His Mother. But I didn't want to get punched in the face again. Just the memory of the punch hurt. I flinched at the thought. My mind revved a bit more, like a computer's hard drive being tested to its limits. I could almost feel the future memories, memories I hadn't even sorted through, being plucked from my mind. A crease grew at the center of Bill's forehead. I wondered if my mother had seen that crease.

Shutting my eyes, I spoke. "I want to—" I held out my hands but dropped them to my sides again when I realized they were trembling. My voice was, too. The pain was intensifying by the minute. I crunched down on the words, biting off each one. "I. Need. To."

In that memory I'd had prior to entering Bill's office, the

one where he'd given the Good Kid speech, his features were a lot softer and, on the whole, more sympathetic. Now he looked disgusted, worn out. "What you need is to go home. Get some rest. Take a breather."

"What I need"—my voice cracked—"is . . ."

I wiped my eye and looked down at my hand. Wet. Perfect. When had I started crying?

He stood up and walked to the edge of his desk. Sat down on it so that his flip-flop dangled off one tanned foot. "Look . . . it's not your—"

I closed my eyes again. Clenched my fists. Sometimes I hated people. They didn't see things the way I did. "You. Are. Wrong."

He went back behind the desk and began to scribble something on a notepad, all the while saying that he recommended I settle down before heading off, as he put it, "half-cocked." My mind cycled a little more, so I squeezed my head between my hands and let the memories fall into place.

"Emma. Emma Reese," I said aloud.

We know who you are and what you did and because of you she is dead you killed our Emma

The words lingered in my brain; a man spitting and growling them in such a way that I could feel his breath on my ear and smell something sour and dank, like old milk, on him. The vision that accompanied this was of a vaguely familiar brick ranch house, surrounded by pretty white pebbles. And there was the taste of lemonade. Lemonade and blood. Even though some of the images made no sense, it was clear that they blamed me. Whoever they were.

More cycling. *You will . . .*

I tried to green-elephant, but all I could see was a picture of the girl lying dead on the sand, surrounded by a circle of onlookers.

When I snapped back to reality, I realized that Bill had come over to my side of the desk. I found a piece of paper, folded, in my palm. I stood and thanked him. A cool ocean breeze greeted me when I opened the screen door and stepped outside.

The pain in my head subsided.

> *You will pick up your bike, straddle it, then open the sheet of paper in your hand.*

I did so, but before I even read the paper, I cringed at what I knew was written on it. Scrawled there were nine words:

> *Get help before you end up like your mother.*

Chapter 4

I was eight the first time I was called Crazy Cross. It was by a chubby red-haired girl named Carrie Weldon who lived next door and had only a day earlier come over for Oreos and milk. Nan had beamed, excited because I had found a "nice friend," as she had called Carrie. But the next day, my new nickname was all over the playground. Carrie had told everyone at school that my family was a bunch of monsters.

Until that moment, I'd thought the kids at school were the weird ones for having mothers who would walk them to the bus stop and come to their holiday concerts. To me, that was a job for Nan. Nan was also responsible for feeding me, clothing me . . . well, basically for everything. She did the same for my mother.

When Bill said, "Get help before you end up like your mother," he really knew only a part of what being "like my mother" meant. He knew that my mom was a recluse and never left the stuffy second floor of our cottage. Only Nan really understood what was up with my mother and me. Most people would just cross to the other side of the street whenever they saw us coming. They thought we were harmless, but they didn't want to take any chances. They figured we had something going on, but they weren't sure what.

I trudged into our house, stuffing the pink sheet of paper from Bill into the pocket of my SPBP Windbreaker. Three months. Three months I'd managed to keep myself together, keep that nice, comfortable future intact. And it was all gone in the blink of an eye. It had been foolish to think I could keep it. My head still throbbed, and I hadn't yet been able to fully unclench my fists. I kept them in tight balls at my sides. As the door slammed, three competing thoughts popped into my head: spilled milk, clown hair, and Bruce Willis. A You Will sliced through them, and I braced myself for the sound I dreaded.

Immediately, I heard it. Moaning from upstairs. It was the same low buzz of anguish that Carrie had heard ten years ago. Often, it wasn't bad, and I could block it out. But on the worst days, it nearly drove me mad, echoing in my nightmares.

Nan was playing Journey in the kitchen, which she usually did to drown out my mom. She had a dish towel in her hands, and something that smelled strongly of fish was sizzling in a fry pan behind her, right under a row of tomatoes and cucumbers ripening on the windowsill. She must have been working in the garden today, judging from the circles of dirt on her bare knees. There were bobby pins holding down three almost-fluorescent orange curls at the base of her forehead, over a big, toothy grin. Though the hair was shockingly different, the smile was a constant. You'd think we'd won the lottery with the way Nan smiled all the time.

She caught me staring at her hair and sighed. "Don't say a word. Must have picked up the wrong color at the supermarket. You know how my eyes are. I've already bought new color. I'll dye it back this week, when I—"

There was a moan, like the hum of an engine. Nan swallowed, but the smile returned, bigger than before.

"How long has she been going on like that?" I asked, even though I already knew. Mom and I were like two sides of a coin. Whenever I cycled, she did, too. Whenever my future spun out of control, her future, which was tied to mine, did, too.

"Since lunchtime. You must have done a doozy."

I shook my head. I didn't want to talk about it. Mom moaned again. It made my eardrums rattle. "Why is she so melodramatic? It doesn't hurt that bad anymore."

Nan clucked her tongue and turned down the radio. The band, her favorite, was singing something about holding on to a dream. When I was younger, she used to sing the song to me before I went to sleep. She leaned in as if telling me a secret. "You know how your mom thinks. Why just react when you can overreact?"

She said that all the time. Usually it got a laugh out of me, but now I looked at the ground. "Nan, I screwed up something big. A girl died. I killed her."

She drew in a breath and crossed herself. Her voice was gentle. "Oh, dear. How?"

"I got sidetracked. It looked like someone was in danger, and by the time I finished with her, the girl I was supposed to save had drowned."

She exhaled. "You didn't kill her. You just didn't save her. There's a difference."

"I was supposed to be at my post. And Pedro was—"

"You are always too hard on yourself."

Her words didn't comfort me. Because I knew the truth. I gnashed my teeth and dug my fingers into my sides just thinking about it. And then there was the words—*You killed our Emma*—that echoed in my brain. Her parents, I guessed. "Her parents think I killed her."

Nan's eyes narrowed. "They told you that?"

I shook my head. "They will. I'm not sure if they know now, but they will. I saw it in my vision."

"Your vision? Are you sure? It could have been your imagination. Remember Ginger?"

I nodded. Ginger was the puppy I'd been convinced I was going to get when I was ten. I took him everywhere, and I really loved him . . . but I never got him. He wasn't real. Sometimes I would think so much about something, want it so badly, I convinced myself that it was in my future. But those were only things I wanted, and I definitely did not want Emma's parents hating me.

"Don't let that bother you, honey bunny. I know you did the best you could." She whipped my thigh with the dish towel. "Get yourself on course. Give her time to breathe."

She turned back to the stove and started to season the fish.

I realized at that moment that the fish would be too salty, but I didn't tell her. She didn't want to know the future, and would usually stop me midsentence whenever I tried to explain anything. Plus, Nan's life was hard enough, since she constantly had to care for us, so I always tried to tread lightly around her. And I'd like to think I was more sensitive to the living because I could taste the grief that would linger after their deaths. My mother and I both knew Nan would die in just over three years. Despite the many cycles we went through day after day, that was constant. Really, there were only two constants in my life: Mom would never leave her bedroom, and Nan would die in her recliner. She would pass away peacefully, of old age, while watching her soaps. Neither of us had told her that, though, because telling her could change the outcome. And my mother and I figured if there was any nice way to die, that would be it.

Another moan. I looked up the staircase.

Nan, wait—

It wasn't even a fragment of a vision that popped into my mind that moment. It was just those words, and an overwhelming feeling that racked my entire body with chills. I grabbed the edge of the counter for support, nearly knocking over a milk jug. As I did, I caught a glimpse of the dusty, faded mural that had been under the cabinets ever since I could remember. It said, Heaven's a little closer in a house by the sea.

Yeah, right.

Your past makes you who you are. You might not remember

all of it, but even the things you forget can leave a mark. My future did the same to me. Things I hadn't experienced yet weighed on my brain like bricks. At any one time, those images of my future would lie in wait somewhere in my brain, waiting for something to happen, something that would call them up. A lot of times, they were just pieces. But because I hadn't experienced them yet, I couldn't put them in context. They didn't make sense. Like the one I saw as I began to loosen my grip on the counter.

The image I saw was me, standing in the dark hallway, looking down the steps, screaming *No!* In that vision, I couldn't catch my breath. I'd never felt that pain before. Like everything inside me was being sucked out with a straw.

Definitely not good.

After the pain subsided, I let out a string of curses. I threw the jug to the ground, and milk splattered everywhere. Then I tore at my hair until I heard it ripping at the roots, scraped at the skin on my face until it felt red and raw. I hated myself.

It was stupid to think I could hold on to one future for longer than a few months. But I'd liked that future. I'd liked the way I died in it. I couldn't remember much after playing in the sand with my grandson; I'd just gone back to the beach house, collapsed into my favorite rocking chair, and drifted off. That memory was like a dream now. Who knew what kind of death I'd have?

I'd screwed everything up.

Nan stared at me, her eyes warm with understanding, though she really didn't have any idea. She came over and wrapped her arms around me, squeezed me, but I didn't squeeze back because her bones felt small, breakable, like twigs. The top of her head barely reached my chest, so she had to bend her neck all the way back to look into my eyes. "What's wrong?"

"It's nothing," I answered. Really, it was everything, but my head was still cycling dully, which made even talking hurt.

The lucky and the brave, Bruce Willis, rotting inside.

I helped Nan clean up the stupid mess I'd made. She tried to swat me on the backside with the towel again, but this time I anticipated it and skirted away. I climbed the stairs, which were covered in worn green shag carpet. Since all she had was a measly monthly social security check, Nan hadn't brought anything new into the house in decades, save for a bunch of crucifixes and worthless statues of saints, which she put on every available surface or wall. All the furniture was from when she was growing up here in the sixties, Formica, with shapes that looked like germs under a microscope everywhere. My sheets had dump trucks and airplanes on them, and the matching curtains were so worn, they did little to block out the morning light. Not that I cared. I didn't have friends who'd see my room, and I never slept much, anyway.

When I reached her door, there was silence. I stood outside it longer than I had to. Going in there was never fun. I knocked and whispered, "Mom?", then went inside.

The room was hot and dark and stank of incense and sweat. Mom was lying on her stomach on the bed in boxers and a tank. She's young as far as moms go. I think she'd be considered a MILF if there weren't thick dark rings around her eyes that matched the color of her waist-length hair, which was pulled up in a messy loop on top of her head. When I looked at her, I could almost see her resemblance to Nan. They have the same deep-set, fathomless eyes, the same soft, even voice. They laugh the same, boldly, though my mother's laugh is always tinged with bitterness and irony. They have the same thin lips and I suppose they might even have the same smile, but I didn't know my mother's smile. I'd never seen it. I'd always wondered what else she would have in common with my grandmother, had things been different. Would she make great pancakes? Find pleasure in things like gardening and weeding? Go to church every Sunday?

Would she smile?

I kissed the top of her head as she picked up the remote beside her and turned down the volume on the ancient TV set. I looked over at it. *Die Hard* One or Two, I couldn't tell which. She was a slave to action movies—they helped take the edge off her cycling.

"Bad day," I sighed.

Her eyes drooped. "So I felt."

"Sorry."

"I know about the girl."

"Well," I muttered, "you can see the future, so that doesn't make you Einstein."

She sighed. "Do you feel it, too? Like things are going bad?"

I snorted. A girl was dead because of me. It was hard to imagine life going to a worse place than we were at right then, but yeah, I knew what she meant. It was an odd feeling, as if two totally different sensations were competing within me: hunger with queasiness, anticipation with fear. "But what?" Maybe she'd had time to think about it.

She reached down to the foot of her bed and picked up a copy of *Star* magazine. "My horoscope says this is a terrible day to make changes to the status quo. So you picked one hell of a day to—"

"Sorry." I snatched the paper from her hands. My mom loves—no, worships—all things unseen. Good-luck charms, horoscopes, superstitions, all that crap. I think that if our seeing the future wasn't so complicated, like if we could just see one version of the future, and it could never be altered, maybe she would have given it a rest. But as it was, she was constantly consulting the occult.

I turned and surveyed her lunch tray. She'd downed an entire carafe of coffee, as usual, but only taken nibbles of her sandwich. It sometimes pissed me off how well Nan took care of her, and how useless she was in return. Nan shouldn't have had to deal with that. In the mirror, I could see her settling into her pillow, watching Bruce Willis tiptoeing down a hallway in bare feet and a wifebeater. There were little slips of fortune-cookie fortunes stuck in the edge of the mirror, hundreds of them. Mom didn't like to toss them away. The one I saw said, *Love is for the lucky and the brave.*

I shook my head. Luck and bravery were two things that didn't exactly flow through this house. I thought of the day I learned I had something that made me different. I was four. Nan was making me lunch and I was sitting at the table. I could see the can of grape juice concentrate rolling down the counter and splattering over the linoleum, so I stood there to catch it. If Nan was worried about me, which she must have been, she hid it well. She just smiled and called me her hero. I used to be proud of it. I used to call it my superpower.

"Something with the staircase," Mom said. "Right?"

I nodded. I'd seen that, and something with blood. But I didn't want to say it. "But what?"

"I don't know. I need time to sort it out. Are you on script?"

"Yeah."

"It's strong. A strong, bad feeling."

I agreed. Blood was rarely a good thing to see in a vision. "Do you want me to go off?"

"Maybe. You have track tryouts tonight?"

"I wasn't going to go. I don't think I'm going to make the team. And too much has happened." I knew what she was thinking even without consulting the script. "You think I should go?"

"Well, it might help change things."

"All right."

She took the magazine in her hands and began to page through it. "What's for dinner?"

It was a running joke between us, asking each other questions we already knew the answer to. When I was a kid I used to spend hours trying to come up with really disgusting answers to the "What's for dinner?" question, like sautéed horse guts and fried iguana feet, but now I barely smirked. It had been a long time since I'd found it funny.

Chapter 5

Sometimes I wish I lived in the Heights. A guy like me could get lost there.

Though it's just to the south of the Heights, my town, Seaside Park, is like the less popular, more boring twin of Seaside Heights. Both towns are on the barrier islands of New Jersey, a small strip of land surrounded by water. But that's where the similarities end. Nan calls the Heights the Devil's Playground. There are bars and amusements and all kinds of riffraff hanging around the Heights. MTV loves the place. People drink and party and go wild there. Freaks are welcome there. They prosper there. A guy who could see his future would not, by any means, be the weirdest thing that town has ever seen.

The Park is a complete one-eighty. It likes the quiet, and prefers to be called family-friendly. The people who planned the town of Seaside Park had very little imagination. For example, it's split down the center by Central Avenue. One block to the west, you have the Bay, barely a mile wide, and across that, you can see mainland New Jersey. One block to the east, you have the Atlantic Ocean. There is a road that stretches down the bay side called Bayview Avenue, and a road that runs along the ocean called—big shocker—Ocean Avenue. And all the cross streets are either numbered or lettered, so it's pretty hard to get lost here. Unfortunately. It's a vacation town, so during the summer, the hotels and apartments fill up and the roads swell with people, but starting in October, the place empties out and tumbleweeds blow through. Then it's just us regulars, and everyone knows everybody else, and everybody else's business. Unfortunately.

My high school is on the mainland, in Toms River. But Coach Garner, who has been in the position for forty years, lives on the island, and is about as athletic as a bar of soap, can't be bothered to go the nine miles inland to the high school to hold tryouts, so every year he holds them on the boardwalk. There are mile markers, but running on boards can be challenging. Still, the view is nice, so people don't complain.

When I got to Fourteenth Avenue, at the southern terminus of the boardwalk, people I recognized from school were milling about in their singlets and shorts, stretching against the pilings and fence, looking serious. The You Wills told me to go home, to go anywhere but here, but I ignored them and the dull ache they were causing in my head.

The first person I saw when I climbed the ramp was Evan Sphincter. His real name was Evan Spitzer, but when he opened his mouth you knew a bunch of foul crap was going to come out, so I used the other. Not to his face, though.

It took me a minute to recognize him because he looked different, and not in a way that I'd have liked. Maybe it was the tan. No, it was more than that. He'd never been ugly, but he'd never been a movie star, either. His face had always been kind of round, but now his jaw was chiseled. Once upon a time, he'd been kind of thick around the middle, with doughy arms and legs. Now he had muscles. More than muscles. He looked like the spokesperson for home gym equipment. Unreal.

"Hey, Crazy Cross," he said, reaching down like he was going to help hoist me up onto the boardwalk. But it was all an act. The second I'd reach for his hand, he would pull his away and run it coolly through his highlighted hair. I didn't have to pay attention to the You Wills to know that. And—highlights? What kind of dude got platinum highlights?

I just said, "Hey," and pretended I didn't see him wiggling his fingers at me. His forearm muscles were bigger than my biceps. When the hell had that happened? He'd been a jerkwad since fourth grade, but now he was a built jerkwad. Fantastic.

Sphincter jogged across the boards to his dad, who had a terminally serious face. The guy never smiled. He was holding a stopwatch and looking at it like he wanted to kill it.

Runners will make a path for you as you walk to the other side of the boardwalk.

Yep, they parted like the Red Sea. When I turned back toward Sphincter, he was already surrounded by a bunch of hot girls. They swarmed around him like flies. Just completing his journey toward being a total one-eighty from me, I guess. Not that I was jealous or anything. Okay, yeah, I was.

Some guys I recognized from school stretched along the fence, refusing to make eye contact with me and instead checking out the fresh meat. There were a few cute girls, ones I'd never seen before, who might not yet have been aware of Crazy Cross protocol. I was wondering how long it would be before they kept their distance, too, when another memory bubbled through.

You will stretch your quads and hamstrings and then you will hear . . .

I was just starting to relax and stretch my muscles when a tiny redhead's words floated over on the breeze. "Hear about the little girl who died on Seventh today?"

A guy was with her. He said something about an ambulance.

Then she said, "One of the lifeguards went completely nuts. They had to drag him away in a straitjacket."

I wanted to slither between the boardwalk planks. "Hey, wait," the girl said. I turned away but from the corner of my eye saw her pointing in my direction. Whispers were exchanged. "Him?" the guy asked. Then they both laughed. The guy said something that sounded like "Figures."

Great. At this rate, I'd be lucky to make it out of high school without the words "Crazy Cross" printed under my yearbook picture.

I turned back toward Sphincter and saw him breaking away

from the throngs of girls. He strutted right on over to . . . Oh, perfect. The angel was here. Had she seen the rest of the runners avoiding me like the plague? She was wearing the same thing she'd had on when I saw her earlier today—shorts, a tight tank, and running shoes. Duh, of course she was here, she was a runner. Did she go to my school? How had I never seen her before?

I watched Sphincter put the moves on her. He said something—a joke, probably, by the way he raised his eyebrows and laughed like he was the wittiest scumbag on the planet—and she looked at him and smiled, but politely, not like she wanted him or anything. I was impressed. Most girls would have taken one look at those muscles and jumped in his arms. He said something else and she just kind of shook her head, still smiling graciously, then walked away and started to stretch against the chain-link fence.

No goal, Sphinctie.

Two seconds later I realized I was staring at her with this admiring grin on my face and wiped it off. Had to concentrate on my running.

Concentrate. Right.

A few minutes later the tryouts began. Sphincter's group went first. He bopped and hopped at the starting line on the boardwalk, cracking his neck, all ego, Mr. Showman. Every part of his body screamed, *Watch me, watch me.* His dad was standing behind the fence, on the beach, in prime position to see every move. They gave each other a thumbs-up, which looked so fake, like the final scene from some cheesy sports movie. I couldn't believe we'd ever had anything in common. Then, as he lined up among the other runners doing the 100 meter, something came to me.

He's rotting from the inside.

It was a bit of a conversation, but it was so strong I knew it couldn't be my imagination. I'd never heard it before, so it had to be in the future. And whenever I looked at Sphincter, I felt it so strongly that it had to have been about him. Rotting from the inside? He was the poster child for healthy living. The starting gun went off and he pulled to an easy lead right away, pumping his long legs and smirking the whole while. Rotting from the inside. Yeah.

But then I heard the voice again.

You shouldn't be jealous of that. There's more to him than you know.

The voice was familiar. It was one I hadn't heard much of, and yet it was easily recognizable.

The angel. So we'd talk again? She'd want to talk to me after what happened today?

I turned toward her. She was sitting on a bench, not watching the race like everyone else. She was more interested in her fingernails. She inspected her thumbnail, then brought it to her mouth and ripped the top of it off in a sort of savage way. Somehow she made that look cute.

There's more to him than you know.

Well, I knew Sphincter's life wasn't a picture postcard. For one, everyone in school talked about his dad. Yeah, it was nice that the guy came to support his son during tryouts, but he was entirely too serious about everything. In most circles, Mr. Spitzer was known as The Sergeant. I don't think he'd ever been in the armed forces, but it was well circulated how he'd show up at all the meets and give Sphincter hell if he came in second. He'd bring along his stopwatch and argue with the officials and all that good stuff. I'm sure he was just as hard on Sphincter as he was with everything else in his life. So yeah, I wasn't jealous of that.

Just then, the angel looked up and her eyes found mine. She quickly lowered her hand and the remains of her ragged fingernail, blushing, as I tried to look like I was checking out something behind her. There was nothing but a pile of sand beyond her, though, so as you can imagine, it came off really smooth.

The race ended and Sphincter set a new school record. I was sure he'd done The Sergeant proud. But he's rotting from the inside, I told myself.

Didn't really help make me feel better.

Chapter 6

If you have this uncanny ability to see your own future, it's not a good idea to let other people in on it.

After Carrie Weldon moved away, the Crazy Cross thing calmed down. I was nine when I met my first, and only, best friend. He liked me despite my everyday weirdness. Or at least, he tolerated it.

So say you're nine, and your best friend tells you that he's going to Disney World with his family and suddenly you realize that if he gets in that station wagon, he'll never be the same. He's so excited, parading around in his mouse ears and talking about the Tower of Terror like it's his life's purpose, but you just know something bad is going to happen. You can see the vigil at the elementary school, and you know that your grandmother will try, and fail, to hide the newspaper from you, the one with the article about the horrific ten-car pileup on Interstate 95. So you warn him. You scream at him that he can't go. You even go to his house late at night and let the air out of the tires of his parents' station wagon.

Of course, doing that means they have to get the wagon

towed to the gas station so the tires can be inflated again, and when they do leave, two hours later than planned thanks to some stupid prankster, they arrive in Orlando safe and sound. They have a lovely trip and return home with a slew of pictures and one former best friend who thinks that you are a complete nutcase and never comes within ten feet of you again.

Well, unless it's to pretend to offer you his hand to hoist you onto the boardwalk.

Evan Sphincter and I used to be best friends. A lifetime ago. Back when he didn't have rippling muscles that made all the girls line up for him. And okay, maybe it wasn't just that one incident that forced us apart. There were probably a thousand and one incidents where I acted weird or said something weird or looked weird, and each one drove that wedge between us deeper and deeper.

I tried to be normal. I tried to blend in, to not make waves. But this thing affected me every moment of every day. So I learned not to get too involved with anyone. Every year it got easier. Over time, pretty much everyone had discovered Crazy Cross was not someone to associate with.

I don't really know why I wanted to go out for track that year. I loved running, and I was damn good at it, but I'd always shied away from organized sports. I guess I thought it was something normal people would do. Like lifeguarding. I think I'd gotten cocky, managing to keep that same future intact for three whole months. Managing to be not just a lifeguard but also a good one. I'd surprised myself this summer.

When I'd penciled my name on the sign-up sheet for tryouts, I had this new, invincible feeling, like, I can do this. I thought all that Crazy Cross stuff was finally behind me.

Wrong.

I tried not to think of Emma as I started the mile, but of course I did. I couldn't shake the vision of her small limbs sprawled on the sand, lifeless.

Normal. Yeah.

Anyway, I was a good runner. If I'd been normal, I bet I could have been a great one. I ran steadily, navigating around the few late-day beachgoers with umbrellas and chairs. The other runners lagged behind me; even with the headache from hell, I was on track for a record. I wasn't even out of breath. A couple of hot girls in bikinis grinned at me. I'm not bad-looking; I'm tall, with thick black hair and an okay build, maybe not as good as Sphincter's, but I always got looks from girls. After a minute or so, though, my charm wore off. I'd develop a tic or nervously go off in one direction or another, blowing it. This accounted for me being seventeen and never having gotten to second base with a girl. Even my first base was on account of an error; I'd been running on the boardwalk late one night, which I sometimes did to calm my mind, and when I stopped at the fountain to get a drink, a drunk girl must have thought I was her boyfriend because she grabbed me and kissed me.

Kissing soft lips, blond curls in my eyes

The image lit a fire under me. My pace quickened even more. It was the second time this afternoon that I'd had that memory. How could that be real? The picture was so strong I got lost in it. I forgot everything, even the simple rhythm of my legs pumping and my feet pounding on the boards. But when I passed the entrance for the Seventh Avenue beach, everything changed. I lost the rhythm. My lungs constricted and burned. The last image I saw was that of the little girl, lying dead on the sand.

You killed our Emma

Suddenly, I fell forward, onto my knees, so unexpectedly that I didn't have time to put my hands out to stop the fall. I smashed my face against the boardwalk. Then I rolled off, onto the sand, gasping and choking.

Coach Garner was a guy who perpetually smelled like Bengay and probably clicked on his stopwatch buttons in his sleep. He'd never run, even if something with large teeth was chasing him. When he stood over me, his beer gut blocked out the sun. "Wow. Just wow."

I hoped he was talking about how masterfully I'd run that first nine-tenths of a mile.

"That was the most pathetic fall I've ever seen."

Eh. I rolled over and propped myself up on one elbow. Across the way, a bunch a girls giggled at me, but I wasn't sure if they were part of the regular group of people who giggled at me, or new ones, because my vision was blurred. I looked down and saw blood soaking into my white tech shirt. My knees were dotted with blood and sand and little black splinters.

"So, um, does that mean I didn't make the team?"

Coach Garner laughed long and loud, like Santa Claus with a sadistic streak, then turned and ambled away without bothering to help me up. I scrambled to my feet, still feeling woozy. Then I tilted my head back and shuffled over to a bench, squeezing my nose, which by this time was seriously gushing. I think bits of major organs were leaking out. Every runner in school was staring at me, and most were laughing their asses off.

"Good one, Crazy Cross," Sphincter called across the fence to me, flashing me a thumbs-up. He was standing with The Sergeant, who was giving him the ol' New School Record shoulder rub and watching me like I was a glob of gum in danger of getting on his son's running shoe.

Rotting from the inside, I repeated to myself, over and over so that it drowned out the next You Will. Screw them.

Before I could sit down, someone came up beside me. At that moment, I knew who it was. My stomach lurched even before I heard her say, "That looks bad."

I looked up for only a second. She was wearing the same exact expression she'd worn earlier today—a horrified kind of confusion. Was I doomed to always see her every time my head was exploding, or about to? Yeah, that totally explained why she would be kissing me. Maybe that wasn't part of my future. I'd probably wanted it so bad that I'd just been hallucinating.

"Nah ... too ... bah," I said, trying to act casual but feeling the blood course over my upper lip with every word.

She sat down on the bench beside me and handed me a

crumpled tissue. I clamped it over my nose, but it was soaked in a matter of seconds.

"You should go to the hospital."

I waved her away with my free hand. "Naw. I gef nofbleehs all de time."

"Your knees are bleeding, too," she pointed out. "And your forehead. And your elbows. Well, just one of them."

I lowered my head slowly, still covering my nose, and inspected my knees as if that news didn't completely freak me out. Sure enough, blood was running down my knees, pooling at the cuffs of my socks. Rocky had had it better after his fight with that Russian dude. I pointed to the lifeguard stand. "Well, in that caif, I gueff I'll go and geh a few Band-Aids."

She stood up. "I'll go with you."

I knew she would offer to come, and that I would protest. By that time, the pain in my joints was getting unbearable. Not wanting to look like a total wimp in front of her was the only thing keeping me from weeping. "Nof nefeffary."

"Sure it is. You might have a concussion."

"Naw, I'm fine."

"That's what my uncle said after he was rear-ended. And then two days later he nearly dropped dead."

"Uh . . ." The last time I'd met her, I'd also told her to leave me alone so she wouldn't have to witness my breakdown. The script had me accepting her offer and her holding on to my good arm as we limped down the beach. The script had me . . . Oh, hell. The script had me crying in front of her because it hurt so bad. That kiss had to have been a hallucination.

There was no way she'd want to get with me voluntarily after this.

When we stood up, my nose had stopped bleeding, so I didn't have to squeeze it shut. As we passed some girls, they stared after us. I thought they were just gawking at the dumbass who'd performed his own facial reconstruction, but then a short girl with a pixie haircut called out, "We'll wait for you by the car if you're not back by four, okay?"

The girl was looking right at us and there was no one else around, so I guessed they were her friends. She had cute friends, ones I had never seen before. She had to be a freshman, and considering the number of hot girls in that group, a popular one. But the weird thing was, instead of answering, she just kept on walking toward the lifeguard stand.

"Hey, Tar! We'll wait for you! By the car! Okay?" Pixie called out, a little louder, her voice an octave higher with desperation.

The angel just swung her head back and called over her shoulder, "Fine!" then muttered under her breath, "Whatever."

Okay. Didn't know what the hell that was about. They seemed nice enough; some of the other kids nearby reenacted my trip as I walked past them, but one of her "friends," a tall girl with crazy black hair, called after me, "Take care of yourself." I really couldn't think about it, though, because I was beginning to feel light-headed. I blinked a few times, hoping I didn't lose consciousness from the blood loss.

"Don't feel bad. I'm a little bit of a klutz myself," the angel said brightly. I knew she was just saying that to be nice, since her every movement was done with the grace of a ballet dancer. Even when I'd pulled her out of the way of that truck, she'd looked good. I noticed some of my blood had gotten on her bare shoulder, but I felt awkward rubbing it off. In my half-assed state I probably would have grabbed her boob. Sadly enough, that would have been, like, the most action I'd ever gotten from a girl. "And who needs cross-country anyway?"

The script had me completely mute, trying to think of something to say. Finally, I put a sentence together. "You know, you don't have to be nice to me."

"What do you mean?" I noticed she had a little accent, one I couldn't place. Not the annoying kind, but the kind that melts hearts.

"I mean, just because I helped you today. It's okay."

"Oh, I know."

"So, what? Is it Be Nice to Dorks Day or something?"

She laughed. "Are you a dork? You're not a dork."

I nodded. "I am. Ask anyone. I don't have a single friend at the school."

"That's not true. You have me."

"You can have any friends you want. You already have a lot of them. Don't think you need me. Go be with them. I'll be fine."

"Oh, yeah . . . those guys." She motioned to the cute girls on the boardwalk and screwed up her face. "Fake, fake, fake. They want things from me. I try to get away from them and they just follow me. It makes me so sick. You don't, though."

I tried to figure out what she meant. Just what did people want from her? She seemed to like hearing me tell her to get the hell away. I'd heard girls liked it when guys treated them like crud, something which boggled my mind. I didn't want to find out that she was one of those stupid girls, so I just said: "It depends on what you have. I accept monetary donations."

She laughed. Whoa. I'd never said anything that made a girl laugh before. "Do you live around here?" she asked.

"Um. Yeah. Seventh."

"Oh. I'm in the Heights."

The Heights was about two or three miles away from Seventh. "That was a long run you were taking this afternoon," I said.

She shrugged. "Five miles or so." I was just trying to understand what lunatic would run that far, before tryouts, at the hottest time of the day, when it was over ninety degrees, when she said, "I run because it helps me think. I kind of have a lot to think about."

I nodded. Couldn't argue with that.

We reached the lifeguard stand, and I hadn't cried yet. I was silently congratulating myself for that accomplishment when she said, "You know, you are really brave. I'd be crying."

I smirked. Actually, she'd taken the edge off the pain, made it tolerable. I realized I wouldn't be able to shake her; she was planning on coming in with me and watching the lifeguard

bandage me up. This girl was harder to avoid than the flu.
And there was something about her. Something that just
seemed ... right. It was all adding up to one thrilling and
terrifying realization:

I had a chance with this girl.

Geoff, a lifeguard, ushered me into his seat on the stand
when he saw me. He didn't have the gentle, female nurse's
touch my hormones would have really liked, so when he
started to swab up my knee, I winced.

And this girl, this angel, stayed with me the whole time.

I knew I would eventually fall madly in love with her. But
I'd had no idea it would start right then.

Chapter 7

Twenty minutes later, I walked her back to the street. By then it was pretty dead. The sun was starting to slump in the sky. Most of the late-day beachgoers were gone and her friends weren't there. It was completely quiet except for the crash of waves, the ping-ping-ping of the flag's metal hardware striking the flagpole in the breeze, and an occasional screech of a seagull. The angel broke the awkward silence by saying, "Well, I just wanted to say thank you. Um, you know. For saving me this afternoon. You're my hero."

I thought of Emma. Yeah, right, me a hero. My lips moved in answer, but nothing came out.

She took in a sharp breath and moved away from my side a little, like she was about to say "See you" and leave. Like most girls did after a minute in my presence. It was like I could almost see any chance I had with her ticking away in those moments. Before she could go, I opened my mouth, still not sure what I would say, so I looked kind of like a fish gulping water. When I asked the question, I realized I already knew the answer. "Uh. So you—you go to Central?"

I cringed at how unsmooth I could be, while at the same time this creeping sensation overtook me. Something about her, about us, was weird. I couldn't place it, which was why I stared at her with my mouth open, as if trying to pull something out of the far corner of my brain. She didn't notice. "Yeah. Well, I will be." She nodded her head a little like a yo-yo. "Just moved here from Maine a few weeks ago."

"Er. Oh." My hands were shaking so much I had to lace my fingers together. I'd sometimes had a fantasy—and this was definitely a fantasy, there was no mistaking it for my future—of me being smooth with the ladies, of always knowing what to say and when. I'd practiced those slick phrases over and over again in my head, but whenever I had the opportunity to actually use them, I'd failed miserably. Words would pile up over one another, confused in the jumble of future thoughts passing through my mind. This time, I opened my mouth and one of those cool witticisms came out. It didn't even sound stilted. "What brings you to Sleazeside?"

She screwed up her face, confused. "Sleaze? Why? I think it's nice here."

The momentary sense of victory I'd felt dissolved into a pang of fear over having to speak again. But I handled it well. "Well, it's not exactly Falmouth."

"Well, no, but—" She paused. "Wait. How did you know I lived in Falmouth? Did I say that?"

"Um, yeah, you did," I said, but all the while something began to dawn on me. She hadn't. And yet I knew. I knew that and . . . and while she lived there, she liked to go out to the pier at the back of her house and eat peanuts and feed them to the seagulls. She had a red bikini that she never wore because she was always too cold and hated sunburn and sand in her suit, and one day she made the top into a flag and put it on her little sailboat, which she called *The Mouse*, after her first pet hamster she had when she was three. . . .

Whoa.

Her voice broke through then. "Oh. I guess I did." I could feel her eyes on me, heavy, like they were cracking through the flimsy disguise I'd set up.

I expected her to run like hell in the other direction. But again, she didn't. Instead, she plopped down in the sand and motioned me over with her chin. She wanted me to sit next to her. When I walked over, the sun reflected off her eyes; they were almost the color of the sky, so light blue they were almost white. I didn't say anything as I sat. I was afraid of saying something else about her I shouldn't have known. I swallowed, thinking of her in that little sailboat.

She filled in the silence. "My dad lost his job at the semi-conductor factory, and we had to move in with my grandmother." She wrinkled her nose. "Gram's a little whacked."

She had no idea what whacked could look like.

She was quiet for a moment, sifting sand through her fingers. "I heard what happened here today."

I reached over, snatched a handful of black witch's-hair seaweed, and started yanking it apart. "Yeah, it was a bad day."

"I saw the ambulances. The Reeses are Gram's neighbors. They live next door to us. She used to sit for . . ." She trailed off when she saw my body tense. "You probably don't want to hear this."

I let out a short laugh. "Bingo."

She shrugged. "Fair enough. But it's no wonder you fell. You're obviously upset. Why did you . . . ?"

"I just wanted to do the normal thing, I guess."

She snorted. "The normal thing would have been to go home and sleep it off. At least, that's what I would have done." I cringed as she said that. Of course I didn't know what was normal. I couldn't even pretend to know. "Anyway, it's not your fault."

"I know," I lied, not wanting to talk about it anymore. To her, it wasn't my fault, but she didn't know I'd knowingly left an unfit guard in my place.

More awkward silence. I put out my hand, lamely, wondering all the while if that was the way casual introductions were supposed to go, or if I would look too formal, like a bank teller extending her a loan. "I'm Nick."

She looked at my hand and contemplated it for what seemed like a lifetime. Then she sighed and took only my fingertips in her hand. Her hand was soft, surprisingly cool. Mine felt all sweaty next to hers, and probably not just from the run. "Taryn," she said, but I knew that already. That she was Taryn was as obvious as a house being called a house or a bird being a bird.

Before I could search for another slick thing to say, something happened. Something big.

My mind went quiet.

No cycling. No You Wills . . .

Everything. All the future memories. Just gone.

I was too busy trying to figure out what had happened to notice that her smile had disappeared. Her hand trembled, and she wrenched it away from me. It was almost like . . . could she feel it? No, that was crazy. Her blond corkscrew curls whipped in her face in the ocean breeze, but I could have sworn she mouthed the words "Oh, God."

Damn. I knew my palms were sweaty, but they weren't that bad.

"She told me I could feel it when I touched them," she whispered to herself, looking out onto the horizon. "I didn't believe . . . Oh, God."

I squinted at her. Now who was acting crazy?

As if she'd heard my thoughts, she shook her head, scrambled to her feet, and edged back from me, as if she was afraid. Of me. She said something dismissive like "I'll see you around" and then turned away.

As I watched her hurry up the beach, toward the boardwalk, my mind began to rev again, whirring until it felt like the bones of my skull would shatter.

You will stand and make your way back to the boardwalk, slowly.

And so it began again.

Chapter 8

My life was pretty depressing as a whole, but watching Taryn walk away was probably the most depressing thing I'd ever really experienced. My stomach started to churn and then there was this pain—this squeezing pain in my chest. I had an overwhelming desire to run after her, to beg her to stay. In fact, as she walked down the ramp toward Ocean Avenue, I took a few steps after her, stopping in my tracks when I realized I couldn't do that. She would have thought I was a lunatic. We were practically strangers.

At least, to her, we were.

You always hear those stories. Two people meet, get married, live for decades and decades together. When one of them dies from old age, the other one, though perfectly healthy, falls ill and dies a month later. There's always some medical explanation, but at the funeral, most people would nod knowingly and whisper that the real cause was a broken heart.

After Taryn left, all the glee I'd felt from finally being able to say more than three sentences to a girl without completely freaking her out deteriorated into this horrible feeling of emptiness. The squeezing pain inside got worse, like my heart was being stepped on. I spent my walk home rubbing my chest and cursing myself for the stupid thing I'd done to drive her away.

Whatever that was. I'd been running, so maybe I stank. I picked up my T-shirt and sniffed. Not so bad. The salt in the air kind of overpowered any other smell. She'd bolted right after shaking my hand, so maybe my palms were sweaty. Maybe she hated calluses. I looked at my palms, then rubbed them against my shorts. Bits of hardened skin caught on the nylon.

Yeah, that was probably it. Driven to a heart attack at seventeen because of my chapped hands. Fitting end to my life.

By that time, I was sick of the constant headache that came with not doing what I was told, so I followed the script home. Two leather-skinned older women in bikinis glared at me from the porch of their stately mansion as I passed them. Though Nan had lived here decades longer than those ladies, they still treated us more like dirt than like neighbors. The only person on our street who talked to us was the cat lady, but that was because with more than a hundred cats, she had her own issues. Our house was the only tiny bungalow on the block, and surrounded by megamansions, so it was dark and overshadowed most of the day. Sunshine never made the mistake of leaking through our windows. When Nan was growing up, all the houses had looked like ours: tiny and cramped, with rotting black shingles. I'd seen pictures. But now it was common practice to tear down the bungalows and build up to the sky to get that priceless ocean view. These monstrosities either had yards filled with millions of perfect smooth white pebbles, or even worse, lawns with grass so green and unnatural it looked spray-painted. To me, those lush lawns were just plain wrong. They didn't belong here. But I guess from the way those old ladies looked at us, they felt the same way about me.

If people knew we could see the future, they'd probably think we could have had our own mansion. That we could have had a lot of things, if we wanted them. One night, I was sitting in front of the television watching the Pick-6, and I said every number two seconds before the ball shot out of the popcorn popper. Of course that gave me an idea. I thought I could stretch it, so that I saw the Pick-6 numbers early enough for Nan to buy a ticket. But the thing was, I couldn't. Things like Pick-6 numbers were short-term memory. The numbers only occurred to me a few seconds before they were drawn. Before that, they were lost in the muddle of outcomes competing in my head. Besides, Nan was dead against using our power for profit. Every time I thought of a way, she'd just roll her eyes. "We're perfectly comfortable," she'd say, looking out the kitchen window, past the plump red tomatoes ripening on the sill. "Besides, money is the root of all evil." Nan was like a brick wall when it came to certain things, and this was one of them. Eventually, I stopped asking, though she would never get me to believe that only evil stemmed from money. Some good came out of it, too. Like a new iPod. Or running shoes with treads that hadn't been worn so smooth that running sometimes felt like ice-skating.

My muscles and head hurt as I climbed the steps, and once again I couldn't tell if the pain was from the fall on the boardwalk or some horrible future memories swirling in my head, waiting to be unleashed from my subconscious. The thing clearest in my mind, besides the unraveling of the script, was Taryn. Somehow, everything I knew about the future disappeared when I'd touched her hand. Somehow, she already meant so much to me that my chest ached for her, even though we'd only met a few hours ago. As I opened the screen door, one clear thought stood out from all the others rattling around in my head: there was something different about her, and I had to find out what.

Nan lay in her silver-blue pleather recliner. It had a combo of red plaid dish towels and packing tape over the arms to hide the rips there. She kept the packing tape on the card table nearby since a new rip sprang up every time she sat in the chair. It was the same recliner she'd pass away in. She was watching *Wheel of Fortune*. Okay, not really watching. Snoring and staring at Pat Sajak with one glazed eye. Behind her, on the kitchen table, was a plate covered with foil.

The fish.

I pulled off the wrapping and, not finding a fork nearby, tore off a ragged piece of whitefish and popped it in my mouth. The salt stung my tongue. Gagging, I found a Coke in the fridge and downed most of it in one swallow. Funny how my knowledge of the future never seemed to protect me from things like that.

Then I heard my mother upstairs, the creaking of her mattress springs. She couldn't understand why I tried to live a normal life. She thought that in order to truly control her own destiny, she had to remove herself from everything. And I guess it worked, somewhat. It never really mattered what she did in her room; because she always did the same things, like clockwork, it very rarely affected me in such a way that I would cycle. If she did go off script, say, choosing to watch *Die Hard* instead of *Gladiator,* it didn't change her or my future a heck of a lot. But she had learned that even confinement didn't make her immune to pain. If it was up to her, she'd isolate all of us. I could still remember being four years old, and my mom holding me to her chest. Sobbing. Just stay here, Nicholas. Stay with me. It's the only safe place.

She saw that loft bedroom as her sanctuary. I saw it as a coffin.

I'd even told her that, once, a year or two ago. "It just became too much," she'd told me. As if I hadn't seen her and Nan and so many others die over and over again. As if I hadn't lost enough. I didn't care. No way was I becoming a hermit. Not if I could help it.

Just then, Nan turned to me, still bleary-eyed. "Oh, honey bunny. What happened to you?"

"Nan, the weirdest thing happened to me after tryouts," I said, ignoring her question. "My mind . . . stopped. . . ."

"And so why do you look like you just took a beating?"

I'd totally forgotten, but the second she mentioned it my wounds began to sting. "I fell. . . ." I tried to explain, but as I stared at Nan, my mind went into overdrive, forcing the script to the background. It revved for a second, and in that second I stopped talking, the memory popped into my head. A memory of the future.

Of Nan. With that halo of clownish orange hair. Lying in fetal position at the bottom of the loft staircase, surrounded by broken plates and what was likely the remainder of Mom's breakfast.

Her head was perfectly encircled by a large pool of blood.

"Nan!" I shouted instinctively, as if the danger was only seconds away.

She startled and kicked up the recliner. Her eyes ran over my body, probably looking for bleeding wounds.

I slunk backward, feeling guilty. She had diabetes and high cholesterol and all the other things that went along with enjoying food too much; I could have given her a heart attack. And for what reason? The vision could have been of tomorrow, the next day . . . who knew? I knew it would be soon, because in that vision, her hair was still the wrong color, that neon orange she'd accidentally dyed it. But it wasn't going to happen right now. "Uh, nothing. Uh. Have anything for dessert?"

Her eyes narrowed for a second, then softened. She'd long since given up on trying to figure me out. "There's a new half gallon of Turkey Hill ice cream in the freezer."

I opened the freezer door and took the ice cream out.

"That fish was plain awful, wasn't it?" she called into the kitchen. "I don't think I've ever fouled up so bad in all my life."

"It was okay," I muttered, thinking, Just wait. . . .

I trudged upstairs intending to take a shower but stopped as I was gathering my towel and things and threw them against the shower curtain. My toothbrush made a little chip in the ceramic on the tub, almost a perfect square. I sat there for the rest of the night staring at it, resisting the script, which kept telling me to get myself clean. It hurt like hell, but I'd fight everything that was in the script, with every ounce of strength that I had. That useless, piece-of-crap script that was leading Nan to an early death.

Chapter 9

I awoke the next day, knowing I wouldn't follow whatever the script had laid out for me. It had me hanging around the house, moping about Emma and feeling guilty. But that could wait. Now, more than ever, I needed to try to throw the future off course.

The clues from my memory told me that Nan had fallen down the stairs while bringing—or taking away—my mother's breakfast tray. So I decided that I would have to do it. But I met my mom at the top of the stairs. For the first time in I don't know how long, she was out of bed. She was wearing slippers and a flannel robe despite the early-morning temperature being at least eighty.

"I'll eat downstairs," she said, brushing past me.

"Wha?" The shock made me lose my vocal capacity.

"What?" she asked, turning and staring at me like I was the one who'd suddenly decided to make an appearance on the lower level of our house after years of seclusion in my bedroom. "This is my house, too."

Sure it was, but I could count on one hand the number of

times she'd come downstairs in my lifetime. I think the last time, the house was on fire. "You know about Nan," I said as I set the tray down on the kitchen table.

She took a bite of her toast. "Yes."

"If you eat downstairs, that ought to fix it."

She shrugged. "Fix one thing, another breaks. I'm so tired of this."

"I know, but we can't let this go."

She nodded slowly. "So did that change things?"

I tried to think of Nan's death. There she was, lying at the bottom of the stairs. "No."

My mother squeezed her eyes closed. "How could it not? I said I was going to eat all my meals downstairs, so—"

I concentrated on the picture in my mind. Then I noticed that the remains of my mother's meal were no longer surrounding Nan's crumpled, fragile body. So she would still fall, just not carrying the tray. Great. My mother must have noticed that at the same time I began to say, "It doesn't matter. She still—"

"Still what?" Nan appeared in the kitchen. She took one look at the burnt eggs and toast I'd made for my mom and smiled. "To what do we owe the pleasure of you cooking, honey bunny? And why are you downstairs, Moira?"

"How could you tell it was my cooking?" I asked, but I knew the answer the second I asked. I burn everything.

"You burn everything."

It was true. I never cooked because every time I got the urge to, I'd think forward to the vile end result and give up.

Nothing about being able to see my future could stop me from sucking at cooking. Actually, it didn't stop me from sucking at a lot of things.

Mom and I looked at each other. She nodded. She understood the plan.

That was the cool thing about us both being able to see our futures. Sometimes we could have whole conversations without them ever taking place. In my head, I saw Mom pulling me into the living room, telling me, Well, we need to change things up as much as possible. Go off script. And I said to her, I have been, but it's not helping. She said, Well, we just need to change the right thing. It could be something really small. She grabbed her head just then, so I said, But how will you take it? Because I know her headaches are way worse than mine when the cycling starts. At least, her moaning and carrying on is way worse. And she said, I don't know. I have to try.

I nodded back. But the flipping had already started and my head was beginning to ache. This was going to be a long day.

I burst outside into the humid air and gulped it in like a fish. It was already late morning; my lifeguarding job would have had me on the stand at the Seventh Avenue beach for a full hour by now. I didn't miss it. I wasn't cut out for lifeguarding, and at least now, any more Emma Reese incidents wouldn't be my fault.

Holding my head to stop the cycling, the You Wills that were compelling me to turn back and go straight to bed, I headed toward the Heights. I tried to convince myself I was wandering aimlessly once I got up there. But I wasn't. In truth, I was looking for platinum corkscrews. I scanned each car in every driveway for Maine license plates.

Crazy, right? After all, I needed my gift, my power, or whatever you call it, more than ever now. I needed to figure out how to stop Nan's death. I shouldn't have been trying to seek out a girl who, whenever I touched her, made all the visions go away.

But for some reason, I couldn't stop myself. All night long, instead of green-elephanting, I'd thought of her instead. Even the thought of her quieted things. She was my green elephant.

As I rounded the block onto Lafayette Avenue, I stopped.

Almost like an oasis, she was sitting there, on the porch of a little bungalow even smaller than Nan's, staring at her feet as if engaged in some serious thinking. Somewhere between the You Wills sputtering through my mind ran the thought that I should turn around, leave, go anywhere away from her. But I was only half listening to the You Wills. I ran across the street, remembering too late about traffic. A VW Bug screeched to a halt and a brunette in sunglasses gave me a deadly glare, then lay on her horn with a sneer. Taryn looked up, and I realized she wasn't in the midst of contemplating the meaning of life. She had a bottle of red polish next to her and was carefully applying paint to each of her toenails.

The look she gave me wasn't much happier than the VW driver's. I considered backing away, but only for a second.

"Sorry if I offended you."

Guy Law says nice dudes finish last. Girls like guys who

ignore them, who tell them to get the hell away. She clearly didn't want me apologizing. She raised one corner of her upper lip in a part snarl and said, "You didn't," as if I really had but she was so disgusted she didn't want to waste any more of her precious breath.

"Then what's up?" I asked.

Guy Law also says that when a girl's pissed off at you, prying out the "why" is like brain surgery. Again, totally right. She said, "Nothing," and continued to paint her dainty toenails. I moved closer, but she didn't like that. She jumped to her feet and tottered, pale toes raised, up the staircase to her front door. "Look. I'm so sorry. I shouldn't talk to people like you."

She made it sound like I had a disease. "People like me?"

"You know," she whispered. "Touched."

I reeled back, feeling the rejection swell everywhere, from the tips of my toes to my head. Even the new girl, a girl with whom I'd managed to have what I thought was a somewhat normal conversation, thought I was a nut job.

"But get this," I said, trying to keep my voice even, but it was coming out as a defeated mumble. "I have this problem. But all of a sudden, when I touched you, this thing I've had my entire life is . . . just . . . gone."

"I'm sorry, really I am, it must be horrible, but—" She turned to me and drew in a breath, then finally looked me in the eye for the first time today. I expected her to ask a question as to what the problem was, so her next words took me by surprise. "Wait. You've had it your entire life?"

I nodded, then felt the need to explain. "Yeah, you're really not going to believe this, but—" But what? I couldn't tell her. I couldn't tell anyone. I thought of how nine-year-old Sphincter had looked at me when I explained he was going to die. I clamped my mouth shut so fast and hard that I bit my tongue.

"Your entire life?" She murmured it more to the ground than to me. "What are you talking about?"

"It doesn't matter," I said. "It's just—there's something about you that . . ." Okay. Clearly it was impossible to explain why she was different without explaining why *I* was different. And I couldn't do that. I threw my hands down. "Forget it."

She bit her lip. "It doesn't make sense."

"Welcome to my world," I muttered, turning away.

"You're Touched, right?"

I turned back around, narrowing my eyes, frustrated. "Touched?"

Just then, a figure appeared behind the screen door. I could see dark, cavernous eyes, like the empty sockets of a skull, and a pyramid of silvery black hair. In the shadows of the porch's overhang, her skin shone a cold, metallic bronze. She had on a flowered blouse, but they were not cheerful flowers. They looked brown and dead. Actually, her entire presence had an air of death to it, especially those eyes and that mouth, which bore no expression. Her mouth was just a lifeless gash in her brown face. This was the grandmother Taryn had mentioned yesterday on the beach. The "whacked" one. Instinctively, I took a step back.

Her voice was deeply accented; Italian, maybe. "Who is this?" she asked, her eyes never leaving mine.

Taryn turned toward the woman and whispered tensely, "He's one of them." She said the last word as if there was a war going on, and I was on the other side. Then she shrugged. "I think."

Grandma opened the screen door, came outside. Her eyes were so fastened on mine, I had to look away. I saw then that her ankles and wrists were just as thick as the rest of her body, like tree trunks. And that in one of her meaty hands, she was holding a . . . freaking butcher's knife.

Another step back. Suddenly I was shivering, despite the near-ninety-degree heat.

Her eyes narrowed to slits. "What's that you say, *sevgili?*" she snapped.

I wasn't sure who she was addressing, but I wasn't capable of speech at that point, either way. Taryn finally answered, "You're right. I felt it, just like you said. I saw what he has."

Her grandmother's eyes narrowed even further. "Impossible! Not this one."

Taryn looked confused. "But I saw it. I—"

"No," the woman growled. I could see why Taryn didn't get along with her. She was about as much fun as the flu. This woman had a freaking knife and was waving it over Taryn's head as if getting ready to slice a Thanksgiving turkey. If that wasn't God telling me to just play the hand I'd been dealt and go away, I didn't know what was.

"But he—" Taryn protested.

"I've never seen this boy before in my life!" Old scary woman was getting vicious. This was not good.

The You Wills had me turning around and running in the other direction, and I knew I was supposed to go off script, but this time, I couldn't agree with them more. "Sorry," I said, holding out my hands. "Sorry. I mean, I still don't know what the hell you guys are talking about. But I'm just going to go. Now."

Taryn's expression was guarded, remorseful. Remorseful for what? Meeting me? Having to send me away? I couldn't tell. As I mentioned, I sucked at reading girls. But I didn't have any problem reading her grandmother. She waved the knife some more and spat out: "You never come back, you hear me? Never!"

Oh, don't worry about that, crazy lady.

By the time I made it back to Seventh Avenue, my brain was revving like a sports car. But that was good. The more I cycled, the better the chance I'd change Nan's death back to that peaceful one I'd envisioned once before. And I would just have to forget about that brief moment with Taryn. That moment when for once in my pathetic life, I was just like everybody else.

Chapter 10

When I returned from getting reamed out by Old Scary Lady, I thought I'd just go and hang out at the Tenth Avenue beach, away from the Seventh Avenue regulars who would undoubtedly stare me up and down after what happened yesterday. Work on evening out my tan, since the lifeguard uniform's tank top had left me a lot paler on my chest and stomach. Sort out some of those messed-up visions I'd been having. Try to find what would prompt Nan to fall and somehow remove the problem.

Instead, the cycling just made for the kind of headache a cartload of Excedrin couldn't fix. That was the problem with going off script: once I went off, a thousand jumbled next-steps in my life began to compete for attention. I tried to concentrate on the waves, the sand, the sea, which had always calmed me before. Now, every crashing wave whispered Emma's name, and when seagulls cried overhead, it sounded like they were proclaiming my guilt. I couldn't focus for a second on the mystery surrounding Nan's death. The only sane thought I could make out was a picture of Taryn. Touched, she'd called me. What was that supposed to mean?

You will be annoyed by the greenhead flies. You will stand up,
fold up your towel, and put on your T-shirt.

It was a west wind, too, so the greenhead flies were biting. West winds sucked; they meant cold water and flies so vicious and determined, most tourists ran away crying. But I was a local. I could handle it. *Rrrrrvvvvv*, went the gears in my mind. Meanwhile, an insect feasted on my skin and drew blood on my forearm. Pressing one finger into my temple, I swatted the fly away with my other hand. The nasty thing came back to my foot. Once a fly found its target, the only thing that could tear it away was death. I swatted it again, watching an old lady down the hill applying Skin So Soft, and remembering how Nan used to slather me in that stuff when I was a kid. It smelled like old lady, but it kept the flies away. When the persistent little bugger landed on my knee, I smacked it, and its crushed body tumbled to the sand. The victory was short-lived; when I flicked its little corpse away, two more flies appeared in its place.

You will start getting bored, so you will stand up, fold up
your towel, and put on your T-shirt.

Actually, I told myself, I'm not really that bored. I could hang a few more minutes. I need to think.

Rrrrrvvvvv, went my mind.

You will be annoyed by the children playing tag nearby, kick-
ing sand on your legs. You will stand up, fold up your towel,
and put on your T-shirt.

No, I can handle those kids. I'll just hang out here a little while longer . . . and think. . . .

Rrrrrvvvvv...

You will think about standing up and leaving but you will not. A Frisbee will hit you in the head.

What? I scrambled to my feet and tried to get over the cycling that had my mind whirring and my head pounding. More nonsensical images flashed through my brain, which might or might not have become part of my future: pine needles, goopy black tar, a pink smiley face, brown craft paper.

Then, clunk. The Frisbee bounced off my shins. I screamed, unfortunately like a girl, in front of two hot chicks in bikinis. They laughed at me mildly, like I was a bad entertainer planted there for their amusement, and rolled over onto their stomachs.

That was it. Thinking was barely possible on script. How could I expect to analyze the situation with all those possible options whirring in my head like chain saws? Yes, there were bad things in my future, things I somehow couldn't change or prevent, but maybe I just wasn't meant to. After all, that was what the future was like for most people.

But Nan...

Finally I trudged through the sand toward the street, noticing the girl in the yellow bathing suit with the pink smiley face on her round tummy. She was probably Emma's age.

Crap. Step one: I needed to get away from the beach. From everything that reminded me of that little girl.

Nan used to have a boyfriend who would take me fishing off the pier at Fifth Avenue. That would always calm my mind, kind of like the ocean once had. I needed calm. I didn't want to go home and listen to my mom's moans of pain from the cycling. My head ached like there were a thousand needles in my scalp, and I knew she was feeling just as bad. Probably worse.

Almost without thinking about it, I found myself at the bait shop, getting minnows. I must have stopped by the garage to pick up the net, bucket, and poles, but I couldn't remember doing it. I held them in my hands, so tight I knew I'd probably get blisters, and they smelled like brine and old seaweed. The guy at the register gave me a careful smile as he handed over the roll of bait wrapped in brown craft paper: a smile because he'd known Nan for fifty years; careful because every local on the island had heard the Crazy Cross stories.

I was so deep in the thought that I didn't realize how quiet my mind had become until I heard a sweet voice whisper, "What did you get?"

I turned and saw Taryn. Not two hours after her grandmother gave me the tongue-lashing of my life, not two hours after I promised myself I'd never see her again. She was smiling as if that conversation never happened, as if she hadn't called me one of the despicable "them."

I should have been able to say something tough, something to show her that she'd made a huge mistake telling me to leave her alone. Instead, all I could mutter was "Huh?"

She pointed at the board over the counter. "I was going to get a number eleven. The Italian. But number six looks good. And then there's number twenty."

I looked up at the board above the head of the guy at the register. It might as well have been in Chinese. I never bought subs here. "Uh—"

"You're the local." She pointed at the paper-wrapped roll in my hands. "So I'll let you make the decision for me." She turned to the guy behind the counter. "Give me whatever you got him."

I grinned slowly. Revenge.

At the guy's confused look, I said, "You heard her."

He got busy packaging up her "sandwich," as Taryn gave me a shy glance that made me a little remorseful for what I was doing. Just a little. I'd shaken it off, when suddenly my nose began to sting. Out of nowhere, I thought of pine trees.

She asked, "What's in it?"

I pressed my lips together. "It's a surprise."

"No anchovies, I hope."

I shook my head.

She quickly peered over the counter at the worker. "Oh, and make mine without onions."

He looked at me, even more confused.

I shook my head at him. "Doesn't come with onions."

"Oh, good." She looked down at her toes, the nails of which were now painted bloodred, a striking contrast against the paleness of her skin. I had the momentary vision of those pale toes against a backdrop of black-green water. "I'm allergic."

"Um," I began, focusing on a rack of chips and pretzels behind her head, a display of car air fresheners shaped like pine trees dangling near the register, not sure where I was headed. "Fancy meeting you here."

The shy look returned. "I heard this place had the best subs in town."

I shrugged. As if I had any idea.

"Really," she said, as if she had just been caught in a lie. Then she smiled. "Actually, no, I followed you in here."

Too good to lie. God, I was liking her more and more. And she was not what I needed right now. What I needed was to find out what was going to happen to Nan, and try my best to prevent it. Alarms were blaring in my head, but instead of helping me, they were crowding out the You Wills, allowing my hormones to take control. All I could do was raise my eyebrows and savor this new thrill surging through me. It was the first time a girl was admitting to following me instead of running in the other direction.

"I wanted to apologize," she began.

"Order up," the man behind the counter said. He pushed the package over to her.

I took it before she could put her hand on it. "Allow me," I said.

She grinned. "Seriously? Thanks."

It was the least I could do. "It's nothing."

As I paid for the two packages, she inspected the net, poles, and bucket at my feet. When I collected my change, she said, "Look, do you have time?"

I stared at her. Time? Did she want the time? I pointed to a clock on the wall.

She shook her head. "No, do you have time for a talk? I want to explain things."

"Things? You mean the"—I stretched out my hands and wiggled my fingers—"touch?"

She nodded.

"Fine," I said, but then I realized that if I had to be present when she opened that wrapped package, it wouldn't be pretty. Didn't need a vision of the future to know that. She might sic her scary grandmother on me. "After lunch? I'll be at the pier."

"Great," she said, chewing on her lip. "Again, I'm sorry for acting a little crazy, but you don't know . . . well, I'll explain it. After lunch."

She started to shuffle down the stony path in her flip-flops, cradling the fish in the crook of her arm, and then turned. "You really have no idea why you're the way you are," she mused. "That's fascinating."

"What way am I?" I asked, amused by her attempt to understand me. Most people wouldn't bother. There were so many easy ways to fill in that blank. Neurotic. Looney. Obsessed. Pathetic.

She narrowed her eyes. "Duh. Able to see your future."

Chapter 11

I was too stunned to follow her. I just stood there, surrounded by my fishing gear, mouth hanging open.

I spent the rest of the time walking back and forth on the boardwalk, feeling like crap. This was useless. First of all, when I got out there, I realized the reason my nose had begun to sting in the sub shop. It would be fried by the time I got home, but I didn't have enough money with me to buy sunblock. And every time I set out to cast a line, I saw the outcome of my expedition. No fish. It wasn't that they weren't biting. It was that my hands would be shaking too much to steadily reel in the line.

And Taryn somehow knew I could see the future.

All my life, I'd been hiding it from people, doing whatever I could to throw them off. I'd always wanted to have someone understand what was going on with me, but I knew that if I told, they'd never believe it. Or if I showed them what I could do, they'd be so freaked they'd run far away or summon men in white coats to take me to a laboratory for a lifetime of painful tests. But she believed it. She sought me out. And not only that, she acted like it made total sense.

Of course I always wondered why my mom and I were like this. There are pictures in the house of my mom when she was in high school. She was a cheerleader and on the debate team, and you could just tell that back then she was normal. She didn't have the dark circles. She didn't have the worry creases on her forehead. Nan said she "got it" around the same time I was born, whatever "it" was. I assumed it was me. Something about being pregnant with me. My mother would always say it had something to do with my dad, but she'd shut up whenever I tried to pry more out of her. I didn't know who he was, but maybe he had something in his blood. Maybe he poisoned us.

But that was a long time ago. I'd never met my dad, never wanted to. And yeah, there was always something tugging at me, some hole begging to be filled. But he clearly couldn't fill it. By the time I realized that he existed I was old enough to know that if he didn't want to be in the picture, I didn't want him there. I figured he probably saw me like everyone saw me. A freak.

That was my own father. So how could this girl I barely knew not see me that way?

"What is it like?" a voice said gently as I sat there, legs dangling over the side of the pier, staring at the ripples in the brown bay.

I knew she would be coming back, even after she found the fish in her "lunch." I knew she would sit down next to me and her red toenails would glisten in the sun, against the backdrop of dark water. I knew her hair would smell like apples. "How was lunch?"

She wrinkled her nose. God, she was cute. "Great. Thanks."

I didn't apologize. The last time I did that, she told me to go away. I just sat there, feeling my nose baking and wondering if it was already stoplight-red. "Are you going to tell me how you knew?"

"Don't you already know that? I mean, if you can see—"

I snorted. "You'd think."

"So, like, do you know what's going to happen right now?"

I shook my head. "No. Well, yeah. I knew you were going to ask that. But the further you go into the future, the more fuzzy things get. Because little things in the future change— you know, the butterfly effect. So I can see pieces of every- thing that could have happened, all the outcomes based on where I am at a certain moment. And at first, they all fight against each other, so I can't tell which is real and which isn't. After I stay on script for a while, it becomes clearer. I can figure out what's real and what's not. But it's really hard to stay on script."

She gasped. "On script? How do you—"

"You can remember best the things you just did, right? I can remember best things that are right about to happen. They're more real to me. I call it my script. My You Wills. You know, you will start running. You will fall and smack your face against the pavement. . . ."

"Script? So wait. You actually see the phrase 'You Will' in your head, like in a real script?"

I shake my head. "No, I see myself doing those things in my head. If I stay on that script, my mind doesn't get clogged up with lots of possibilities. It just stays on one future. But if I go off script, even a little—"

"So that day when we met, you were—"

"According to the script, I was supposed to save that girl. Emma. I saw myself saving her. Instead I met you. And my mind went haywire with all the new outcomes."

She stared at me, uncomprehending at first. I saw the moment it made sense to her, because her breath hitched. "Oh, my God. Really?"

"Yeah. And now something's going to happen, and I have to fix . . . Oh, forget it." I'd never explained this to anyone, and it felt so foreign coming out of my mouth. Unbelievable, even to me. "Did you make the team?" I asked, trying to change the subject.

She nodded. "You?"

"Nah. Probably better if I'm not on it. I'd know when we were going to lose and just drag down team morale." I meant it as a joke, but it came out bitter and sad.

She stared into the water for a minute. "Well, why did you even bother trying out? You must have known you were not going to make the team, right?"

I shook my head. "You would think. But it's like this: think of the last movie you saw."

"Okay."

"Are you thinking of it?"

"Yeah."

She said it so quickly and dismissively I thought there was no way she could be thinking of it. Without even realizing I was doing it, I said, "Wow, *The Little Mermaid*? Seriously?"

Her eyes grew wide for a second, then she glared at me. "I babysit a lot. How did you know that?"

"I can do it sometimes. If I have something concrete to focus on, I can just go forward into our future to where I find out what I need to know."

Her jaw dropped. "You can do that?"

"Yeah. Sometimes. I mean, I can't go too far into the future. A couple of minutes at most. Anyway, back to *The Little Mermaid*. Do you remember all the lines, everything that happened?"

"Yes." When I raised my eyebrows, she smiled. "Like I said, I babysit a lot. I've seen the movie four hundred times." Then she began to sing, "'Look at this stuff, isn't it neat. Wouldn't you think my collection's—'"

"All right. But with movies you're not secretly obsessed with—"

"I'm not obsessed!" There was a small smile playing on her lips as she punched my arm. "Right. I only remember the really big things that happen."

"Right. Or the dialogue or action or whatever that really hit home or meant something to you. Or just random things, pieces of the whole. But if you hadn't seen the entire movie, and you just saw that random thing out of context, you'd be a little confused, right? That's what I see. So no, I had a strong feeling, but I didn't know for sure I wasn't going to make the team. I guess it didn't matter to me so much. I remember the things that matter more."

She nodded. "Oh."

I took a breath and suddenly I saw red velvet, like from a tent. A gypsy tent, like the ones on the boardwalk in the Heights. Taryn was standing there, beckoning me into the tent. Then, Old Scary Lady at a table, surrounded by red velvet. "Your grandmother is a fortune-teller on the boardwalk? Seriously?"

She gave me a severe look, like it was nothing to laugh about, and it was only then I realized I was kind of laughing. Because the fortune-tellers on the boardwalk were all old crackpots who were so senile they didn't remember their own names. Only idiot tourists went to them. Of course Old Scary Lady was a fortune-teller. It totally fit.

"Well, why not"? Taryn said. "Hey, you shouldn't knock it. She makes a good living. You could probably make a killing doing it."

I shook my head. "I can only see my own future. And I don't even see that very well. Like I said."

"Oh." She bit her lip, another one of the cutest little mannerisms I'd ever seen on a girl. "She's not a fortune-teller, anyway. She's a bibliomancer."

"A what?"

"She can tell a person's future by passages in certain books."

"Passages in books? Sounds shady."

"It's an ancient practice," Taryn said. "Dates back to medieval times, or so my grandmother says."

I raised my eyebrows. "So, like, what does she do? Open up a book and just tell a person's future from it? How does that work?"

"Well, it's a little more scientific than that. Most bibliomancers use the Bible, but my grandmother has people bring in their own books. Whatever book they like best."

I laughed. "I'm partial to Dr. Seuss. Can she do it with *Green Eggs and Ham*?"

It was like I was floating above my body, unable to stop myself. I didn't even have to touch her to be at ease; just being near her made my mind calmer. Yeah, the script was still there, but muted, not so insistent. I was in danger of getting entirely too comfortable with her. Never had the one-liners come so easily to me, never had I felt so witty. Somehow, I was getting cocky again. She had that effect on me, I guess. But bad things had a way of happening whenever I got cocky. The script suggested politely to me to be quiet, and I agreed, stifling the laughter remaining in my throat.

She gave me a look that said she wasn't happy with me taking it so lightly. Like she actually believed in that kind of crap. Then she picked through her beach bag. "Look, I'll show you how it's done. Pick a number between, say, um, one and fifty."

"Look, I really don't need any more help seeing my future, thanks."

"It's just a demonstration," she said, producing a worn paperback.

I couldn't see the title, but I could see a man and woman locked in an embrace, bare skin everywhere, on the cover. "Wait, you're going to tell my future using"—I reached for the book and stared at its cover—"*Sins of Tomorrow* by Rebecca Stanhope? Epic."

She turned a flattering shade of red. "I said, it's just a demonstration. And it's a very good book, despite the cheesy cover. Don't make fun until you've read it."

"Okay. Can I borrow it from you?" I said, studying the back cover. Something about a young woman who loses the love of her life in the war and then, after marrying another dude, discovers her first love is alive! He has amnesia and has no idea who she is, but "can her undying love rekindle the flame of their passion?" That's what it said on the back cover. Definitely epic.

"When I'm done." She stood and said, more insistent this time, "Pick a number."

"Okay. Twelve."

She closed her eyes and threw the book into the air. It landed on the boards on its back cover. "Wait." She ran to it, picked it up, and did it again, with the same result. Then she did it again. It landed on its front cover this time. She sighed. "It's easier with a hardcover. It's supposed to land on an open page. Oh, well, let's just pretend it landed on page . . . um . . ."

"Two-ninety-three?" I offered.

"Yes. Great." She flipped the book open. "And starting with line twelve, it says, '"Oh, Holden," she murmured, as her kisses trailed down to . . .'" Taryn stopped and looked up, her face redder than ever.

"So what does that mean?" I asked, trying to keep a straight face. "Am I going to get it on with some guy named Holden?"

She stomped her feet on the boardwalk, but because she was so tiny and wearing rubber-soled flip-flops, it didn't have any effect. "It. Is. Just. A. Demonstration!" She threw the book down again and this time it skittered toward the edge of the pier. I lunged to the side as it was happening and it landed in my waiting hands. "Saw that, did you?" she began, astonished by my foresight, and for a second, I felt proud of myself. Maybe even a little cocky. But it only lasted a second. The next thing I knew, I saw what was going to happen, clear as day.

You will lose your balance and fall backward into the water.

Damn. I couldn't steady myself in time. I tried to save her book as I splashed into the bay, but it was no good. The water was over my head.

The water was slimy and gross, and fingers of seaweed entwined themselves around my toes. I surfaced, hair over my eyes, spitting out a mouthful of salty green water, then stroked as quickly as I could toward the rickety wooden ladder. Crabs that had been feasting on my bait were probably now looking at my ankles. "Are you okay?" I heard Taryn ask. When I wiped the veil of hair away, she was bending over the side of the pier, looking worried, either for my safety or for her reputation, being seen with such a spaz.

Did I say I felt cocky? Suddenly I felt like a spider must, trying to scurry up the side of the toilet bowl before it's finally flushed.

When I climbed up, she laughed. "So, you *didn't* see that one coming?"

"Um, sort of," I said, water dripping off the end of my nose. "Too late, though."

"Anyway, that passage might mean you're going to have

a whirlwind romance. Or something," she said, blushing, as she waved the book in the air to dry it. The damage had been done, though. The pages were already starting to ripple. "Thanks for rescuing my book."

"No problem," I said, thinking how ironic it was. I might not be any good at saving toddlers, but dime-store paperbacks, I could handle. As I looked at the cover, with those two entwined semi-naked bodies, I was hit with a feeling that nearly knocked me back into the bay.

Her favorite color is red. She likes to make construction paper snowflakes. She lost her favorite aunt in a car accident. Her first pet, a goldfish, was named Harry. She has a bright-red birthmark on her upper thigh. The list went on and on. I'd known there was something about her, something that crushed my chest every time she turned to walk away, and here it was. I knew her well. Better than Sue, my former wife. Better than anyone. The weight of all that knowledge that a day ago hadn't been there pushed me down to the rotten planks. She looked at me, lying on the boards like a dead fish, and I opened my mouth to speak, but I couldn't find the words. What could I say? Nice birthmark? The script had me fumbling around, tripping over my words again. And if I went off script, if I messed anything up, she could just become a stranger to me again.

But I had to go off script, as much as possible. I had to save Nan.

So we sat there for a moment, not saying much, while my mind was working overtime. Follow the script? Veer off a little and hope she still liked me? It wasn't hard to follow the script; it just had me sitting there, next to her, quiet, afraid to say anything and mess things up. When I was almost dry, the script had me packing up to go home. I started to pull in my lines.

"Why don't you just come with me?" she said, tugging on the sleeve of my T-shirt. "I want to show you something."

There probably was nothing I wanted more than to follow her. But the thought of my grandmother kept intruding. That and the nagging suspicion that this undeniably cute girl couldn't be so into me after all the stupid things she'd seen me do. There had to be something behind it. Maybe I'd wanted to know her so badly that I just made it all up in my head.

That was it. She was the one talking about how people always wanted things from her. Maybe she was thinking she could use me. Maybe she thought I could provide her with the winning Pick-6 numbers or tell her who was going to ask her to the homecoming dance. "Why?" I asked.

She shrugged. "Because. I might be able to help you."

"You? Help me? Don't you mean the other way around?"

"No. I mean, you can't help me. No one can—"

"And the idea of picking winning lottery numbers never entered your mind?" I asked, crossing my arms.

She swallowed, looked away. She could have said something. She could have denied it. Instead, she said nothing. Her silence told me everything. The sun was so hot I was already almost dry, but because of the salt, my skin felt tight and itchy. Of course she wouldn't be interested in me. How could I even think that? Stupid, stupid, stupid.

Something stuck in my throat, making my words come out clipped and distorted. "Your grandmother used her"—I wiggled my fingers again—"powers to learn that I can see my future. Great. The secret's out. I can fulfill my lifelong dream of appearing on national television as America's Biggest Freak."

She stared at me, confused.

"Don't you get it? I can't help you become a millionaire. And I can't help you find true love or whatever. It doesn't work that way. It sucks." My muscles were so tense and my body so hot that I had the momentary compulsion to bolt out of there, leaving her, the fishing equipment, everything far behind. But then I took a breath, counted to ten. Exhaled. Felt better. My voice was calmer when I spoke next. "Look. I'd rather people not know. I just want to be normal."

The confusion wasn't leaving her face. And that's when she said it. Well, she didn't say it, because she didn't have to. I heard her next words, clear as day in my head, before she even thought them. My grandmother did this. They were crazy. Absolutely insane. I interrupted her as she opened her mouth to speak. "That's not possible."

She stopped, her jaw slowly falling.

"How can your grandmother have anything to do with this?" I muttered, getting more and more disgusted by the minute. What the hell did she think this was? Some nifty little parlor trick? Our seeing the future was more than a living nightmare. It was constant, unstoppable, and wholly devastating. Something so terrible could only be explained as an act of God. It couldn't be something that one being, one human created. That would make it seem so trivial, so silly, so small. And it was big. Big enough to ruin my life a thousand times over.

Taryn swallowed. She didn't have to say it, but I let her words come out anyway, because maybe if they were outside of my head, that would make them more believable. And so she said it, exactly as I had imagined. But when the words were out there, hanging in the humid summer air, it didn't help.

"Say that again," I murmured.

Her face was serious. There was a hint of remorse in her eyes. "Nick. It's true. My grandmother made you this way."

Chapter 12

I needed to get away from Taryn. Taryn, who was just as crazy as her grandmother, her all-powerful grandmother who somehow made me this way. Yeah, right. Once I scurried across Bayview Avenue and past Charlie's ice cream shop, the cycling became a little steadier and I could make out some of the visions passing through my head. I could see my grandmother lying in that now familiar position at the bottom of the stairs, almost as if it had just happened. Somewhat more faded was the image of sunlight glimmering on the deep mahogany cover of a closed casket.

The sun was still hot enough to roast my shoulders and create a haze on the streets as I climbed the decaying concrete steps at the front of the house, flung open the screen door, and let it slam behind me. My mom had retreated to her bedroom, of course. I didn't think she could stand being outside her tomb for longer than a few minutes. I climbed the stairs two at a time and they creaked as if the house was going to fall down. When I burst into her room, I realized I was sweating, out of breath, and still holding my fishing gear.

Salt water sloshed from the bucket onto my feet and the hardwood floor. I knew Nan would scream bloody murder if she saw.

My mom looked up from the latest issue of *People*. I didn't know how she could read that trash, but she had piles of celebrity tabloids in her room, littering the chairs, floor, and the tops of the dresser and night table. Who seriously cared what celebrities did in their effed-up lives? Most of them had everything going for them and still couldn't manage to hold it together. But hey, I guess anything that worked to keep her mind off the future. She stared me up and down. "You got sunburned."

I looked cross-eyed and saw that my nose was the exact color I'd seen in my vision. I wiggled it a little and it stung. Perfect. "Mom. Why is some fortune-teller on the boardwalk claiming that she's responsible for making us the way we are?"

Her eyes went back to her magazine. "No idea," she murmured.

I used my index finger to push the magazine down to her knees so that she'd look at me. "This girl knows I can see the future. I never told her. She just knew."

"Is that so?" she asked, clucking her tongue. She shrugged and went into the same speech she used to give me when I was a kid and wanted to show off my abilities at show-and-tell. "Don't be ridiculous. I would stay away from her. You know what could happen if you say too much. If you trust too much."

"But she knows. I didn't have to say a word. She just knows."

"Oh, Nick. She doesn't know. She *suspects*. That's dangerous. The curious ones are always dangerous. Maybe she's just perceptive. Some people are. Bill Runyon was. I still think that he might know. But they don't have any way of proving it. And it's not like this is of any use to anyone. If you keep your distance, she'll leave us alone. We don't want people coming around, asking questions. Believe me."

"I got the feeling that she really understood it, though," I said, sitting on the edge of bed. "And Mom, if she knew what started it, she might be able to tell us how to stop it."

She shook her head. "That isn't possible."

"How do you know?"

"Don't you think I already tried everything possible?"

Actually, I didn't think that at all. From my earliest memory, she'd been confined to this bed, hopeless. She'd never once talked to me about finding a way to stop the visions. "Did you?"

She sighed. "Do you really think I wanted you growing up like this? I did everything I could before you were born. And then I just prayed that it wouldn't be passed on to you. But of course, I knew it would be. When I was pregnant with you, I went to fortune-tellers and gypsies and all those charlatans, hoping one of them could help me reverse the curse. But none of them could."

"Curse?" I stared hard at her. It was the first time I'd ever heard it referred to as a curse. Usually it was just "the thing." The thing I got, somehow, when she was pregnant with me. "But why did you say that Dad—"

She looked away. "We've been over this before. I don't know what it is. I did a lot of stupid things, though, before I knew I was going to have you. One of those things was being involved with your father. You know it started around the same time I met him. Maybe . . . I don't know. But I do know that there's a good side to it, too."

"Good?" She always insisted this, and yeah, she was right. Sometimes, every once in a while, we could juggle our futures and prevent bad things from happening. But ninety-nine percent of it sucked. That cool one percent never seemed worth it.

"Look, I'm tired. Can you please—"

"But what could Dad have done? And why does this girl know about it? What if she knows how to fix—"

"She doesn't." My mother cut me off, fuming. She leaned back in her bed. "And I said I'm tired."

That was one problem with us communicating. We could have whole conversations without them ever taking place, but so many topics were completely closed to discussion. My dad was one of them. Nan was better about it, but every time I asked her how Mom and I ended up this way, I got the same story. My mom was normal until she was my age. She was pregnant and planning to marry my dad that summer. And then, something changed. Something intervened. This illness, this curse, whatever it was. It tore everything apart. By the end of the summer, my dad was gone and my mother, six months pregnant with me, had locked herself in her bedroom.

Nan opened the door to Mom's bedroom then. Her eyes

focused on the net and dripping bucket before anything else. She gasped at the water puddling on the hardwood. "This is not a bait shop!" she said to me, disappointed, and suddenly I had that feeling. The prickling feeling on the back of my neck, whenever something big was about to happen. I whirled around and Mom must have felt it, too, because her eyes were wider than silver dollars and her face paler than its normal pale.

My grandmother stepped toward the staircase, muttering something about how I needed to be more responsible and how she was always cleaning up after me like I was some three-year-old, and the entire scene flashed before my eyes.

You will hear her muffled groans as she slips on a puddle of salt water and falls down the stairwell. You will rush to the top of the stairs and slip once yourself on the water you spilled. She will be dead before you get there. You will see the pool of blood already—

I'm not sure how I ended up at the top of the stairs. I slipped twice on the salt water and kicked up the worn braided throw rug on my way, but before I could take even one breath I was beside Nan. She'd just begun to lose her balance on the top step and I saw her bare feet slipping out from under her. She turned her head toward me with a frightened look in her eyes, her mouth shaped as if letting out a silent scream, at the same time I moved toward her. I reached out and grabbed her by the upper arm, using, in my overexcitement, far too much force than common sense would dictate I should use with her. When I pulled her up toward my chest, toward safety, there was a sickening popping sound.

But she was safe. I hoisted her in my arms to the other side of the banister and set her down on steady ground, while she let out a little terrified squeak. "My arm," she said.

It hung down at her side, limp. She tried to lift it but winced. The cycling began at once in a torrent, a hailstorm thudding against my eye sockets, but I knew for sure that her arm was broken. Despite the pain in my head, I sighed with relief. The alternative was a lot worse.

My mother stood in the doorway to her room, clutching the side of her head with one of her hands and wincing a little despite a small, contradictory smile on her face. "See?" she said to me. "The good side."

Chapter 13

If I really wanted to give myself a headache, I can think back to what exactly it was that put Nan's life in danger. I wouldn't have dripped water up the stairs, making them slick, if I hadn't been so rattled by my talk with Taryn. I wouldn't have gotten rattled by talking to Taryn if I hadn't met her on the boardwalk the day I was supposed to save Emma. I wouldn't have gone fishing if I hadn't lost my job and had nothing better to do. I wouldn't have lost my job if it hadn't been for Taryn.

Taryn, with her innocent angel face, had already wrought havoc on my life. That was enough of a reason to forget about her.

Instead, though my mind was again screaming with visions being threaded out and replaced, the one thing it kept hitching on was her. Nan was safe now. Taryn had the power to make me feel normal somehow. Being with her felt right. And she was the only person in the world who knew what I had. So what if she'd somehow deluded herself into believing her grandmother caused it?

Maybe her grandmother *had* caused it. Maybe Taryn was telling the truth. Why would she lie about that? What else did she know?

I sat in the hospital room with Nan while her cast set, itching to get out of there and find some answers. The vision of her at the bottom of the steps was nothing more than an image from a vivid nightmare. It was realer than if I'd just imagined it, but now when I thought of her death, I saw her back in the old recliner, dozing peacefully into oblivion. The thought was a pile of bricks off my chest, yeah, but my hands shook and my mouth tasted sour, thinking of what new bricks would be laid down, one by one, as the images settled. Right now, all I could see was this: red velvet, LUVR, powdered sugar. I heard a tick-tick-ticking-ticking sound.

I really hoped my new future didn't suck.

Nan sat on the hospital bed, looking so fragile and small in the fluorescent light. Her bones were delicate twigs, so it was no surprise I'd broken her arm in two places. She needed one of those giant casts that covered everything from wrist to underarm. It looked mega-uncomfortable. "Don't worry yourself, honey bunny," she said to me. "If you can just help me pick tomatoes when we get home? That was what I was heading out to do when . . ."

"Oh. Yeah. No problem."

She put her hand on mine and patted it. I was supposed to be there to soothe her, but as always, she was the one doing the soothing.

"Nan, it was—you were going to—" I started to explain, but

she raised a finger to shut me up. She'd come to accept our weirdness without question.

"I understand," she said. "No explanation needed."

The cycling still whirred through my brain a mile a minute, making all the outcomes impossible to see. I guess it was pretty obvious to Nan that something big was up, considering I was resting my head in my hands, massaging it to lessen the pain. I would bet a thousand dollars that back home, my mom was doing the exact same thing.

"Why does Mom never want to talk about Dad?" I asked.

"Too painful for her," she said, sticking out her foot to rein in her massive leather purse on the floor. Her first attempt to hook it failed, so I grabbed it for her. She reached inside and pulled out a few hard candies in yellow wrappers. They were covered in specks of dust like they had been there a while. From the time I was a kid, she had a never-ending supply of those candies on hand. I think I sucked on them continuously from when I was in preschool until I learned they would put me in dentures by age fifty. I stopped eating them, then. Seemed like every pleasure in my life got sucked away by this "curse." "I need a butterscotch," Nan said. "Want one?"

"No. You didn't know him?" I asked, already knowing the answer. I'd asked her before. When she murmured yes, I said, "I thought he was the reason we're like this. That's what she told me whenever I asked. I would say, 'Mom, why can we see the future?', and she would say, 'Maybe it has something to do with your father.' But she wouldn't say anything else, so I didn't know what to think. I thought that his blood poisoned us or something. And so I'd ask you, and you would tell me that my father was a good man in a bad situation. She wanted me to hate him so I would accept he was the reason for this and wouldn't ask any questions. But you didn't think that was fair, right?"

She removed her bifocals and massaged her eyes. Without her glasses, she looked like a completely different person. "Wow. You've certainly been thinking a lot about this, Nick."

It wasn't a direct answer, but I could tell she agreed with my assessment. "Today, someone told me something. . . ."

She stared at me. "Told you what?"

"I was told this fortune-teller on the boardwalk made us this way. Is that true?"

She looked at me for a long moment. Finally she pressed her lips together. "Could you scratch my left shoulder blade? I have an awful itch there."

I stood up, reached behind the pillow she was propped against, and scratched her back. The line of her shoulder blade was so sharp it could cut through her T-shirt.

"The weirdest thing happened when I shook her hand, though. Just being near her, I feel calmer," I said. "But when I touched her hand, I could think clearly. I couldn't see the future. I felt—I think I felt what normal was like."

"Whose hand? The fortune-teller?"

"No. This girl. Her granddaughter. So it made me think that this fortune-teller knows something." I rubbed my eyes. They felt sore. "Also. It's crazy, but I think I'm in love with her."

"Who? The fortune-teller?"

I sighed. "The girl, Nan. The girl. My whole future is tied to hers now, I think. I feel like I know her. Like, really well. I know her favorite color. I know about the birthmark on her—" I stopped. Too much information. Nan just smiled at me as if she understood the whole thing. "But ever since I met her, things have started to turn bad."

Nan cocked her head. "Bad?"

"I can't explain it, but the future is changed. Monumentally. It started with meeting that girl. It led to you falling down the stairs, but I get the feeling there's more. Mom and I haven't made it out yet, but something is just wrong. The girl is going to hurt me. Maybe she's like a drug. Bad for me, but I'm already addicted. Probably because I think she has the answers to why I'm like this, or because she's beautiful, or because I'm stupid and I like asking for trouble."

Nan shrugged. "Maybe a little of all those things. But how do you know that she's responsible for all that?"

"I don't, but I also don't know if a butterfly flapping its wings in Brazil can set off a tornado in Texas," I muttered, then threw up my hands. "She may be indirectly responsible, but I don't know anything for sure. As usual."

"Look, honey, I don't know what's true anymore. Your mother used to be a very free spirit. Funny to think that when she was your age, I had trouble keeping her home at night. The day she graduated from high school was the day she told me she was pregnant with you. She was so happy. She had such plans. She was going to marry your father and move inland and start a curio shop. And then, one day, in the summer, I remember it so clearly . . . you know all this, though."

I nodded. "This thing couldn't have just happened to us, though, right? There's got to be a reason."

She nodded sadly. "I wish I knew, honey bunny."

I thought about it some more as my mind slowed to a dull thrumming. Some things did just happen. People developed weird diseases. Bridges crumbled. The good died young. Crap like that. And nothing, nobody caused it. All my life, I'd never dug too deep because I thought our curse was likely one of those things. And maybe it was.

But if there was a reason for it, I had to find out.

And I had a good idea where to start.

Chapter 14

I'd wanted to seek Taryn out the minute I got home, but by the time Nan's cast was set and we found someone willing to drive us back to Seaside, it was after ten. We didn't have any money for a cab, so one of the orderlies who had just gotten off work offered to drive us. The guy had a shifty look to him, like a snake, and a vanity license plate that read LUVR. Plus his ancient Pinto smelled like pot, but Nan was so drugged up she kept beaming at him and calling him a "nice young man."

She also wouldn't stop muttering to me about how the tomatoes needed to come in. She was probably so out of it she didn't realize how late it was. But I went outside with a bucket and a flashlight anyway and picked as many as I could from the little plot of earth by the side of the garage. I knew I'd have other things I wanted to do in the morning.

All night long, I had visions of Emma. With everything else going on, I'd managed to bury most of the thoughts of her that were lingering in my brain. But when the lights went down and I lay in bed, they surfaced like jellyfish. All I saw was a once beautiful face, bloated and misshapen. I could see those cold blue lips. In my vision, her lips opened and this eerie whisper came out: Why? Why? When the light of day finally streamed through my window, I saw these things: smiling potato, ugly blue dog, fingertip kiss, bad lemonade. The constant sound of clicking, like teeth chattering, felt buried as deep within me as my heartbeat, and when I shook my head it only seemed to get louder. I could smell something sweet in the air, like sugar doughnuts, so when I got downstairs I was confused to find Nan cooking eggs and bacon.

Two days had passed since Emma's accident, and I knew those night visions were my subconscious, telling me I needed to go the Reeses' house, to offer condolences. Even if they hated me. Whatever. It was the civil thing to do.

I remembered that Taryn had said the Reeses lived next door to her. So after breakfast, I rode my bike to Lafayette, where I found a bungalow near Taryn's house. I saw a lady in a pink terry housecoat, absently watering a bunch of dying flowers in front of the bungalow. Her aim was totally off; most of the water was falling on the white pebbles and rushing down the driveway, into the gutter. I knew that had to be Mrs. Reese.

I stopped in front of her, not doing a very good job of ignoring that Taryn's house was right next door. It was closed up and looked empty. I wondered where she was, what she was doing, when I saw the smiling potato again. I shook it from my head and concentrated on the frail lady who was now staring at me. "Um. Mrs. Reese?"

She nodded. She looked like she was my mom's age, and

her blond hair was in a tangle on her head, as if she hadn't run a brush through it in days, which was like my mom, too. She still had a tan, though. She'd probably loved the beach up until two days ago. "Yes?"

"I'm Nick Cross. I was one of the lifeguards on duty when your daughter . . . um." I couldn't bring myself to say more. Her expression never changed, as if she wasn't even listening. "I just wanted to say I was sorry."

"I remember you." She looked down at the flowers, and I braced myself for the attack. But it never came. I sighed with relief before she spoke, when I realized what she was going to say. "It's not your fault. I only wish you had been there instead of the other one." Her voice was fragile. "He shouldn't have been there."

I knew that. I knew that, and should have said something to someone. But I didn't. What she didn't know was that I was responsible. I stood there, trying to think of something else to say that could be of comfort, but guilt ate away the words. The You Wills just had me fumbling around for a few moments and turning awkwardly away, so very me, even though I'd been envisioning this confrontation for the past few hours. I'd come up with better words, then, but now they failed me. I caught my eyes trailing once again to Taryn's house. "I live on Seventh. If there's anything I can do, I just wanted to—"

"Would you like to come in? Have some lemonade?"

I jumped back to reality and planted my eyes on Mrs. Reese. She ran a suspicious eye over me and pointed inside her house. The You Wills had me halfway down the block. "I . . ." Lemonade. I took her daughter from her, and she wanted to give me lemonade. "All right."

I followed her inside, lamely, all the while thinking that I'd rather be anyplace else. She led me through the kitchen, which was painted a cheerful lemon yellow but still seemed sad, because it smelled like rotting garbage. There were drawings covering every bit of real estate on the fridge, each one signed by the little girl. I swallowed as I passed them, hoping the next room would be free of memories of her. But it wasn't. I nearly tripped over a puppet-show stage in the living room, and when Mrs. Reese sat me down on a worn lime-green sofa, I immediately faced a wall of photos. Dozens of Emmas, baby Emmas with little hair and no teeth, toddler Emmas in overalls, little-girl Emmas in pretty dresses and pigtails . . . they all stared at me, smiling. My throat was sticky and dry by the time Mrs. Reese placed a glass in my hands. I lifted it to my lips. The lemonade tasted strange, like artificial sweetener. Emma's mom noticed my stare, and her eyes trailed over to the picture wall, but for only a moment. Then she looked down. "Where did you say you lived?"

"On Seventh." I pointed, but realized that where I was pointing was in the opposite direction. "As I was saying, if you need help with anything, I'm happy to—"

"Seventh. Where you were lifeguard?"

I nodded.

She nodded almost imperceptibly and sat down next to me. I could tell she had other things on her mind because she sat uncomfortably close and I had to move over. "I loved that beach most of all. My grandparents had a house there. That's why we went there. I know it's a drive, and why should we drive when there's a beach just up the street? But we got badges for Seaside Park because of the family atmosphere. It's not as crowded, too, so I thought Emma would be safer."

She trailed off, and in those silent moments my stomach twisted and turned until I thought something would snap. I really had nothing to say after that, because I hated myself. She thought Emma would be safer at my beach. And what had I done? A thousand Emmas watched me, silently smiling, like she enjoyed seeing me unnerved. The biggest one was a portrait of the whole family. It looked pretty recent. Emma's father had gray hair and looked much older than her mother. Emma was sitting close to a boy who had to be around my age. "You have a son?" I asked.

"Yes. He was away at college. He left last week for Penn State. But he's coming back for the service." She smiled at the picture of him. I noticed she had a crumpled tissue in her palm. "Emma was very special to him. They did everything together. She was devastated when he left for school. And now . . . well, my son's the one who is devastated. He blames himself for not being here."

I looked at the glass of lemonade. It was still full. "I don't want to take up any of your time. Just wanted to offer help, if you need it. I'll give you my phone number."

She got a pen and paper and I quickly scribbled my information on it. She whispered thank you as she led me to the door. By then, the gnawing guilt in the pit of my stomach had done a number on my insides. I wanted to throw up. I wanted to go home and crawl into bed and die.

Suddenly I heard the tick-tick-tick of the gears of a ten-speed bicycle, and a flash of blond hair and pale white skin whirred by. I jerked my head up in time to see Taryn round the corner onto Ocean, heading toward the Heights. Immediately the You Wills told me to follow her, but that was a given. I couldn't not. Even if she was bad for me, I needed to find out what she knew.

Mrs. Reese came out and started to water some other patch of asphalt while I took my bike and followed. All the while, the tingles popped up on my shoulders, like it was so obvious I was chasing after my doom.

Chapter 15

Taryn really was going into the heart of Sleazeside. I should have known that. She biked furiously toward the boardwalk with a little bag slung over her shoulder, wearing an oversized white T-shirt with a giant smiling potato on the back. It said:

MUGSY'S
BASKET O' FRIES
BEST FRIES ON THE BOARDWALK
CASINO PIER—SEASIDE HEIGHTS, NJ

When I biked up to the boardwalk, it should have been no surprise to hear her voice calling behind me, "How may I help you, sir? Basket o' Fries?"

I turned toward the Mugsy's stand. She was standing next to the big smiling potato, wearing a ridiculous paper sailor's hat and grinning like she wasn't ashamed to be seen in it.

Crap. I hadn't expected her to notice me first. I thought maybe I could just . . . watch her from afar. Stalk her. Still, it was a thrill to have her smiling at me.

I tried to turn and navigate toward her but there were kids

having a water-gun fight and I nearly took them both out with my bike. I weaved my way around them, trying to look swift, but I accidentally jabbed a pedal into my shin. Pain sliced through my leg. Fighting back tears, I managed, "You work here?"

You would think that being able to tell the future, I could have come up with something less moronic to say. She just giggled. "Funnel cake? Please let me clog your arteries."

"I didn't know you worked up here."

She shrugged. "It's a job. All my friends back home were so jealous when they heard I was going to work up at the Heights. They thought I was going to have a boyfriend named Guido who talks like *dis*." She sounded a little like the Godfather and made a gesture like she was kissing her fingers, like the guy in the pasta sauce commercials does before he says *"Delicioso!"*

"This is Jersey," I said. "Not Italy."

She shrugged. "Okay, so my accent's not the best. But you know what I mean."

"I know that your friends watch too much reality television."

She bit her lip. "Aw, who cares what they think, anyway? They're not my friends anymore." Then she smiled and held out a crinkle-cut. "Mmm. Hungry?"

I stared at her as she sucked the fry into her mouth. I didn't know if she meant to be seductive, but she was. My heart thudded, and it wasn't for the grease. Everything about her was putting me in an early grave. I thought about those lips, the lips I was, at least the last time I checked, destined to kiss. The breeze coming from the ocean did nothing to calm the heat in my face.

I guess I wasn't doing a good job at hiding it, because she crossed her arms and asked, "What?"

"Oh. Nothing." It wasn't like I could tell her the truth. There were about three hundred flies swarming on the whitewashed wooden counter, so to change the subject, I said, "Has the health inspector been to this place lately?"

It didn't work. She said, "You were totally undressing me with your eyes."

I thought about the birthmark. Now I felt the heat flushing across my cheeks. "No, I was . . ." In my eyes, you were already undressed.

She cleared her throat. "Did you come to find out more about my grandmother? About what I said?"

I ran my fingers over the counter. There was a splotch of ketchup there, dried and crusty, that didn't move when I touched it. "Nah." Yeah. "Where is the charming lady's booth, by the way?"

She pointed her chin toward the next booth. There was the red velvet I'd seen in my visions. It wasn't totally a tent; it was a regular storefront, but the thick lush fabric lined the windows and door. There was a sign above the entrance:

READINGS BY BABE,
BIBLIOMANCER EXTRAORDINAIRE.

I stared at it. "Babe? That's her name?"

Taryn nodded.

"What happened to something mystical, like Madame Paulina or the Great Zoltaire? Babe? That sounds like a little pig."

"It's short for Erzsebet or something. Most people can't pronounce it. It's Hungarian."

"It kind of ruins the mystique. I don't know if I can trust a bibliomancer named Babe."

She shrugged. "Fine. Your loss. I thought maybe you wanted to find out why you are the way you are."

"I do. But I doubt Babe over there has the answers." I hitched a thumb in that general direction and checked out her digs. There was a neon sign that said WORLD FAMOUS and a paper sign that said: SPECIAL: PALM READINGS $10 TODAY ONLY! It was so sun-faded and covered in cobwebs it had probably been up there for years. The red curtain was open a sliver, but all I could see was blackness. Looked like a closet. Or like a place you went into if you wanted to get mugged. "Has she ever read your palm?"

Taryn nodded. "Yeah. Plenty of times."

"Was she ever right?"

"Oh, well . . ." She smiled a little. "Of course. Always."

I couldn't tell if she was fooling with me. I looked at the placard outside, which said: GUESS YOUR WATE OR YOUR FATE! COME IN AND GIVE BABE A TRY. I smirked. "She spelled 'weight' wrong."

"Okay, so she's not book smart. But she knows things."

I stepped a little closer to the booth and smelled some nasty spicy incense. Gagging, I was about to turn away when I noticed a smaller sign, only the size of a business card, in the other window. ABSOLUTELY NO REVERSALS. I pointed to it. "What does that mean? Reversal of what?"

"If you meet me after my shift ends, I'll show you. Okay?"

I got that feeling again, that familiar feeling that always seemed to happen around her, like being torn down the middle. I needed to run away. Fast. And yet I found myself nodding. What the hell was I getting myself into?

She leaned forward, about to speak, when I felt a presence behind me. "How can I help you? Basket o' Fries?" she asked cheerily, as a man in a wifebeater sauntered up to the counter. He placed his order and she got it for him. He was kind of an idiot, asking for ketchup and salt and napkins when they were right there in front of him, but Taryn helped him out, the courteous smile never leaving her face. When he started to walk away she turned to me and opened her mouth to speak, but I suddenly saw the guy coming back to ask for her phone number.

"What time is your boyfriend coming to pick you up?" I asked in a really loud voice.

She stared at me, her mouth half-open. "Um."

"You know, Butch? To take you to the STD clinic?" I motioned to the guy, who was waiting nearby.

She looked over my shoulder at him for a moment, then said, "Um. Four?"

"Cool." I looked over my shoulder. Idiot was meandering away.

Her eyes widened. "What was that all about? Was he . . . did you . . ."

"He was going to ask for your number."

"Oh. Really?" She pressed her lips together, flustered. "Well, I could have just told him no."

"I know that's hard for you."

"No it's not. It's—" She wrinkled her nose. "What do you know about me, anyway?" She got even redder as she thought about it. "You know a lot about me, don't you?"

I nodded. "I'm sorry."

"What else do you know about me?" She seemed sort of angry. "No, forget it. Don't tell me. I don't want to know."

"You're angry?"

She shrugged. "It's not your fault, is it? But it's really weird." Then she smiled. "You are right. It is hard for me to say no sometimes. When I like someone. But I could have said no to that guy. He's not really my type."

"He looked a little like that kind of boyfriend your friends back home expect you to have, though. You know, the one that *talksa like dis*." I did the *"Delicioso!"* fingertip kiss.

She thought for a second. "You're right. Maybe I should try to get him back." Then she leaned over the counter and said to me, "Four is when my shift ends."

"I'll be here." I tried to be nonchalant, but then I thought of the birthmark again and knocked over the condiment tray. Taryn just shook her head as if to say, "I don't want to know."

She was right. She didn't.

Chapter 16

Since it was six hours until her shift ended, I could have biked back home. I should have. Nan was disabled and could have used my help. Instead, I spent a good chunk of the time aimlessly meandering down the boardwalk, taking in all the sights. Sure, I was a local, but the truth was I hadn't been to the Heights since the idea of cotton candy sounded good, which was years ago. The farthest I ever ventured up there was to the Seaside Park Beach Patrol headquarters, which was right on the border between the two towns. Here, though, the crazy people and steady clicking of the big wheels and the whir of rides combined with the scent of saltwater taffy and pizza to make it virtually impossible to hear the You Wills.

Now I worked extra hard to hear them. Something was making me cling to them. Of course it was Taryn. I strained to hear the You Wills, which led me to a stand in the corner of the boardwalk that was raffling off ugly dollar-store stuffed dogs. I blew eight dollars trying to win one by throwing darts before I realized I was a sucker, since I already knew what was going to happen. What the hell would I do with a stuffed dog, anyway?

By the time I returned it was 4:05. I'd timed it perfectly. I didn't want to appear too overeager by showing up early or right on time. So I figured five minutes late was good, even though I spent those five minutes staring at the clock on the boardwalk and watching the seconds tick away. When I got there, she was sitting outside the stand, hat removed, tapping her foot and looking anxious. "You're late," she said.

"Sorry."

She grabbed me by the wrist and immediately the You Wills stopped. A gust of air flooded my lungs at that second because I gasped and choked a little. She led me toward her grandmother's booth. "You don't get it. My grandmother starts working at five, but she always arrives early. And she can't know we're here."

With my mind calm, I could really concentrate on her for the first time. She had little crinkles around her eyes and freckles over the bridge of her nose. I realized I'd already had the map of those freckles committed to memory—a dark one under her left eye, a constellation of three at the side of her nose. She didn't wear any makeup and her hair was in a ponytail, but she still managed to look beautiful. She always would, even when she was older.

"Why are you staring?" she asked, sounding annoyed. I probably would be, too, if someone was studying me as closely as I was looking at her.

"Nothing. Um, why? I thought your grandmother and I really hit it off that last time."

She smirked, then jabbed her finger at the tiny sign that said: ABSOLUTELY NO REVERSALS. "That's why."

"But what does it mean?" I asked again, as she lifted the velvet curtain and pulled me inside. This was right from my vision. The room was barely the size of a closet, with a small table in the center, a crystal ball atop it. Everything was dark velvet, hot and cramped, like the inside of a coffin. The stench of incense was so strong I had to swallow again and again to keep from gagging.

Taryn reached under the table and pulled out an old book. "This," she said, "is the Book of Touch."

I stared at it. It wasn't anything remarkable. It was small with a simple black leather cover, kind of like one of the ancient Bibles Nan kept by her bedside. "What is it for?"

"I'll show you."

At first I thought it was a how-to manual for massage or something, but I wasn't lucky enough to have Taryn wanting me to give her a backrub. Not yet, anyway. She hurried to a small dusty bookshelf and slid her hand behind a picture of a man who looked about a thousand years old. She pulled out a key. "That's my grandfather," she said, motioning with her chin as she turned the book on its side, revealing a half-rusted lock. "He's dead."

"Nice."

She shrugged. "He didn't speak English."

She put the key in the lock and it clicked open. For a moment I could have sworn the temperature in the tent dropped, but that was probably just the result of watching too many episodes of *Scooby-Doo*. Taryn opened the book to the first thick, yellowing page and motioned me over. "Each page is a Touch."

I watched her flip through. The book must have been crazy old, because it smelled moldy and almost every page was mostly blank, with just a few foreign words in bold print and a signature on it. The ones that were full had an ornate, slanting gold script that was somewhat faded or smudged. But I couldn't make a thing out. "That's not English."

"Duh. Hungarian."

"What does it say?"

"It tells you what to say to perform the Touch. First you have to sign on the page. It's like a contract. And then once the Touch is performed, the words of the spell fade—look." She opened to a page that was blank except for a heading and a signature, Ernesto Pugilini, at the very bottom. "This Touch has already been performed."

"What the hell is a Touch?"

"Oh. Sorry. It's like a spell." She stared at the page. "And this one is . . . Paws of the Bear. Ernesto received unnatural strength."

My jaw just hung there. "Wait. You can read Hungarian?"

"Duh. Isn't that what I just did?"

"Okay. So you're telling me that this book can make someone—strong? Or whatever? Give me a break." I studied her face. It was completely serious. "You don't believe in that crap, do you?"

"Um, of course." She stared at me. "Wow. Didn't think I'd have to convince you."

"Okay. Prove it."

I was already getting that feeling, as if the You Wills were saying, *Great thing to ask, Captain Obvious.* She flipped through a few pages and turned the book around to face me. It was an almost blank page, I guessed from a Touch that had already been performed, or whatever. Under the heading I saw a very familiar signature. A name I'd seen signed on every absentee excuse I'd ever brought to school, usually after a bad bout of cycling. Moira Cross.

Taryn pointed at the heading in Hungarian. "This one says Sight of the Eagle," she said. "Three guesses what that will do."

Chapter 17

Outside, a balloon popped, making me jump so high I hit the cobwebbed chandelier above us. A child's cries echoed in the background as I stared at the name on the page until my vision blurred.

Of course. Of course.

It was like the vital missing puzzle piece, and as soon as I fit it in, everything else became clear. I wondered why I didn't think of it before. It seemed so like her. Always wanting to know her future, always being tied up in superstitions. I'd bet before this, she'd visited every fortune-teller in the Heights.

"So you're saying . . . ," I sputtered, collapsing in a black pleather armchair and ignoring the farting noise it let out. I knew what she was saying. I just couldn't form the right words.

Taryn crouched beside me. "This book has been in my family for hundreds of years. There aren't very many Touches left."

"Wait. She let your grandmother . . ." I tried to say more, moved my mouth in a thousand different ways, but the words didn't come out.

"She paid to do it. Probably a thousand dollars or more."

"Paid? Your grandmother ruined her life, my life, and charged her for it?" When Taryn nodded, I realized I couldn't breathe anymore. I doubled over, feeling like I had been kicked in the gut.

Taryn pointed to the date, which was in July, eighteen years ago, a month after my mom's graduation and a few months before I was born. Eighteen years ago. I stared at that date until my eyes burned. The exact date our nightmares began.

"And it transferred to me, because my mother was pregnant with me," I muttered, rubbing my eyes.

"That's where the 'No Reversals' comes in."

I dropped my hands. "You mean, she could reverse a Touch if she wanted to?"

Taryn shook her head. "No. I just told you, that's not possible."

"You didn't say it wasn't possible. You just said she wouldn't do it."

"It's not possible," she said firmly. She took the book and closed it, then locked it with the key. "But Grandma warns people. She doesn't just take all their money and give them a Touch. She has seen that, while some of these Touches perform miracles, some of them destroy people's lives. She tells them that sometimes a person's greatest desire can be the most terrible curse."

Of course we would have the luck to fall into the "curse" category. "So let me get this straight. My mother paid so that she could be this way?"

She nodded. "Every one of these Touches is something really cool. Something people would kill for. And long ago my ancestors realized that certain people would not only risk their lives to be Touched but they'd also fork over huge sums of money. Charging a lot also helps to ensure a person is serious about it. Grandma doesn't want just anyone waltzing in and getting a Touch. When people put together that much money, they're usually serious. Plus it pays her bills."

I leaned my head against the table and muttered my mom's name. "Why?" I whispered, and no sooner had I done that then I saw the answer. I saw my mom, explaining, tears running down her face. I was so scared when I found out I was pregnant. And there was so much uncertainty with your father. He said he loved me, but I couldn't be sure. When he asked me to marry him, I was so afraid that one day he would leave me, like my father left your grandmother. So I pulled together my life's savings—a thousand dollars—and went to her. The first thing I saw when I got the Touch was me, alone. Your father was gone. And then the worst thing—I saw I'd given this curse to you. I destroyed every chance of us having a normal—

At that point I started to green-elephant. I didn't want to hear her whining anymore. She knew. All this time I was searching for answers, and she already knew. It was her fault. At that moment, I didn't want to see her again.

"What is that?" Taryn asked. "The green elephant?"

I groaned through the pain, through the memory that came up at that moment. Really, anything would work, but I started saying that because when I was seven or eight, I bought my mom this necklace for Christmas that had a jade elephant pendant. I bought it for a buck at school, so it wasn't real jade, but she wore it every day. On bad days, when my head really hurt, I'd sit with her and she'd hold me to her and I would see nothing but that green elephant, with its trunk in the air. It meant good fortune. Good fortune.

She didn't wear it anymore. It was probably in a landfill somewhere. That was one of the few times I'd experienced cycling because of something she did. One day the cable had gone out, so she reached behind the set to jiggle the wires, and the necklace's black cord, which had been fraying a bit, got caught on a screw and snapped. The jade elephant fell to the ground and the trunk broke off in a pile of green chalk dust. That day, it was as if every future memory I'd have of my mom changed just a bit and felt slightly strange, like new shoes that needed breaking in. In each of those visions, the elephant was gone from her neck.

I leaned back in the chair, feeling something close to the numbness I'd get after a night of bad cycling, when my head had been thrashed so much it couldn't feel anything anymore. "It's just a nonsense phrase. It doesn't mean anything. I say it to keep the future memories from invading. To calm my mind. If my brain is concentrating on something else, it doesn't have time to dwell on the future."

Taryn nodded as if it wasn't the stupidest thing in the world, and I loved her for that.

The picture of my mom sobbing kept invading, and I pushed

it away. She was lucky we could carry on conversations in our minds, because if I'd been in the same room together, I didn't know what I might have done or said. "So, what other Touches are in there? What else can this book do?"

She flipped through the pages. "Like I said, there's only a handful of them left. Um, this one is Poison Arrow. Architect of Time. Small Army . . ." She kept flipping pages.

"Any Touches that will undo previous Touches?" I asked, hopeful.

She shook her head. "No such luck."

"Well, can you, like, say the curse backward and—"

"Uh-uh. Absolutely no reversals."

"But is that because it can't be done, or because your grand-mother doesn't know how to do it?" I asked, getting desper-ate.

"It can't be done. Touches are permanent," she said, mak-ing my heart, which was suddenly twittering with all these new, thrilling sensations, turn to lead. She looked at her watch. "We'd better get out of here. Grandma will be here any minute and she does not want me talking to you about the Book of Touch."

"Why not? Isn't it good business for her?"

"Sure it is. Like I said, it pays her rent. But I don't think local law enforcement would be too happy about it, so it's very hush-hush." She walked to the opening of the booth and stopped short. I didn't have to look out; I immediately saw what was coming. Her grandmother plodding up the ramp, her thick sausage cankles visible under that same shapeless dress of dead brown flowers. I grabbed Taryn by the wrist and the vision dissolved in my head. We needed to hide. But when I turned, there was nothing, just mounds of red velvet on the walls. Sure, there was the little table, but it was too little to hide both of us, and did I really want to spend any length of time with Taryn's grandmother's cankles in my face?

Taryn led the way, pulling back one of the curtains. "In here," she said. I climbed in. There was a cinder-block wall about three feet behind the curtains, but it was a good hiding spot.

"How'd you know this was here?" I whispered.

"I used to spend a lot of time back here when I was a kid," she answered. "Grandma thought it would be good for me."

"Good for you? You mean, she wanted you to see people get this . . . Touch?"

She nodded, then shrugged.

I laughed bitterly. Her grandmother was totally whacked. Letting a little girl see people curse themselves was the perfect playdate, right up there with Chuck E. Cheese's. Taryn let the curtains fall behind us. From where we stood, I could look up and see neon lights from the arcade next door. The bells and chatter of the electronic games were loud enough to make me realize they were probably right on the other side of the wall. It only went up seven or eight feet. I could probably hoist myself up and escape that way. As I was looking for a way out, Taryn cursed. Really loudly.

"Shhh," I said. "What?"

"Forget it. Grandma's practically deaf," she explained, and not in a whisper. She held out the key to the book.

I stared at it. "You forgot to . . ."

"I was in a hurry. It's no big deal. She probably won't perform any Touches tonight, anyway. I'll just put it back tomorrow." Then she put her hand on my knee, steadying it. I hadn't realized it, but I was fidgeting, something I did all the time. "You are a jumpy one, aren't you?"

"Yeah," I said, not really thinking. "Sue always says I'm so jumpy I make kangaroos jealous."

"Sue?"

Oh, hell. Usually I was good about keeping my future under wraps, especially with complete strangers. But like I said, she put me at ease. Why else would I be bringing up my no-longer-wife-of-thirty-years? Sue, who was probably now going to marry some other guy and have a lot better future than she would have had with me. "Forget it," I mumbled.

I watched as her grandmother lumbered into the tent, breathing heavily. She was nothing like Nan, who was barely sixty. This lady looked ancient. "How old is your grandmother?"

Taryn studied her from the slit in the curtain. "I have no idea. But I'm her twenty-ninth grandchild. Her last grandchild." She exhaled slowly. "Lucky for me."

"What does that mean?"

She motioned to the wall with her chin. "I'll tell you later. Let's go."

Chapter 18

We walked through to the rear of the arcade, looking for a door. If we could get out onto Ocean Avenue, we could get around the booth and to the bicycle rack without any possibility of Old Scary Lady seeing us. "So, who is Sue?" Taryn asked.

And I'd thought maybe she'd forget. I cleared my throat. "No one. Really." Which was the truth. Now she was no one to me.

"Old girlfriend? Current girlfriend?"

I just mumbled, "My wife. In a different lifetime."

Her eyes widened. "What do you mean, different lifetime?"

"Like I said, every time I do something off script, I can throw things off. And once, before I met you, I had this future where I was going to marry a girl named Sue." I had a momentary reflection back to that feeling, that feeling of safety and happiness I'd only had in that life, and cringed at the thought of losing it. Could I ever get that back? "It was a good future. A perfect one."

"And the one you're going to have now?"

I shrugged. It was hard to explain. That last future, I'd had time to settle into. It took a while, but eventually I learned all the ins and outs, and the more I learned, the more perfect I realized it was. I knew this new one didn't feel right, but it was too soon to tell. All new futures felt that way. It felt like standing on the edge of a cliff. Maybe I would fly, maybe I would fall. It always took a few days or weeks to fully understand it. "I don't know. I need time to sort it out."

"It could be even more perfect. You don't know."

"I guess." I didn't bother to tell her I had had hundreds of futures set in my mind before. None of them was as good as the one I'd just lost. Sure, there had been okay futures, but in a good majority of them, I ended up alone. I understood that; I'd been alone most of my life so far. Nobody got me. Nobody could stand me for too long. Sue had been a miracle, even though I hadn't met her. And Taryn . . . Taryn was another miracle, with a difference. She was here, in the flesh.

I looked at Taryn, filled in that moment with the urge to grab her and hold her against me and never let her go. Suddenly, she stopped and looked at me. "You look like you're going to throw up."

My throat was desert dry. I shook my head and started to say something to blow it off when she caught sight of something beyond me. "Oh, Skee-Ball! Let's do just a couple of games."

I agreed, even though I hadn't done Skee-Ball since I was, like, five. Taryn fed all the quarters she could find in her bag into the machine and the balls fell down the chute. I did the same and then realized I was playing next to a master. One after another, she popped those suckers into the little circle in the center marked 50. I kept hitting the gutter. The You Wills kept repeating the same thing to me, like a record skipping:

You will hit the gutter, you will hit the gutter, you will hit the . . .

"So you've seen people get Touched, huh? What's that like?" I thought maybe conversation would take the focus off my sucktastic abilities.

She straightened and threw her first gutter ball, then swallowed. "It's . . . horrible. I don't want to think about it."

I stared at her as my brain quieted from the You Wills. "Then why would your grandmother make you watch from behind the curtain?"

She threw another ball. "Because I am the last grandchild. And in the lore, the last grandchild inherits the power."

"Power?"

"The power to use the book. And . . . other things." She looked away. "Not nice things." She blushed a little. "I am afraid if I tell you this, you'll think I'm a freak."

I grinned, surprised. "Look who you're talking to."

"Well, I also attract certain people. People with a certain wanting or void in their lives. And people like that aren't usually the best people to hang out with."

"Like me?"

She finished throwing her last ball and shook her head. "You're different. You didn't ask for this. But I kind of lied to you about why we left Maine."

"Your father wasn't laid off?"

"Oh, no, he was. But it was because of me." She bit her bottom lip. "I'm an only child and my mom and dad wanted me to be a doctor. They weren't too keen on me growing up to be a fortune-teller."

"Understandably."

"Right. So when I was six, Grandma started taking me to see the Touches performed. And as I said, they were horrible. Then the nightmares started. When my parents found out what I was going through, there was a huge fight. My grandmother told them I'd never be able to escape my destiny, but they thought she was crazy. They dropped everything and moved me to Maine. And everything was okay for a while. My dad started doing really good. He was one of the top executives at the factory. Everything was great. I think my parents thought we'd escaped it. But like I said, I have these powers. The power to attract certain people. I had friends up there, or at least, I thought they were friends before I came here and realized they were just being drawn by the Touch. And you know how I am about saying no."

"So you were a troublemaker, huh?" I said, raising an eyebrow.

"Uh-huh."

"Seriously?" I asked. She just didn't seem the type.

"I was! I was terrible. It started when I was thirteen or fourteen. My friends and I would stay up all night, doing things. Mostly little, stupid things that bored kids do when they have nothing better to do. Breaking into houses. Destroying property. Stuff like that. I refused to listen to my parents, and no matter what they did, I found a way around it. They barred my windows, for God's sake. And I knew it was stupid but—"

"You couldn't say no."

"Right. And I couldn't shake them. Just as they were attracted to me, I fell for them, too. They kept following me around, worshipping me, and I never realized that it was because they were attracted to what I could do for them. The Touch. I kept running away from home and my dad took all this time from work to go looking for me or deal with the trouble I'd gotten myself into. So he was fired. And we were forced to move here. The funny thing was, all those great friends I had back in Maine never emailed me, called, texted . . . not even once. They didn't want me, they just wanted to be Touched."

"That sucks."

"Like my grandmother said, I can't escape my destiny. I have to take over for my grandmother and perform these Touches, or else things will get bad. Really bad. My parents are finally accepting that, I guess." Her face had paled past its normal pale, to an unnatural and deathly bluish-white. "They have no other choice."

"What do you mean by 'really bad'?" I asked.

She wrinkled her nose. "The worst. But I don't want to talk about that. I get really nervous thinking about it. That's why I like hanging out with you. I don't think about it constantly when I'm with you."

I ran out of balls, so I stood there and watched her throw her second gutter ball. When she threw a third one, she grimaced and massaged her arm. As soon as she started throwing again, she hit the 50.

"And that's why I knew you were Touched. The second I felt your hand, it was like I understood everything. But it's more than that. We're alike. Usually, people get Touched of their own free will. But you didn't. We're both cursed, but it's not our fault."

I nodded. "When I touched your hand, I couldn't see the future anymore. It made me almost feel normal."

She stopped throwing balls and straightened. "I guess that makes sense." Then she said, "Do you like it?"

"What? Touching your hand?"

She grinned. "Feeling normal."

I smiled. It didn't matter which question she had been asking; either way, the answer was yes. "Of course."

She reached over and grabbed my hand. "Better?"

My mind stopped in the middle of a You Will and I just nodded. "Yeah. Much. It's like ... almost ..."

She squinted. "Like what?"

"Almost too quiet. I'm used to multitasking. Doing things while seeing what's coming next. You know, like if you have two televisions tuned to the same program, but on different signals, and one is a few seconds ahead? That's what it's like. I'm used to it. This is ..."

"Exciting?" she said, giving me this coy smile. "For once in your life you have no idea what is coming next."

I was going to say scary, but then I realized that made me sound like a wuss. "Um, yeah. I guess normal life can be exciting."

Never letting go of my hand, she ripped her tickets from the dispenser and dragged me to the prize center, where she traded in her twenty-five tickets for two neon slap bracelets. She gave the blue one to me and kept the hot pink one for herself. Then we walked onto the boardwalk, away from her grandmother's tent and toward the rides. I felt two feet taller. I'd never held hands with a girl before, much less a hot one. Other guys were checking her out, and each time I stuck my chin out farther. It felt freaking phenomenal.

"So," she said as we walked. I guess we were walking aimlessly, because our bikes were in the other direction. I didn't care. I could have walked all night like this. "What else do you know about me?"

I smiled. "I thought you didn't want to know."

"Well. I'm curious. It's nothing bad, is it?"

Holding hands with Taryn did nothing to erase the image of that birthmark, of the curve of pale skin on her lower back, leading to her backside. It didn't matter how many girls I cycled through; I knew that would be etched in my brain permanently. "No. It's nothing. Really."

"Well, I think you must know something. Your face keeps getting red every time I bring it up. Do we get really close or something?"

I swallowed, fully aware that anything I said now could totally destroy that future. "I don't know."

"Yes, you do," she teased.

"Look," I said under my breath. "The future isn't set. And I don't want to . . ."

"Oh, you don't want to blow it. I get it. But you know, normal people don't worry about these things. They just take it naturally."

Even though the ocean air was cool, my hand was sweating in hers. How the hell did I know what normal people would do? All that confidence I had a second before drained away and I found myself wondering again why she'd want to be seen with me, the abnormal person who didn't even know how to take things naturally, whatever that meant. "Okay," I mumbled.

"We can go on a ride. Like the Tilt-a-Whirl? Or the haunted house?" she suggested. "What do you think?"

"Surprise me." She was still contemplating, unaware, so I said, "Get it? Surprise me? That's a joke."

She gave me a look. "Oh, right, because you can't be surprised. Funny," she said, like it wasn't. "Wait, can you be surprised? When you fell into the water at the pier, you were surprised."

"Nah. I knew it would happen. But by then I couldn't stop myself. It's okay, though. I don't really like surprises."

"You don't? Are you scared of them?" she taunted.

"No, I'm—I like to be in control as much as I can."

"Booor-ing!" she singsonged. "You should forget about that. Live a little. What's the worst thing that could happen?"

She didn't get it. I could see the worst things that could

happen. A lot of them would make her lock herself in her bedroom for the rest of her life. "Most surprises are bad."

"That's not true. There are lots of good ones, too." She surveyed the amusements and her eyes widened. "Oh yes, the haunted house. I love it. Don't you?"

"I—I've never . . ." I clamped my mouth shut. It was obvious I was a dork. That I led a sheltered life because of the curse. I should just take things naturally and tell her. But from the way she was looking at me, I think she already knew.

"Don't worry. It will be fun. Lots of surprises in the haunted house."

"Bad ones," I answered, reluctant, as I tried to understand what about the concept of surprise could be good. Surprises sucked. It was so much better to be in control.

Taryn dragged me toward the stucco housefront at the end of the pier, with the fake wrought iron fence and cobwebs everywhere. There was a raven with a skeletal hand in its beak perched on the sign that said 6 TICKETS, but even that looked pretty pathetic. Taryn must have come here a lot because she had a book of tickets in her bag. She handed the attendant twelve and we squeezed into a car.

Then she clutched my hand tighter. "I'm scared," she said, but in a way that I couldn't tell if she was joking. Before I could look at her face, the car jerked forward and we careened into darkness.

It was pretty dumb. The scariest thing was how the ride twisted us around, almost dislocating my spine, and our car shook back and forth so much I was sure the whole thing was going to collapse. The squealing of the wheels on the track drowned out any scary noises we were supposed to hear. Occasionally someone in a scary mask would jump out at us, but it wasn't dark enough to make it a complete surprise. I think Taryn was disappointed, because the first time it happened, she let out a high-pitched, deafening yelp, which dissolved into laughter, but after that she just muttered things under her breath.

When the ride found daylight again, we squinted at each other and then said "Lame" at the same time. I shrugged at her as we got off. "Oh, well. At least you paid."

"Hey!" she began, but stopped short. She was walking in front of me, so I couldn't see her face, but then I looked up and saw him.

Terrific. Sphincter.

He was with—of course—two girls from school with too much in the way of hair and makeup and too little in the way of clothing, the kind of girls who never gave me the time of day. They were his bookends. His smile disappeared as he took us in. "Well, hello, Taryn," he sang in a game-show-host voice. Then he nodded at me. "Cross."

I nodded back. Taryn gave a little wave. "Hi, Evan!" she said in her typical bubbly way, but there was something weird about how she stiffened.

"How are you doing?" he asked, not casually, but in a tone you would use if you knew a person's close family member had just died. I knew the question was just for Taryn, because he stood so that his back, and the backs of the other girls, were to me. The perfume and cologne and whatever else they were wearing smelled worse than the incense at Babe's tent, but the view of the girls' asses made it tolerable. "How's your grandmother?"

"Fine. We're all doing good," she said.

Both girls looked away, bored or annoyed or a little of both. One fed herself a long string of sticky blue cotton candy; the other inspected her nails. I suddenly had the feeling I was listening in on a private conversation. Like maybe Taryn knew Sphincter. Like, really knew him.

They talked a little more about school starting next week and doesn't-it-suck-that-summer's-almost-over? Even though it was a really generic, safe topic, the more they talked, the more my stomach churned. Sphincter moved in really close, probably just to piss me off. It was working. How did they know each other? I stared at the lame "his" slap bracelet on my wrist and silently wished Sphincter would crawl back into whatever hole he came out of. When they parted, Taryn just said, "Let's go on this Rock n' Roll thing. I have more tickets."

I shrugged and we walked to the ride. I heard him mumble something about "Crazy Cross," and the girls tittered. They headed off toward the haunted house. While Taryn reached in her bag for tickets, I turned and caught Sphincter staring.

I thought maybe I could get her to admit what they had going on. "He totally wants you," I said as we settled into the car.

She shrugged, not impressed. "I'm sure he does." She shifted in her seat. "They always do."

I thought she meant guys, but I couldn't remember when she'd last been so full of herself. So I just let out an amused "Oh, yeah?"

She nodded, biting her lip. "Yeah." The ride started to pick up speed then, so I couldn't be positive, but I was pretty sure there were tears in her eyes.

Chapter 19

Meeting Sphincter was like throwing a bucket of water on whatever fire was going between us. Taryn still held my hand, which would have been a good sign if it hadn't grown cold, stiff. I thought about asking her what was wrong, but I really didn't want to know the answer. What about Sphincter had gotten her crying? I don't think I could have looked at her the same if she and Sphincter had . . . well, if she and Sphincter had anything.

We got off the ride without a sound and stopped at the rack to get our bikes. Taryn had to let go of my hand to unlock her bike, and when she did, the You Wills began immediately. She saw the look of pain on my face and offered to hold my hand again, but it didn't matter. I was going to have to deal with it sooner or later anyway. So we walked our bikes all the way back to her street, not talking much. By then I was feeling a little better. Still woozy, but the stabbing pain between my eyes was gone.

"So," she said when we got to her driveway, tipping her head in the direction of the Reeses' house. "Funeral's tomorrow. Are you going?"

"Yeah, I think so," I mumbled as my head pounded away. I felt that pain in my stomach again. Of course I would be there.

She narrowed her eyes. "I know it was probably traumatic for you. Are you blaming yourself?"

I didn't want to tell her, didn't want to talk about it at all, but I nodded. "I saw the other future. The one where I saved her."

She put her hand on my shoulder. "Don't beat yourself up. You did everything you could."

I shook my head, shook her hand away. A You Will popped through immediately, wanting me to get home. Instead, I looked at my feet. "I knew Pedro was not fit to be on watch. But I did nothing. I should have said something. But I didn't, because I wanted to stay on script. You see? It was my fault."

Her hand found its way back to mine. The cycling stopped again. A wave of exhaustion swept over me, as if my mind was sick of starting and stopping again and again. She whispered, "It's Pedro's fault. Not yours."

I nodded. I didn't believe her, but I didn't want to talk about it anymore. She just held my hand for a while. Then I said, "I'd better go."

She nodded, and I dropped her hand and started to walk away. Immediately these things found their way into my head: beauty, harder to kidnap, Saint Christopher. That was when she called after me. "Have you ever been to one?"

I swallowed and, for some reason, tasted grass. I could feel the blades of grass and earth on my tongue. I brought my hand to my mouth and licked it, expecting my hand to be black, but it wasn't. Instead, my eye began to pulsate with pain. I moved the muscle in my cheek up and down. Yeah. It felt like I'd been punched there. What the hell? When I turned back to her, she was staring at me with an expression I'd come to know so well: horrified confusion. I tried my best to cover it up. "I, um, had a hair in my mouth. Been to one of what?"

She let it slide. "A funeral."

I started to say yes and then shrugged. I'd been to dozens, in the future. Lucky for me, none of them had worked its way into my past. The real thing was probably a lot more unpleasant than the memory. "No," I finally said.

She laughed. "Which is it?"

"Long story," I said, not able to say more. My head was aching so much, I felt it down to my jaw. Probably my mom was having the same feeling. Good. For the first time, I was glad. This time, I wanted her to hurt.

"Okay. You can tell me later. So want to go together?"

My heart thumped. She wanted to see me again. Yes! I hadn't screwed everything up yet. And whatever history she had with Sphincter, it didn't matter. But then I thought about Nan's boat of a car, sitting in our dusty driveway. I thought of the way my hands shook on the steering wheel, of how I had trouble most times meeting the speed limit, even on residential streets. I started to sweat. "I, um, don't . . . I mean, I guess I could pick you up. . . . Ten-thirty okay?"

"Oh, great!"

We spent another long moment standing there, outside her house. I counted four anthills in her driveway.

Here was the point when a normal guy would have gone in for the kill. Instead, I froze up. Sure, Taryn came off as innocent and angelic. But I found myself wondering what trouble she'd actually gotten into in Maine. Most likely she was a lot more experienced than me. Didn't take much to be that way, but still. The opportunity to majorly screw up that future I'd seen of her, of us together, was right here. Right now.

And so I blew it. "See you," I tossed over my shoulder, as if I'd been talking to just anyone. I cringed almost immediately after I pulled my bike away from the curb.

And then I went back to face the future memories that had been flapping around in my mind like wounded birds.

Chapter 20

Nan had this 1976 Buick that was the color of calcified dog crap. It was built like a tank, all square edges, and had one of those bench seats that took a team of oxen to move into position. The Buick turned more heads than a car accident when it came down the road. It was so god-awful, people would crane their necks to see the unfortunate owner. Not like they could see little Nan behind the massive steering wheel, which was the size of a monster truck's tire. The Buick wouldn't fit in a regular garage, but that was fine with Nan because, as she would proudly tell you, we had the only three-car garage in town. Our garage was bigger than our house, so the car was very comfortable among Nan's strange collections of things, like the scoops from coffee cans and used pop-up turkey timers. It only had twenty-three thousand miles on it, "a classic!", as Nan would say. She only used it to go to the A&P and church every Sunday. She walked everyplace else.

As the sun began to melt orange against the horizon, I got Nan into the passenger's seat and slid behind the massive wheel, where Saint Christopher stared at me from a placard on the dashboard. I gripped the wheel and inched out of the garage like an old man.

Wow. I really needed the practice. Taryn would be wanting me like crazy after this ride.

It went without saying that I didn't like driving. Before that day I hadn't driven since I passed my driver's test at the beginning of the summer. Something about seeing all the accidents I could cause rubbed me the wrong way. Once, when I had my learner's permit, I thought about flipping on the radio but saw a ten-car pileup. There were just too many opportunities to cause bad things to happen on the road. But today Nan was drugged on something that had her snoring between sentences, not to mention she was down an arm, so it looked like I wouldn't be able to avoid driving. She'd cornered me the second I got home and told me I had to take her to the pharmacy on the mainland, because she'd realized this afternoon she'd run out of heart pills. She'd called Ocean Pharmacy on the island for a delivery, but they didn't have the kind she needed, and she was desperate.

But that was okay, I told myself. Normally I would have been a wreck. Despite the weird way it had ended, the afternoon with Taryn had me feeling good. Like maybe I could live a seminormal life, with someone who finally understood what I was going through. Getting there, I was fine. I joked with Nan about how she looked like she had been in a prizefight and how she could tell everyone "the other guy looks worse." I turned up the modern-rock station on the radio and drummed my fingers on the steering wheel in time to the music. I thought about how soft and small Taryn's hand felt against mine.

On the way back, though, I lost it. It wasn't simply the act of driving, of pressing on the gas pedal, that freaked me out. I made it over the bridge from Toms River (can't tell you how many times I envisioned the Buick careering over the railing and into the bay) and all the way down Central, carefully following the You Wills right down to the letter. But when I was navigating around town hall, not half a mile from Nan's cottage, it hit me.

Glass shards spraying in my face icy water droplets the smell of peanut butter

What the . . . ?

Instinctively I squeezed my eyes shut, and doing so, I slammed on the brakes. Nan grabbed the armrest. A car horn blared behind me and a red pickup swerved around me. The driver gave me the finger.

It didn't seem real. It couldn't be my future. First of all, I hated peanut butter. The smell made me so sick that I couldn't stand it. And the car was all wrong. It wasn't the easily recognizable Buick, with the tan pleather inside and St. Christopher staring from the dashboard. Nothing about it was vaguely familiar. It could have been something that would happen fifty years in the future, or maybe it wasn't real at all. Maybe it was just me getting all worked up about driving, as usual. I needed to stay away from Skippy, which was no problem since just thinking about it made my stomach churn, and stick to my bicycle; again, no problem because I hated driving anyway.

I looked over at Nan. For someone who'd missed her last heart pill, this was probably not the best experience to have. She started to say something to comfort me and then began snoring again.

I clenched my jaw. No matter how good things were with Taryn, nothing could protect me. This curse always found ways to remind me who was boss.

Thanks, Mom.

Carefully, I pulled into our driveway and inched the boat into the garage. I helped Nan out and drew the massive wooden doors closed, then stared at the cottage. Something was going to be off in there. I felt the tingles already.

I helped Nan up the three stairs to the back of the house, and when the screen door slammed, I heard my mom's voice. She sounded angry again. I couldn't tell what she was saying, though, and I didn't care. Was it me or did the tingles feel like a thunderstorm, like a thousand times worse than before Emma drowned?

"Up here," she called. Floorboards creaked. There was a floorboard right in the doorway to my mom's room that groaned whenever someone was standing on it. It made that noise now. She was out of her room, but just barely. Calling to me from the doorway. "Come up here."

I figured she wanted to tell me something about what I'd found out from Taryn. She knew, obviously, since our futures were tied to each other's. Maybe she wanted to explain herself. Apologize in person. Whatever. I wasn't going to listen, even if she begged forgiveness. I was steel. Stone. Finished with her.

"I don't want to hear—" I started, but stopped when I saw

the look on her face. She had made it to the top stair with one white hand on the banister and was staring down at me. The shadows dug into the creases on her forehead, making her look about twenty years older, or like one of those skeletons in the haunted house at the pier. Her eyes were heavy with worry.

I started to say "What?" but before I could she whispered, "You haven't been able to see the future yet, have you?"

I shook my head. "No, I have, I've seen—" Did I really want to tell her about seeing Taryn naked? Or about what happened in the car? "Why?"

"Have you seen anything from next year? Or even next month?"

I shrugged. Weird question. She knew it was so hard to tell when these future memories took place. I just inexplicably felt my bones aching in the ones where I was an old man. Or I'd catch a glimpse of my grandchild and feel this overwhelming love and pride. No, I hadn't had any far-off memories of my future since the Emma accident, but I only caught them once in a while, when everything was still. And things had been really screwy lately. I tried to call up a memory of the future, but they never came when I wanted them to. Usually, when I least expected it, I'd see or hear or smell something and the memory would pop into my mind. "I have no—"

"You can't, can you?"

I didn't like the tone. She should have been begging forgiveness. Instead, she sounded like she was accusing me of something. It was the tone I should have had with her. "No, but—"

"That's because you have no future," she said. "Whatever you did to change things, Nick . . . now you're the one who is going to die. Soon."

According to my mom, Christmas was really going to suck this year. Because not only might I not live out the year, I might not live out the summer. She said that because first, she knew I had trouble remembering anything in the future anymore, and second, she saw Nan dressed in the black dress she only wore to funerals. She was wearing the cast on her arm. The only other thing she could recall was extreme grief.

Well, that was good. I'd hate for anyone to be happy at my passing.

Oh, and that it was a closed casket. Not like she would get the guts to go to her own son's funeral, but that was what Nan told her. Which probably meant that my body would be mangled beyond recognition.

All really awesome things.

I could almost feel the jagged glass shards digging into my cheeks. An accident. The car accident I'd envisioned on my ride home.

I knew it wasn't the Buick. The inside was all wrong. I silently told myself I wouldn't set foot in a car again. That would do it. I hoped.

But the more I tried to see my future, the more I couldn't.

No wonder Taryn made the memories of my future go away. No wonder she made me feel normal.

This all started when she entered my life. For some reason, because of her, I had no future.

Trouble was, the more I tried to resign myself to stay away from her, the more I felt that big hole, that emptiness. My chest tightened and ached when I thought about it. It didn't help that I kept seeing myself kissing her, feeling my hands working through her thick platinum curls. For some reason, I couldn't see anything in the future but that, the most improbable thing in the world.

The morning of Emma's funeral, I put on my suit and tie. The suit was too tight. I looked like a major loser. It was only ten in the morning, and it already felt like a hundred degrees. There was no ocean breeze. I contemplated staying home about a thousand times. Then I opened up the door to the garage and climbed into the Buick.

You know those cartoons where a character is contemplating doing something, and a devil appears on one shoulder, trying to tempt him to do the bad thing, and an angel appears on the other, telling him why he should do the right thing? It was totally like that. But this time, Angel-me was telling me I needed to go and pick up Taryn, because I'd promised and it was the right thing to do. And Devil-me said I needed to go straight to the funeral, because something about Taryn was seriously screwing with my future. I went back and forth, gripping the steering wheel and mumbling to myself, until eventually the devil and the angel looked exactly the same.

Finally I just shoved the car into reverse. Gritting my teeth, I headed for the cemetery.

I knew it was a cruddy thing to do, leaving her there. I imagined her sitting on the front stoop, waiting for me. But I could explain it away. I was going to die in a car accident, right? Even though I kind of knew the Buick was safe, she'd be a moron to accept a ride with me.

It was a bright, sunny day. My limited knowledge of funerals from television and movies seemed to suggest that this was wrong; it was supposed to be raining, so much so that we would all huddle tightly around the casket in a dense forest of umbrellas. In the backseat Nan had a massive black thing, almost the size of a beach umbrella, that didn't fold compactly like new ones did. I'd expected to use it. It would effectively seal me off from the rest of the mourners; nobody would be able to tell who was under it.

Instead, the sun shone like a spotlight pointed right on my head as I stepped out of the car and made my way across the cemetery, to the crowd. I spotted Pedro. I hadn't seen him since that day on the beach. I didn't think he'd have the nerve to show up, but he was probably feeling as guilty as I did. "Hey, man," I said when I'd made my way over to him. "How's it going?"

He nodded, looking stiff in his suit. Funny how clothes could change a person. There was a sheen of sweat mingling with the pimples on his forehead. Finally, he mumbled, "Rather be anywhere else."

There was no doubt about it. I seconded Pedro's emotion.

He sniffed and brought a wadded tissue to his face. Allergies, I guessed. He wasn't the type to cry. But when he pulled the tissue away, it was covered in blood. When I looked closer, I realized there was blood on the collar of his shirt. He didn't turn to face me, but I could see a swollen, bluish pocket on his temple and under his eye. One thing about Pedro, he was almost girlish about his appearance; he didn't get into fights. "Whoa, man. What's going on?"

A few people turned, saw me, and whispered. I knew it was probably, "There's the guy who tried to revive her. The crazy one." One old lady gave me a reproachful look and shook her head.

I'd definitely rather be anywhere else.

We stood in the last row, as far away from the rest of the mourners as possible, but suddenly Pedro faltered, almost like his knees gave out. He staggered backward. "I—can't," he whispered, staring at the ground.

I stared at him. For the first time I noticed there wasn't just blood on his collar. It was all down the front of his shirt, spattering his pale blue tie. Bits of dried grass clung to the knees of his dark pants. "What? Who did that to you, man?"

"I shouldn't have come," he hissed. I was aware some people were beginning to turn, but then Pedro just broke into a sprint toward the line of cars. It was like he was being chased by the devil. He even looked back a few times, as if he was expecting to see Satan.

It was over ninety degrees, but I shivered. Wow. What the hell had happened to him?

The priest began to speak about finding comfort in one another. He said, "It is unexpected tragedy that brings us together today."

"The unexpected in life is often the most difficult to deal with," I mumbled under my breath, along with the priest. I

looked over and saw Mrs. Reese with her head against someone's shoulder. Mr. Reese, I supposed. When she pulled away,
I saw that it was a younger guy. Emma's brother, the one at
Penn State. He stared ahead, unblinking, as Mrs. Reese continued to sob into his suit jacket. Mr. Reese, a white-haired
version of his son, stood next to him.

The crowd parted for a split second, and I managed to see
the coffin. It was a little one. Too little. I bowed my head and
rocked back on my heels and wished for it to be over. In my
peripheral vision, I could see two pale feet in black stringy
sandals coming up behind me. The toenails were painted red.
I knew those feet. Hell, I worshipped those feet.

I cleared my throat. I would not look at her.

She stepped beside me and paused a beat, as if to say,
Look at me, I'm here, I came anyway, and then kept right on
walking, as if being at a funeral didn't scare her as much as
she'd said. Another girl was with her, the girl with the pixie
haircut from track tryouts. The crowd accepted them, made
room for them, making me feel like I was the one who had
been left behind. After a minute, the boy with Mrs. Reese
turned and looked hard, right at Taryn. It was the same look
Sphincter had given her. She stared straight ahead, at the
casket, but it was clear that there was something between
them.

Great. First Sphincter, now this guy. She's going to drive
me to an early grave, I thought, before I realized I probably
shouldn't tempt fate.

After the longest twenty minutes of my life, the funeral
ended and the crowd spread out. I kept looking around for

some hint as to who had messed with Pedro, wondering if they'd pick me next. I meant not to look at Taryn, but I found myself staring right at her when she spun around to leave. I thought she would give me eye daggers. Instead, she smiled. And not a wicked smile, either; a hey-how-are-you? smile. The kind that's out of place at a funeral. She made a beeline over to me, her friend following at her heels.

"Did you forget about picking me up?" she asked, still not sounding angry.

"Um. Yeah. Oh." I tried to play it off as if I had forgotten, but realized too late that I should be apologizing. I mumbled a "sorry," but I didn't think she heard it.

"That's okay. You've got stuff on your mind, I understand."

I nodded. Why the hell was she being so nice?

"Anyway," she said, "I made it. How are you doing with all this?" She motioned toward the coffin.

"Fine. I was just . . . leaving . . . ," I said stiffly. Yeah, I had to leave. Pronto. The You Wills agreed with that.

"Oh." Pixie grabbed Taryn's wrist and started to pull her away, but Taryn shook her friend loose, looking annoyed. Then it was as if she regretted it, because she smiled, embarrassed, and made the introduction. "This is Devon."

Devon and I mumbled hi to each other. She looked about as excited as I was. She stood close enough to Taryn to be her Siamese twin, like she wanted her all to herself.

The only one who seemed interested in conversation was Taryn. But she didn't notice this. "I had to drag Devon along. Didn't want to go myself. I hate these things."

I looked away, feeling like crud. She was too damn cute. I

couldn't take it anymore. "So you got a ride with Devon?" I finally asked.

"No, believe it or not, I have my own car."

"You drive?"

She nodded. "But I hate it. I know, most people can't wait to get their licenses, but I have this big fear of driving. I always have this feeling like I am going to die in a horrific car crash."

I thought about the glass shards spraying in my face. It scared me, too. Another thing we had in common.

"Anyway," she continued, "my parents wanted me to drive because they're too busy to cart me around everywhere I need to go. So I got my license a couple of weeks ago. I'm sixteen. Almost seventeen."

"Really? For some reason I thought you were a freshman."

Now it was her turn to shrink back. Her face turned red. "I am. Well, I was born on the cusp and so my parents kept me back. And then I had to stay back because of . . . well, forget it. Long story."

"That's cool," I said, dropping it. I figured it had something to do with that wild past she'd spoken of. I knew she was trying to escape that, because really, it wasn't her. She was a good girl. A good girl with a bad curse. Probably as bad a curse as mine.

"So you want to see my ride?" she asked, motioning Devon along. "My dad bought it for me as an early birthday present."

"Sure," I said after a while. I didn't want to because I had to get going, and because I wondered if it would be a better ride than mine. Then I realized that any ride was better than mine. Some Schwinns were better than mine.

We walked toward the parking area, and she and Devon talked about how sad the funeral was. Well, Taryn talked about that; Devon obviously wanted to get away from me, like most every girl in the world, because she kept saying under her breath, "We really should go." I kept looking at the headstones, wondering how the people in the ground had died. One stone said MOMMY'S LITTLE ANGEL and from the years engraved into it, I realized the kid was only five. Like Emma. Soon, she would be in the ground, and I would be—

Headlights flashing car horn blaring No no Tar watch ou

"Isn't that crazy?" a voice said. I turned my head. Taryn had said something and now she was waiting for a response.

"Oh. Yeah," I fudged.

"I thought that it was, but then, like, why was I waking up in the middle of the night?" she said with a sigh, which made me really want to know what the hell she was talking about. Instead I started thinking of kissing her. I could taste her lips. I knew I was turning red, so I muttered an "I don't know," which didn't fit into the conversation at all.

She looked at me curiously for a second, and then said, "Anyway. Here it is. I call her Beauty."

It was an old, and I mean old, dusty blue Jeep Cherokee. Nothing about this ride could be considered beautiful, since it was coated in dirt. It was also on a lift and looked too tough to be a Tarynmobile. As I moved around it, I saw a sticker on the back: BAD GIRLS LIKE BAD TOYS.

"Bad girls like bad toys, huh?"

She shrugged. "It was there when my dad bought it. Haven't had time to remove it yet."

I laughed. "Sure. You like your toys bad." I studied the other bumper stickers. FAT PEOPLE ARE HARDER TO KIDNAP. And NICE TRUCK. SORRY ABOUT YOUR PENIS. Wow. If you put me in a room with a thousand cars and asked me to pick which one belonged to Taryn, this would be my last pick. I was just about to point that out when I peeked into the driver's seat and my blood ran cold.

Dark seats. A center console brown with spilled Coke or coffee. A dream catcher dangling from the rearview mirror. In that instant I was transported to a rainy night, to headlights swirling around me, to the low, grating blare of a truck horn. To small, pale feet with pretty painted toenails pressing against the dashboard, and blond ringlets thrown forward over her face as she screamed and screamed. Suddenly her words played in my head like a recording at too slow a speed: I always have this feeling I am going to die in a horrific car crash.

This was it.

This was the car I would die in.

And worse yet, Taryn would be there, too.

Chapter 21

"No."

I hadn't meant to say it out loud, but it must have broken through my lips. My numb lips, useless as the rest of me. Because Taryn, who'd been talking about how her father had picked up the car from some lady in Island Heights, stopped midsentence, baffled. "No what?"

I took a small, feeble step backward.

She turned to Devon, shrugged, then alarm flooded her eyes. She tried to move closer. I backed away again. "Do you . . . did you see something?" she whispered.

I held out my hands in protest, and as I did I stumbled on a rock or a curb behind me. I nearly threw up my breakfast when I looked over and realized it was the gravestone of Mommy's Little Angel. Devon was looking at me as if she was rubbernecking a horrible, ghastly car accident on the side of the road. "I think we should just go," she muttered for the thousandth time to Taryn, but Taryn didn't even sway.

I couldn't breathe. I didn't care what normal was; I knew this wasn't it, and yet I didn't care. "No. I can't do this. I really can't be near you," I sputtered.

I half-expected the ground to open up and swallow me. After all, Mom and Nan would bury me here when I died. When we died. So I turned and broke into a run, back into the cemetery. A blind run, not really sure where I was headed. The cemetery was surrounded by a small line of trees. I didn't know what was behind them. Maybe I could go and live the rest of my life there. Away from Taryn. Away from everyone.

Like my mother.

When that thought hit me, I slowed down, breathing hard once I reached the chain-link fence by the trees. By the time I turned back, the girls were gone. A minute later I saw the Jeep heading toward the exit. So Devon had finally convinced her to leave. They were probably still watching me, wondering what was up. Well, maybe not Taryn. She knew. She knew what was bothering me. Most of it, anyway. Devon obviously thought I was two cashews shy of a nuthouse.

I realized I could have just taken Taryn aside and told her. She would have understood. We could have vowed to stay away from each other, and that would have been the end of it.

Or would it have been? Maybe it would have been like when we decided not to let Nan bring my mother breakfast anymore. She was still on course to die, but the pieces of Mom's breakfast were no longer around her head in the memory. Maybe Emma's death put the wheels in motion for something terrible to happen. Maybe evil would always follow us now, no matter what we did to prevent it. Maybe we were destined for bad things, and nothing could stop it.

I started walking back to the Buick, still breathing hard. As I walked, I loosened the tie, which felt like a noose, and undid the top button of my dress shirt. The collar was damp with sweat. I knew I should stay away from Taryn, but not a minute had passed before my mind kicked into overdrive, and between the You Wills, I began imagining all the different ways I could apologize to Taryn. I was probably paying more attention to my apology than to the You Wills.

That's probably why I didn't anticipate the punch. Out of nowhere, a force slammed against my cheek, throwing me to the ground.

Wondering what the hell had hit me, I tried to turn over and prop myself on my elbows, but the weight pressed on me, holding me down. A hand smashed against the back of my head, grinding my face into the hard earth so that all I could taste was dirt.

"You're the other one," a voice hissed. "Why did you come? Do you think Emma wants you here?"

The other one. Pedro. Fear curled in my stomach. I'd come out of this looking as messed up as he had. Maybe worse. I tried to open my mouth to speak but got a mouthful of grass instead, so only a muffled sound came out. The hand loosened its grip and I could turn my head a little. I tried to look up, but my eye was swelling and the lid felt heavy and useless. Birds twittered happily in the trees, as if what was happening to me was a good thing, as if this was how it was supposed to be.

"Who are you looking for?" I muttered, trying to be tough.

But I'll admit it. I was scared crapless. I hoped it was just a simple case of mistaken identity.

"Nick. Nick Cross? That you?"

Crap. One thing became clear to me: I was going to die if I said yes. "No." I tried to think of a fake name, but my mind whirred with You Wills, proving utterly useless once again. Suddenly something spat through. A name. Bryce. Bryce Reese. "Bryce Reese," I breathed.

There was a pause, and I thought maybe he was going to go for it, pick me up, dust me off, apologize for the misunderstanding. Suddenly a screaming pain whizzed through the back of my head. "That's my name, you idiot," he said.

Oh, hell. Thanks, brain. Reese. Bryce Reese. As in, Emma Reese. Emma's brother. Her mother had said they did "everything together." She'd said he'd been devastated. Of course. The visions I'd had of someone blaming me for Emma's death weren't of her parents. Mrs. Reese didn't blame me.

Bryce was the one who hated me.

He leaned over, his breath in my face. It smelled like stale coffee and cigarettes, making my stomach lurch. "I know who you are and what you did. Because of you, she's dead. You killed Emma."

I tried to take a breath but my lungs were being crushed by his weight. "I . . . tried—"

"You left that drunk SOB alone to watch the beach, didn't you?"

I swallowed. So they did know. "I'm sorry," I muttered, tasting grass. "I feel—"

He pushed me down, harder, into the dirt, then let go. "I hope you feel like dirt. You're a murderer. You'll get yours soon."

Then, quiet. I lie there after the sound of him faded away, too scared even to turn around and watch him leave. It was a good thing Taryn had left when she did. Once I got up, the cemetery was empty, except for Emma's casket, sitting there alone beside the burial site. The front of my suit was covered in dirt; I tried to wipe it off but smeared it in instead.

I walked back to the Buick, my cheek and all the teeth underneath aching from where Bryce's fist had met them. I tried again to think ahead. I focused hard on graduation. I usually could remember that.

But there was nothing. Hell, I couldn't even think of graduation. I don't think I'd ever not been able to remember something about graduation. Sure, things would be different every time I called up the memory. Once, I'd tripped going up to the podium; another time I got a sloppy kiss from Norah Cracowiczki, who sat next to me and was so drunk she thought I was her boyfriend. But graduation was always there. Nan was always there, smiling at me from the bleachers.

My mom was right. I had plenty of time to change it, and I would. Somehow.

You'll get yours. Soon. I thought about those words and how fitting they were. He was right. I would get mine. If everything continues the way it was going, I'll get the same thing Emma got, I thought, turning back to her gravesite.

I swallowed and let out an uneasy breath. Bryce was

standing there, head down, near the pile of freshly dug earth, holding some pink stuffed animal with floppy ears and weeping. Weeping so hard, his body shook with his every breath. I couldn't look at him for more than a second. He didn't have to punch me to make every part of me sting.

And maybe that was what I deserved.

Chapter 22

I drove back home at a slug's pace. It was the middle of the day on the Saturday before Labor Day, and though some of the rich folk with summerhouses had already packed up and gone to their winter residences, the tourist activity was in full swing. I kept imagining the Buick plowing into beachgoers with their brightly colored umbrellas and beach chairs, which always brought me back to Bryce, at graveside, weeping. Which brought me back to Emma. The day she died, something big had been set in motion. I couldn't get it out of my head that whatever had started needed to happen, that it was right. That it was my punishment.

When I got home, the first thing I did was run up the stairs. I already had my tie and jacket off, but I starting ripping at the buttons of my shirt as soon as I got in the door. I was halfway up the stairs when my mom called to me. "What?" I snapped, still clawing at my chest.

"We were just wondering where you've been. We were worried," she said, all innocent. It made me all the more angry because she knew very well where I'd been. Whenever she was even the least bit worried about anything, she'd just think into the future and find out the answer she was looking for. She couldn't not look.

"You know," I muttered, slamming my bedroom door behind me. At that moment, I hated her. Hated her for having to meddle with everything instead of just taking things as they came.

I threw my sweaty, dirty clothes in a heap by my hamper and lay on my dump-truck sheets in my gym shorts, staring up at the cottage-cheese ceiling. With the door closed, the room felt like an oven, but I didn't care.

I thought that getting away from Taryn would do it. She'd never want to talk to me again after that, right? But no, as I lay there, I could still see my future with her, so clearly it had to be real. I knew so much about her, and could feel that she was the peg in my life that held all the pieces together, and without her there, everything seemed to be loosening. I hadn't really even cycled much. But though I knew her as if I'd spent a lifetime with her, for some reason, I still couldn't see anything more than a few weeks into the future.

As I was contemplating what it all meant and what I could do, the door opened, blowing an ocean breeze into the room that dropped the temperature twenty degrees, making me shiver. Nan walked in. "Honey bunny?"

"Yeah?" I snapped. I was so angry at Mom, it was carrying over to Nan, even though she'd done nothing wrong.

"How was the funeral?" she asked, sitting down on the side of my bed.

It was a stupid question. Coming from anyone else I would have told them that. Instead I just rolled over and answered her. "Like a funeral."

Then she saw my face. I hadn't looked in a mirror, but my check still felt raw from where I'd been punched and smashed into the ground. She reached out her hand, but I flinched. "Who did that to you?"

I laughed bitterly. "Okay. It was like a funeral . . . with a gang fight thrown in for added excitement."

"What is going—"

"Mom didn't tell you? I found out why we're like this. There's a stand on the boardwalk where a freaky lady sells spells called Touches. Mom spent a crapload of money to be given a Touch that would make her able to see the future," I said, watching with satisfaction as Nan's face stiffened.

"Who told you this?"

"A girl named Taryn. Her grandmother gave Mom the Touch." I exhaled.

Her face didn't change. "Is this the fortune-teller you were talking about yesterday?"

"Yeah."

"That still doesn't explain why your face looks like it was—"

"She effed up my life. I hate her."

"Who?"

"Mom! Who else?" I clutched handfuls of the sheet and threw them back down. "She knew it was her fault. She knew all this time and she never told me. 'Hate' is too nice a word."

"Oh, you don't mean—"

"Yeah, I do. I really do." I sat up and touched my face, thinking about how she was even responsible for that. For everything bad in my life. "All this time, I thought Dad was the bad guy. That he was somehow responsible for our messed-up lives. Now I totally get it. He's normal. I don't blame him. Hell, I would have left, too."

She shook her head. "No. Well, I don't know what went on between your mom and dad. But I do know that when your mom became pregnant with you, she changed. She was usually so crazy—she'd go on crash diets and drink and smoke and, oh, just about everything I'd tell her not to do. But when she found out about you, she quit smoking and drinking and made sure she ate well. She worked on the boardwalk and she used to bring a container of fruit and a bottle of water with her so she wouldn't have to eat the greasy food up there." She smiled. "You were—you *are* everything to her. Whatever she did to you by getting this—this Touch, as you call it, she didn't mean it."

I studied her. I knew what she was doing. Trying to keep the peace. She wouldn't let me think my dad was the bad guy, and she'd do anything to keep me from thinking my mom was a villain, too. "But my dad—I mean, you met him, right? What's he like?"

She gave me a surprised look. On the rare times I talked about my dad, I always did it with a glower, with hate, and she would always reply, "Your dad was a good man in a bad situation." But coming from her, "good" meant nothing. To her, nobody was downright bad. You could steal her purse and whack her over the head with it, and she wouldn't think you were bad. And she'd say the same thing about a roast she picked up at the supermarket. "It's a good piece of meat." It meant zero.

Now, she opened her mouth, and I knew what she was going to say, so I stopped her. "But what was he like?"

"You got your eyes from him. And your dark skin. I only met him a handful of times. The first time, he made quite an impression. I could see why your mother was charmed by him. He had that wild side to him, too. He was a rocker. The typical teen back then. Had blue hair. Wore tight leather pants. Pierced and tattooed all over. Your grandfather almost threw him out of the house!"

I knew some of this, but before, I didn't care. Before, I wished I could have emptied my head of any bits of information that had to do with my father. Now, I listened intently. He was wild. Nothing like me. I wondered if I might have been the blue-haired rocker type had things been different.

"But he was an athlete, too. I remember he played basketball. He had all sorts of talents. And I liked him. Deep down, under all the tattoos and piercings, I knew he really loved your mom." She looked down at the shag carpet, her mouth moving but no sound coming out, as if she was trying to figure out how to put her thoughts into words. "And I know that is why he left. He couldn't stand to see your mom so weak. She was falling apart. It was difficult to see her so sick, so afraid. But it was as much the fault of your mother as it was his. She refused to speak to him. Partly she hated herself, but she also saw something in the future with him . . . something she didn't want. So she shut him out, too. He left before you were born. But he was a good man in a bad situation."

"You always say that he was a good man. Past tense."

She sighed. "I think he desperately wanted things to work out between him and your mother. I don't think he got over losing you both. I don't know what happened to him, but he's never tried to contact us since that day. I don't know what your mother knows."

Of course, Mom would know better than anyone. We had ways of finding these things out. Knowing her, she probably created futures in her head all the time that had her tracking him down. She was just so . . . She couldn't leave anything alone. I sat there, surprised at how numb I felt. I guess nothing where he was concerned would matter to me now. He'd already been dead to me for too long.

"She didn't tell you because she feels so terrible about what it's done to you," Nan said. "Haven't you ever wished you could undo something in your life?"

Of course I thought of Emma. Of Bryce weeping at the graveside, of Mrs. Reese watering the asphalt. I'd ruined them. With one stupid decision, I'd ruined them all forever. When Nan patted my hand and left the room, I couldn't get out of my head how strange it was that the smallest decisions in our lives can leave the biggest scars.

Chapter 23

That night I had a dream. It's not unusual for me to dream when I sleep, but it is unusual for me to sleep very much. This time I dreamt of slivers of pale blue light, breaking through a spiderweb in the darkness. Of glass raining down on me. Of me reaching for someone and grabbing handfuls of wet hair. Of pain.

I woke up with a scream caught in my throat. When I came to, I was sitting up in bed, sheets twisted around my legs. My hands were out in front of me, as if I was bracing myself for a fall. My heartbeat echoed in my ears.

It was just a dream. But it felt real. More like my future.

The worst thing was, I hadn't been on script in days. I'd been ignoring most of the You Wills or doing the opposite of what they instructed, hoping to shake something up. But nothing had changed.

I'm not going in a car, I told myself.

Sometimes, all I needed to do to change the future was to convince myself I was going to change. When I saw the future of me at the dentist, getting all my teeth pulled because of too many butterscotch candies, I just told myself, "I will no longer eat them." And the more I thought that, the more that memory of me at the dentist faded, became less real. So telling myself I would not drive a car should have worked. Instead, though, the memory seemed clearer. I could make out the pretty spiderweb pattern on the windshield, I could feel the zip of the seat belt on my chest, my fingers digging into the soft plastic seat.

But I am not going in a car. You got that? No car!

But there was no cycling. No new memories. Nothing to suggest that I'd changed the future. It was useless and crazy, arguing with my own mind. Like arguing with a girl. No matter what my position was, I could never win.

I changed my shorts and pulled an old surfing T-shirt over my head as I ran down the stairs. The You Wills whispered and I tried not to pay attention, but random things floated through my mind: unmentionables, lighthouse, fire-engine red. Something smelled like strawberries. When I reached the screen door, Nan was standing by the washing machine. "It's laundry day," she said, a tinge of defeat in her voice.

I realized why she was upset when I saw the cast on her arm and remembered her injury. Nan was one of those people who would keep chugging along even with every bone in her body broken. I rushed to her side, despite the fact that on the few occasions I'd helped with laundry in the past, I'd almost been scarred for life. Something about having to handle my mom's and grandmother's silky, giant underwear, knowing that Nan handled mine, hanging them up on the line outside for the whole world to see. I'd much rather believe they just dried and folded themselves and jumped into my drawer. But with one arm, Nan was pretty helpless. "Yeah, I can help."

"Oh, perfect," she said, to my dismay. She pointed to a big wicker basket of damp whites, all ready to go out on the line. Perfect. Her unmentionables, or at least, that's what Nan called them.

"How is your arm feeling?" I asked, hoping she'd say it was miraculously cured and she could take off the cast. I wasn't sure I could handle more than one week of laundry.

"Oh, fine," she answered through gritted teeth. She waved me out the door.

I walked outside and grabbed the bucket of clothespins, then started with my socks. The easy thing. Unfortunately since I'd only gone running once this week, I only had one pair in the laundry. I moved on to my boxers, hoping that by the time I got to the more serious stuff, a rainstorm would come or the world would implode or something. I was just clipping the last pair to the line when the world did implode. Because she started coming up the pathway. Taryn. And here I was, surrounded by my underwear, all flapping happily in the breeze.

Okay, maybe a real man wouldn't have felt weird about it. It was completely third grade to be embarrassed. But I was. Like I said, I didn't have much real experience with girls. And it was embarrassing enough as it was, being accosted in my ugly backyard, which was all overgrown and filled with rusting, peeling patio furniture. There were faded green aliens and army men (you really couldn't tell the difference) painted on the clamshells that surrounded the cracked walk. I'd made a bird feeder out of Popsicle sticks and that was there, too, lopsided and pathetic, by Nan's garden. Nan saved every weird creative endeavor from my youth; they were valued trophies to her. The garbage cans were nearby, and they still reeked from the fish from a few nights before. All my surroundings reeked too much of me, of things I didn't want Taryn knowing about.

She approached cautiously. She was wearing sunglasses and her hair was up in a bun, making her look older and even more out of my league. "Are you better now?" she asked. "I just came to check on you."

Could she be any nicer? How many times would I have to freak out on her before she left me alone? But I was glad she was persistent. I was so happy to see her it was only then I realized one of Nan's silky white skivvies had landed on my foot. I plucked it off and said, "Yeah, thanks. Thanks for asking."

"Whoa, you don't look better. What happened to your eye?"

I'd almost forgotten about the run-in with Bryce, despite the constant sting where his fist had met my temple. I thought maybe she'd been lingering to witness it, so I was glad to learn that she hadn't. And I really didn't want to go over it again. "Nothing. Just a minor misunderstanding with a door."

She raised her eyebrows and I knew right away she didn't believe me. But she gave me a pass. "So how are you doing?"

She had that look, the one doctors gave to their patients who only had three months to live. Like I was a charity case. Right. That's probably what I was to her. She felt guilty about what her grandmother had done to us, and this was her way of making it up to me. "Why do you keep asking me that?" I said.

"I just"—she shrugged—"care."

"That's warped. I've been a total jerkwad to you. You should be running in the other direction." I looked away, toward the clothesline, then mumbled, "Save yourself."

"What's that supposed to mean? You saw something. Something with me? That's why you don't want to see me anymore. Right?"

She was inspecting the shells on the ground. So while she wasn't looking, I quickly flung the undies back into the wicker basket. She raised her head just in time to see them make a safe landing and raised her eyebrows again but said nothing. I played it off by nodding and saying, really nonchalantly, "Yep."

"Bad, huh? How bad?"

I was still trying to block her view of the basket. I gave her a smirk. "Terror, pain. Death, dismemberment. All that good stuff."

"Really?" She gulped.

I expected her to make herself scarce, like I had when I found out. Instead, she just stood there. Staring, directly, at the row of boxers behind me. "This is the part where you run away, screaming," I prompted after a minute.

"Is it?" She seemed reluctant to move. Almost like she liked the idea of dying.

"Yeah. Why? You don't want to?"

"Well, I was just thinking. You can change it, right? You said your future changes all the time?"

"Sometimes. Not always. Like my mom says, fix one thing, another breaks. And sometimes you can't fix things."

"Why?"

I shrugged. "I told you. I only see part of things. If I don't know what's wrong, I can't fix it. And some things can't be prevented."

She frowned. "So what is it? A car accident?" I didn't answer, but my face must have given it away. "Soon?"

"Pretty soon, I think."

She covered her mouth with her hands. "Oh, my God. Not Beauty. I just got it, and my dad keeps getting on me because of what happened in Maine. He'll kill me if I total my car!"

I waved her away with my hand. "So run away. Save yourself."

But again she just stood there. I checked to see if she was growing roots under those pretty red toenails of hers. Then she just hoisted her bag over her shoulder. "I am not afraid," she said.

I laughed. "You should be."

"We can change it."

I shrugged. "Not always. Not if we keep . . ." I stopped. Not if we keep running into each other. I didn't want to say it. I didn't even want to suggest it. "Look. This is not your fault. You don't have to be nice to me. If there's anyone you should be able to say no to, I'm it. Why don't you start practicing?" I exaggerated the word. "*No.* Say it with me."

She just stared at me.

"And then you turn and walk away."

"You really think that I'm bothering with you just because I feel guilty?"

I nodded. "Isn't it?"

"No. I like you, Nick. When you're not being weird, I like spending time with you. That's the truth."

I shook my head. "I'm never not weird."

"That's not true. We had a good time on the boardwalk." She moved closer, so her next words were almost whispered. "And listen. You know things about me. Things that you never would have been able to find out about me if you were a total jerk, through and through. If you were that person, if that was truly who you were, I would have shut you out. But for some reason, in some version of the future, I let you in. I let you get close to me. Right? That proves to me that there is good in you."

I considered it for a moment. "Maybe in that version of the future, you were stupid. Maybe you kept trying to convince yourself there was good in me, even though there wasn't. I've done really stupid things in some of my futures. I know how to freebase coke," I said, thinking of my short life in Vegas, married to the stripper. "That's pretty stupid."

She shook her head. " I know you're pushing me away just because you're trying to protect me. That's a noble, good thing."

I just stood there, unable to meet her eyes. Unable to meet

the eyes of the one person on this earth who knew me better than I knew myself.

"And so your vision says we are going to be in a car accident. If that can't change, if we are doomed to this future, then how can you know me so well? Maybe because we don't die in it. Or maybe because that future isn't set. Maybe seeing two different versions of the future. You just need to pick the right one. The one that doesn't end in tragedy."

It's obvious she'd put a lot of thought into it, and she was probably right.

"All I am saying is that you don't have to shut me out completely."

"That would be taking a chance." I swallowed and looked away. "I'm sick of taking chances."

"But I'm not," she said, looking over her shoulder. "Look. You said that touching me made you feel normal. Right?"

I sighed. "It's a joke. I'm not normal."

She frowned and started to speak again, but thankfully, just then, a car horn blared. She looked behind her nervously. "I do have to go."

"So, go," I said, surprised at how gruff I could be. I wondered if it would be the last time I'd ever see her. If so, I wouldn't blame her. That would be the smart thing to do.

But that would kill me. In other ways.

She turned and walked back down the path, her head lowered. I felt this weird sense of dread in the pit of my stomach, like a hole inside of me gaping open. I reached down to pick up the wicker basket and when I stood up, I saw a car speeding away from the house, a red convertible. Sphincter's Mustang. Two blond heads, a his and a hers, poked out from the front seat. Sphincter and Taryn. Taryn and Sphincter. No, he didn't have his arm around her and her head wasn't nestled on his shoulder, but in my mind, as soon as the car turned the next corner, it would be.

That wasn't the future. That was just me.

Being paranoid.

Being a sucker.

Watching the best thing I'd ever had, in any of my lifetimes, moving farther and farther away.

Chapter 24

When I got back upstairs, the hole in the pit of my stomach had grown to a canyon. That would have happened anyway after hanging rows of silky underpants on the line, but I felt even worse because of Taryn. Sphincter was parading around with my girl, and I was hanging my mom's and grandmother's underclothes. Something was wrong with this picture. I started thinking there was no way that what I saw with Taryn—me kissing her, being with her—could be real. After all, she had Sphincter, who was, looking at the way hot girls hung on his every word, the highest goal one could aspire to in the game of love. She had Mount Everest. I was just irrevocably and unequivocally too lame for her. The Grand Canyon of Lame.

I guess it must have registered on my face, because Nan took the wicker basket from me and tried to knead my shoulder with her good hand. I pulled away from her. I didn't want anyone to touch me.

"Why are you two so upset?" she asked. "Your mother didn't eat any of her breakfast, and you're walking around with the biggest scowl on your face, you'd think someone peed in your lemonade."

I started to open my mouth, but then I remembered how Nan felt about me revealing the future. "Forget it. Has to do with my future."

"Doesn't it always? Something bad?"

"Pretty much the worst."

Her eyes narrowed. "Car accident?"

"I think so." Now I was surprised. "How did you know?"

"On the ride home from the hospital. You saw it, didn't you? That's why you were upset."

"Yeah. I think it will kill me. Me and a girl. The girl I . . ."

"Oh. The one who was outside just now?"

Nan had probably been listening in on the whole thing. For someone who didn't want to know the future, she sure was nosy. "Yeah."

"She's cute. Is she the one you're in love with?"

I cringed. "No. I mean, yeah. I mean, I think I could be. But I have to stay away from her." I pressed my lips closed.

"But?"

"Well . . . my life is one disaster after another. But being with her makes me almost happy. It makes me feel normal."

Nan looked at me for a long time. Then she put a hand on my cheek. "Well, why do you need to stay away from *her,* then? You said it was a car accident. Stay away from *cars,* honey bunny."

"I know. But what if it's just meant to happen, and messing

with it just means it will happen some other way? Why should I take chances?"

"You said it yourself. Because she makes you happy. That makes it worth it."

I sighed. "Okay. If I just say there's no way I'm going to get into a car with her again, it won't happen. Right?"

Nan nodded.

Just as my spirits started to pick up, I thought about her driving away in Sphincter's Mustang. "But she's with Sphinc—Spitzer now. I think they might be together."

She shook her head. "Evan Spitzer? Oh, Nicky, you're every bit as worthy as he is."

Sure, in her warped world, a world where bifocals were a necessity and everyone who breathed was "good," I was. That's what I got for discussing my love life with my grandmother. Some things were better kept to myself. "Right." It was better just to agree with her.

"You deserve to be happy." She reached into the pocket of her apron and pulled out a hard butterscotch candy. "Want one?"

I took two and unwrapped them, one for me and one for her.

"School's Tuesday," she said. "And your underwear is in a sorry state. Thought I'd go and pick up some new ones for you."

I muttered a thanks. I didn't want to think of underwear any more than I had today.

"Oh, and pens and notebooks." She ruffled my hair. "You need a haircut, too. You look scruffy."

I nodded like I'd take that into consideration, even though I knew there was no way I'd get a haircut before school. I didn't feel like it. I liked scruffy, anyway.

"Anything else you need?" she asked.

"A million dollars."

Nan launched into the same speech I'd heard a thousand times before, so I muttered, "I know, root of all evil, blah blah blah." By then, I was already out the door of the kitchen, headed upstairs. The last thing I wanted to think about was school, where my life would suck even more if Sphincter and Taryn were a couple. In my head, I could see them walking down the hall together, pinkies intertwined, then stopping at her locker to have a massive PDA. It seemed pretty vivid. Could have been the future. Now, the thought of her and me together was faded out, like an inactive menu option on a computer screen. "Whatever," I said.

As I climbed the stairs, my head ached. Things were cycling again, because I'd been ignoring the You Wills. Once it quieted, I tried to see my future. After all, if Taryn and Sphincter were a couple, there was no way we'd die in a car crash together, right? I tried to call up my graduation, but again, my mind just went blank. As soon as I got up to my room, though, I saw the image, felt the darkness and humidity in the Jeep. It would be raining. Steel folding in on us. Glass showering down.

What the . . . how could that be?

My stomach flopped. The walls of the house, like the steel walls of Taryn's Jeep, seemed to press in on me. I needed air.

I ran back downstairs. "Nan, I'll go get those things," I said, huffing like I'd run a marathon. "You should sit. Rest your arm."

"You okay?"

"Yeah, just need something to do." She tried to hand me a twenty, but I waved her away. "I've got it."

As I crossed the street, following the You Wills, I noticed the cars were packed against one another like sardines, up and down the block. People were everywhere. When I came to Central, I realized why. The Labor Day weekend arts and crafts show was going on at the grounds of City Hall. Right. Nothing brought the throngs of people out more than the opportunity to blow money on stupid knickknacks.

As I navigated the crowds scavenging the racks of the B&B Department Store's annual sidewalk sale, contemplating whether I should get underwear, I had this really weird feeling. Like I was going to see Taryn again. Soon. In my mind, I could see her blond head poking out from between a display of Seaside Park lighthouse and seagull souvenir magnets at the Ocean Pharmacy. No local would be caught dead looking at them. But Taryn was no local. In my head I saw her reaching for the seagull.

I had to stop her. Stop her and save her, and in the meantime, beg for forgiveness about how wrong I was. We'd just stay away from her car and everything would be fine. My future would have to change, how could it not? I'd taken three quick steps when I realized something else.

Not twenty minutes ago, I'd seen her speeding toward Ocean Avenue with Sphincter. There was no way she could be in the pharmacy. Not unless she left him a few minutes later and went right there. No. She was probably lying on the sand with him now, in a tiny bikini, looking so . . . forget it.

I thumped the side of my head as if that would make it work right again. As if it ever worked right. But even before I knew it, I was running toward the store. I pulled open the door and a blast of arctic air from the AC hit me as a little bell above the door jingled, startling me. Some lady glared at me over her reading glasses. I could still feel her staring as I ran past the aisles of cold remedies and tissues, looking for the souvenir magnets.

I saw them at the end of the paper products aisle. A big display of them, right next to the rack of personalized bicycle license plates. But no Taryn.

I turned away, chewing on my lip. Staring Lady was still doing what she did best, making me forget what I'd come in there for. I pretended to be really interested in toilet paper while I tried to remember. When the bell above the door tinkled again, the lady broke her death glare on me to check out the new customer, and I relaxed enough to let it come to me. Pens. Notebooks. School stuff.

I started to book it to the stationery aisle when I looked up and saw Taryn.

"Hi," she mumbled.

I was cleaning my throat to say something when I realized that for the first time, her voice wasn't chipper. She actually grumbled. And for the first time, she didn't look happy to see me. She brushed past me, as if she didn't want anything to do with me. As she should have done all this time. Her face looked red. Like she was upset. What had Sphincter done to her?

Of course, she wandered off toward the magnets. I followed her in time to see her pick up a seagull. "Locals call them beach vermin," I said. "Do you really want a rat on your refrigerator?"

She shifted her gaze to me for a nanosecond, and then made a "hmph" noise and put the magnet back. Then she picked up a lighthouse.

"False advertising," I said. "There are no lighthouses in Seaside Park. That's Barnegat Head Lighthouse, in Island Beach. Every painter in the free world has tried to reproduce it."

She shrugged. "So?"

"Well. You would think artists would have a little more creativity, right? Isn't that the whole point of being an artist?"

"No. The whole point of being an artist is that you can take something everyone has seen before and make them see it in an entirely new light."

What was this? The girl was getting a backbone. Really, what had Sphincter done to her? "You're angry," I remarked.

"Maybe," she said, turning and walking away.

I stopped her. "At me?"

She sighed. "You're the one who can tell the future, right? Figure it out." Then her face softened. "You know it's not about you. It's about . . . I don't want to—"

"Evan? Trouble in paradise?" It just kind of slipped out. I couldn't help myself.

A second later, I wished I could have. Her eyes narrowed. "It's not like that. We're not . . . anything."

I doubted that. If they weren't "anything," why was she looking angrier than I'd ever seen her? "Uh-huh," I said.

"It's true. I can tell you don't believe me, but it's true. He was driving by when I dropped Beauty off at the gas station on Eighth for an oil change, and asked me if I wanted a ride. I told him I was going to your house to see you, to make sure you were okay, so no thanks. But he was kind of insistent. He said he'd wait in the car while I talked to you. If you didn't notice, it's really hot today, and I really didn't feel like walking the three miles back home. Really. You don't have to be jealous."

I snorted. "Me? Jealous? Why would I be? You and I aren't together."

"Yet," she said, her voice low. She had me there. If I could grieve for children I never had, miss a woman I never even met, then of course she knew I could have jealousy for a relationship that hadn't even started yet.

"Whatever," I said, trying to play it cool. "Okay, so you and Sphincter aren't anything."

She started to speak, but then stopped short and burst out laughing. "Sphincter?"

"It's a term of endearment." I looked over her shoulder, to where Staring Lady was watching us like someone would watch one of those caught-on-tape shows. This time she was standing up, as if readying to throw herself over the cash register in case we tried to start any, as people her age called it, "funny business." "Can we . . . go?" I whispered, motioning to the woman.

Taryn turned and saw her, then said, a little amused, "Oh, so now you're okay with being seen with me?"

"Until I get a better offer, I guess," I answered, and she followed me out the door. Five minutes later, we sat outside on Central Avenue, watching the first of the beachgoers making the trek back home as we shared an iced tea from the Park Bakery. I liked sharing it with her because I knew her lip gloss tasted like strawberries. It reminded me of how it would be when I, or *if* I, got a chance to kiss her. Maybe I let my lips linger on the mouth of the bottle too long, maybe it was obvious how much it excited me, because she allowed me to drink most of it.

"I don't even like sunbathing," she said, watching a family of beachgoers trudging down the block. She winced and pulled a pair of dark sunglasses over her eyes. "I can never get comfortable. I try to read and I get sand in my book. The sun hurts my eyes. Parts of my body always fall asleep. I end up burning in places and being completely white in others. I never tan. Of course, you know this already."

I looked at her legs. They were perfect. White, yeah, but sunbathing couldn't improve them. One of my most prominent memories of Sue was her lounging in a beach chair, wearing big sunglasses, her red hair tossing in the wind. I'd never had a memory like that of Taryn. Most often when I thought of her, I thought of her indoors. "Whatever happened to it? *The Mouse.*"

She raised her eyebrows. "What?"

"*The Mouse.* Your sailboat. You told me that was what you used your red bikini for. You made it into a flag for your sailboat, since you never went to the beach."

"I never told you that," she said. At first I thought she was so weirded out she was going to run away, but then she said, "It got smashed in a nor'easter. When I was nine or ten. But by then I didn't really want it anymore. I was kind of done with it, just like I was done with sunbathing."

"And the whole sunbathing confession is because . . . ?"

"Sphincter, like you call him. That's all he does. He lives to tan. His life is so pathetic and empty. I can't believe you would think I'd . . . Please."

I laughed. "I bet every other girl in school would *please* him."

She wrinkled her nose. "Ew."

"Well, he totally wants you."

She didn't seem impressed, just played with her bracelet. "Duh, they all do."

"Conceited much?"

"It's not conceit. I told you. I told you that people like him are drawn to me." She seemed really annoyed. I must have stared at her too long, confused, because she finally spelled it out for me in a whisper. "He's Touched."

I nearly choked on my own tongue. "Hell he is."

"He is."

"I've known Sphincter for years. We used to be best friends, back in the day."

"He wasn't Touched then. My grandmother did it for him last spring." She stared at me. "If you don't believe me, I can show you his signature in the book."

"No, hey, I do," I said. After all, it made total sense why he changed seemingly overnight. "What Touch did he get?"

"Physical perfection," she answered, seeming bored. "Well, outwardly, he's perfect. But as you know, a lot of those Touches have a catch. His has a really bad one."

Suddenly the wind picked up, just as a thought caught in my brain. "Let me guess. He's rotting from the inside."

She nodded and smiled at me, but it was an empty smile. "It's just sad. I want to warn him, but what do I say? 'Hi, my grandmother made you perfect on the outside, but you're also filled with a hundred tumors and won't live to see Christmas.'"

"If I was him, I'd want to know. You have to tell him."

She nodded and rubbed her temple with her free hand. "I know. I keep trying to. But it's so terrible. Grandma tells me to stay away from the Touched, but I feel bad for him."

Another group of tourists wandered by, and one, a girl of about thirteen or fourteen, looked at me and giggled. I realized my mouth was hanging open wide enough to probably spot my tonsils and clamped it shut. Wow. Evan Spitzer, my former-best friend. Dying. Hadn't seen that one coming. Maybe if we still traveled in the same circles, I would have. Maybe I would have noticed something about him, something that would have hinted at the havoc being wreaked inside his flawless body. I thought of him racing down the boardwalk the other day, pumping his arms and legs, the picture of physical health. Of perfection.

Suddenly it seemed like we had a lot in common. We could have started our own Dead Before Next Year club. Except . . .

"It was his choice," I said.

"No. He chose something else. Not this."

"So, you were trying to explain it to him?"

"Yeah, that and . . . well, you know how when I touch you, you said you feel normal? Well, I thought maybe I could touch him and heal his tumors."

"Oh, sure you were," I said. "So did it work?"

She shrugged. "I have no idea. I touched his cheek, like, pretending to wipe something off it, but I couldn't feel anything. Anyway, he thought I was coming on to him. He was all over me. We didn't even make it two blocks. I wanted to help him, not be his newest conquest. So I told him to pull over and let me out."

"So, you do feel guilty. For things your grandmother did."

"I guess I do. A little. Otherwise, why would I be hanging out with you?" She grinned.

"Funny."

She motioned across the street. Some of the artists were already beginning to pack up their wares and leave. "What's going on there?"

"Arts and crafts show."

"Oh. Cool. Let's go," she said, tugging the sleeve of my T-shirt. She was already halfway across Central when I tossed the empty iced-tea bottle away and hurried to follow her. "Is this like an annual thing?"

"Yep. Every Labor Day weekend."

"Oh, cool," she repeated, then walked a few steps, wrinkling her nose. "You are right. People do paint that lighthouse a lot. Do you come to this thing every year?"

I shook my head. Actually, the last time I'd come, I begged Nan to get me a beanbag frog. It was the only thing there that a seven-year-old would want, the only thing that wasn't a reproduction of that lighthouse. I loved that frog, took it everywhere with me. But a couple of weeks later there were weevils in my bed, and Nan inspected the frog and told me she had to throw it out. I begged her not to, but then she showed me a little black bug popping out of the seam. She wrapped the frog in two plastic bags and stuck it in the trash. Sometimes I wonder if that really happened, or if it was just part of a future that might have happened, but anyway, I never went to the festival again after that. It was just another reminder of how everything good in my life was always laced with bad.

Taryn said, "Oh, well, it's cool. Anyway, I've got to go. I've got to . . . Listen." She bit her lip and suddenly I knew what she was going to ask me. She was afraid to, but I would eventually pry it out of her. She wanted to ask me to meet her tonight. At the boardwalk. Yes!

Before she could answer, I found my lips spreading into "yes."

Her surprise melted into a smile. "You mean it? You can?"

"Sure. What time?"

"Like, six?" She bit her lip again. "I can't stop myself from shaking. I need to start now. I should have done the last one, but I bailed."

I squinted at her. What? What had I just agreed to? "So you're . . ."

"I don't really think I'm ready, but I've put it off long enough. Too long. So you will?"

Wait . . . wait. Suddenly it all became clear, all of it. Everything I'd agreed to. And the answer was no. No thanks, never. By that time I felt too stupid to change my reply, to tell her I'd just agreed to it because she had the most amazing . . . the most amazing everything and it wasn't possible for me to turn her down. "Sure."

"Great. I'm a little nervous. Actually, really nervous."

I nodded. I would be, too. She was going to perform her first Touch tonight. For whatever reason, she wanted me to be nearby for it. I didn't know how I could do that. Be in the same room with someone as his life was ruined. As Taryn ruined his life. I opened my mouth to speak and a bunch of nonsensical syllables streamed out before I finally managed, "You, like, want me to wait outside?"

She nodded.

"Um. Why?"

"It's not easy," she whispered, and her eyes got all glassy. "Just . . . can you?"

I shrugged. "All right. I'll wait in the arcade next door, and you come out when you're—"

"Actually, I thought maybe you could hide in that place I showed you? That way you can watch it."

"I don't know how that will help. But okay," I said, digging my hands into the pockets of my shorts. "But I won't get . . .

uh . . ." "Hurt" was the word I said in the You Wills, but I couldn't push it past my lips. It made me sound like a gutless wonder.

"Oh, no way. You'll be behind the curtain. And besides, you can't be Touched twice."

"Really?"

She flinched at my surprise. "Why, did you want to get another one?"

"Why would I want that? The good is always accompanied by bad."

She shook her head. "Not always. Sometimes it's all good. Bad things happen a lot. But sometimes it just does what people want."

I snorted. Just my luck. "But now it makes sense why your grandmother isn't too concerned with providing stellar customer service. No repeat customers."

She wasn't paying attention, though. She had wandered over to a display of little wire figurines, made to illustrate different professions. "Look," she said, picking one up. "A fortune-teller. Looks just like my grandmother."

I stared at the figure, hunched over the table with a deck of tarot cards in front of her. "No it doesn't. She's smiling."

She turned it over, checking the price. "I think Grandma would get a kick out of this."

I eyed it, doubtful. "She gets kicks out of things?"

She sighed and put the figurine down. "You're right. So, um, today? At six? You'll be there?"

I dug my hands deeper into my pockets, rubbing the grains

of sand that always seemed permanently buried in the seams of all my clothing against my palms. "Yeah."

"And you won't blow me off again?" she asked, nudging me.

She came in so close I could smell the apples in her hair, and it made me wonder how I was ever Superman enough to find the will to blow her off the first time. "Promise," I mumbled.

We followed the crowds of shoppers out of the green and she waved goodbye, then headed across Central Avenue, in the direction of her grandmother's house. And as usual, the second she left, I missed her.

Chapter 25

I didn't want to go home again, but I did. I had a lot of time to kill before six, and after Taryn left me, I realized I looked like a slob. I wanted to brush my teeth, wash my face, and change out of my holey gym shorts and T-shirt so I could look halfway presentable. I opened and closed the screen door carefully, then quietly climbed the stairs and did all I needed to without my mother noticing. Well, maybe she did know I was there, since she could see the future and all, but if she did, she didn't come out of her room or call to me, and I was glad for that. Quickly, I threw on some cargo shorts and one of the few clean plaid button-downs I had lying around, and was still buttoning it when I ran into Nan downstairs. "Don't hold dinner for me," I said.

"Oh, it's that girl, isn't it?" she said, beaming. "A date?"

"Not exactly," I said, nerves tweaking as I thought about what it was. "But we're . . . hanging out."

"Not exactly," she repeated, mimicking my voice, then swatting my backside with a dish towel. "Dating, hanging out. It's the same thing. You kids and your funny expressions."

"Whatever," I said with a smile, then went out the door, this time not caring if my mom heard the slamming. When I straddled my bicycle, in my mind I saw these things: pizza, smiley face, strings of disgusting peppermint. I was halfway down the street in a matter of minutes, heading toward the Heights, when I passed the badge-checking station at the Seventh Avenue beach. A thought of Jocelyn, my old baby-sitter, popped into my mind. I figured it was probably because that booth was where she worked, but I'd passed it a hundred times before and never thought of her once. I shook the thought away, stood on the pedals and pushed harder, past the piles of sand on Ocean.

It was a weird night. The wind was blowing steadily from the east and thick clouds, like a pile of charcoal, were hovering over the mainland. I could see the white outlines of the seagulls against them. Somewhere, far away, thunder rumbled. That meant a nasty summer downpour, the kind that raged for a few minutes and then disappeared as quickly as it had come, leaving a rosy sunset and a rainbow as a parting gift. I crossed my fingers and hoped I wouldn't be drenched by the time I made it to the stand on the boardwalk.

I didn't have to worry. When I got there, the storm was still rumbling in the distance. Taryn was sitting on one of the green benches overlooking the beach, her backside on top of the backrest and her feet planted on the seat. There were seagulls swarming around her. As I got closer, I noticed she had the fabric of a long skirt bunched up around her knees and a scarf over her shoulders. Hoop earrings and a tambourine would have completed the picture so nicely. She was feeding the birds funnel cake. She shrugged as she saw me. "I know, rats of the seashore and all, but we're all God's creatures."

I sat beside her. "Will you still think that when one craps on your head?"

"As a matter of fact," she said indignantly, "one already did, on my knee. Anyway, this stuff is pure grease. It will probably kill them."

I stared at her knee. She was probably the only girl in the world who wasn't bothered by seagull crap. "Nothing can kill them. They're like cockroaches."

She turned and held the plate out to me. "Want some?"

I grinned. "Are you trying to kill me?"

She stood up and let the skirt fall over her knees. She caught me looking and said, "Grandma says people expect us to wear this stuff. It makes us seem more authentic, more dark and mysterious. But"—she lowered her voice—"I feel like a total idiot." She tossed the plate in a trash can, then licked the powdered sugar off her fingers. Thunder boomed in the distance, and a jagged edge of lightning slit the sky beyond the bridge. "We'd better get inside. It's going to pour."

I noticed as I followed her toward the tent that she was wearing rainbow-colored flip-flops with smiley faces on them. So much for dark and mysterious. She stopped. "Wait. I'm hungry. Want to get a slice of pizza with me?"

"Didn't you just have funnel cake?"

She shook her head. "That was left over from the Mugsy's stand. It fell on the ground. So I fed it to the seagulls."

"Wait. You offered me food that fell on the ground?"

She blushed. "I didn't think you'd accept."

"What time do you have to do the Touch?"

She looked at her cell-phone display. "Five. Plenty of time."

I was hungry, too. We'd started to walk to the Sawmill when she stopped short. I followed her gaze down the boardwalk. Devon and a couple of other cute girls were coming our way. Her friends. I thought she'd wave or go up to them, but instead she started looking around the stands nearby. It wasn't crowded, so I know they saw us. Finally Taryn grabbed my wrist and pulled me into a surf shop. She pretended to inspect the hemp necklaces on the wall, but kept peeking out the door every two seconds. She gasped and hid behind me, then drew me even farther into the store, to the very back. The shop was so crowded with stuff that I rammed various body parts into three racks of T-shirts and smacked my forehead into a fake parrot hanging overhead before the trek was over. "Hey," I said, as she stood on her tippy-toes, peering out the opening. "Inspector Clouseau. What the hell do you think you're doing?"

"I just can't take them anymore."

Her friends? What girl didn't want to hang out with her friends? As I stared at her, the answer came to me. "What? You don't want your friends to see you with me?"

She snapped her eyes to mine. "No, that's not it at all. They're not my friends, anyway."

Okay, now I was confused. "Did you get into a fight with them? Devon—"

"She's okay, I guess. But all the rest of them drive me

bonkers. I guess I can understand why you'd think I was friends with them, because they're constantly following me around. Didn't I tell you before? I attract them. They're drawn to me, but they don't know why. They all want something from me. After the great friends I had in Maine, I don't want any more."

"You mean, they want something, like a Touch?"

She laughed bitterly. "Yeah. 'Taryn, can I get you this?' 'Taryn, you look so pretty today.' 'Taryn, can I rub your feet?' It gets old really fast. But the problem is, I don't have any Touches they'd want."

"What do you mean?"

"Well, there's a limited number. There's only a few left now." She glanced quickly outside. "Come on, I'll show you."

We got slices at Five Brothers, the next pizza place on the strip, which was a little more private. We sat down in a booth that wasn't splashed with too much pizza sauce or swarming with too many black flies. She folded her slice up and took a bite, letting a long string of cheese hang down to the plate, then scooped it up with her finger and piled it into her mouth. "Yum. Jersey pizza is the best. I missed it like crazy. In Maine, it's like raw dough. Gross. So the night I came back here, I ate an entire pie by myself." Then she shivered visibly. "I am so nervous."

"Yeah." I laughed as she took another huge bite. "I can see. You can hardly eat a thing."

She blushed. "I eat when I'm nervous." Then she reached into her flowery backpack and started to pull something out.

I thought it would be her phone again, but it was old and dusty and completely conspicuous . . . great. The Book of Touch. She'd actually taken it with her.

"Why do you have that?" I asked, raising my eyebrows.

"Well, I need to practice. Duh." She took the key and opened the lock. For some reason, I'd thought that the book was this big secret, that the only people who could lay eyes upon it were people like her. That she'd entrusted me when she let me look at it. I didn't know that she could whip it out at any pizza place on the strip and not have to endure the wrath of her grandmother. In the bright light I could see the book much better. There were a few small red tabs sticking out from some of the pages. She flipped through the pages until she came to one of the red tabs. I could tell that it was a Touch that hadn't been performed because there were more words inscribed on the page, and the signature line was blank. "This is the one I have to do."

I stared at it. It was all nonsense to me. "What is it?"

"Flight of Song. The ability to make people do what you tell them to."

"Like . . . you mean, anything?"

She nodded.

"Are you serious?" I couldn't believe how nonchalant she was being about the whole thing.

"Yes. Why?"

"Because, that's dangerous. Right? I mean, whoever gets that Touch could just say, 'Go jump off a cliff,' and you would have to do it. Right?"

She thought for a moment. "I guess."

"Then, how can you just go ahead and—"

She bit her tongue and threw the pizza down on the plate. "You think I want to do this? I have to! This book has been our curse since the beginning of time. We have to give people their deepest desires. We're tied to this book. If we don't perform these Touches, all of them, Grandma says we'll die. There are only five Touches left in this book. Once we finish with them, we're done. We're free."

"Why doesn't your grandmother do them and leave you out of it?"

"Because she's dying, that's why," Taryn said, her face reddening. "She has pancreatic cancer, and the doctors gave her fewer than three months to live. That was two months ago. She needs to train me so that I know what to do in case she dies before the Touches have been used. If I'm not properly trained to carry out the Touches by the time she dies, I won't be able to do them, and I'll die, too."

I just stared at her. "Wow. How did you guys ever get so lucky?"

"It was over two hundred years ago. Back in Hungary. Basically one of my ancestors pissed off a Gypsy. Supposedly my ancestor was a charlatan, and a very gifted actress. She used to go from place to place and promise she could perform miracles, but she used cheap parlor tricks and stuff to make people believe in her. Even so, she thrived. She was very successful at fooling everyone, and it was majorly cutting into this other woman's—the real Gypsy's—business.

To exact revenge and prove who the real mystic was, the Gypsy placed this curse on her. She would have to perform these spells on people—her very life depended on it. Her last grandchild inherited the book, and that grandchild's last grandchild, and then Grandma, and now me. And here we are." She turned back to the book. "I really hate this," she whispered. "Don't think I don't."

"I know. I'm sorry."

She shrugged. "Well, maybe this will be a good one. Maybe this person will do amazing things with this Touch."

"Maybe," I said, thinking, Not possible. It was too volatile. There was too much room for bad things to happen. After all, how often do people say things they don't mean? "Do you know who is getting it?"

She shook her head and hunched over the book for a minute, quiet, and I watched her, her blond hair pooling on the pages.

"Do you have to memorize it?"

"Yeah. Well, I can always refer to the book, but it's tricky because it's in Hungarian. If I say one syllable wrong, the Touch won't work and both the person receiving the Touch and I will . . ." She cringed. "I don't want to think about that right now. But anyway, that's why I want you there. If anything happens, I'd hate to be alone."

She didn't have to complete the sentence. I knew what she meant. If she didn't do it, she'd die. If she didn't do it right, she'd die. Death was a pretty big part of the whole thing. For some reason, the thought comforted me. Like maybe I'd finally found someone with a curse worse than mine. "Your grandmother—"

"Not the same," she muttered. "She would probably just stand over me and curse my stupidity in Hungarian."

She studied the page, her brow furrowing and her lips moving slowly. Every once in a while some strange syllable came out of her mouth. Then she exhaled heavily and took another bite of pizza. "I am so not cut out for this. You know when we moved to Maine, I had it in my head I was going to be a veterinarian."

"Oh, yeah?" I said. Explained why she liked seagulls so much.

She nodded. "But my parents just patted my head and said, 'That's cute.' I guess because all kids under ten want to be veterinarians."

"I never wanted to be one," I pointed out. But then again, I never wanted to be anything. I never had any plans for the future. I just wanted to be . . . normal.

"Okay, so you're the only one. But really, I still wish I could be one. I love animals. And I really think I could be good at it." She looked at the book in front of her. "Not this. I never wanted this."

"Who would?"

"Well . . . I get the feeling my grandmother doesn't mind doing it."

"She's probably just been doing it so long, it doesn't bother her." I leaned forward. There were four more red tabs sticking out from other pages. "Are the tabs the Touches that haven't been used yet?"

"Yeah."

"Not that many."

"I know. Only five. And when I was saying that I didn't have any Touches my 'friends' would be interested in, it's because there aren't that many left. I'm sure they would have clawed each other to death to get ahold of Evan's Touch, even if they knew it would cause them tumors. That's how shallow those girls are. That's another problem. I attract all these weak people. But I can't help them all." She snorted. "Help. I know. Hilarious, right?"

I said, "Which ones are left?"

She didn't need to look. "Flight of Song. Open Heart. Broken Ice. Invisible Assassin. Architect of—"

"Whoa. Invisible Assassin? That sounds brutal."

She swallowed. "It is. I don't . . . it's the ability to kill whoever you want, in . . . It's—"

As she spoke, I suddenly had this really uneasy feeling that made me grip the edge of the table. My thumb got stuck in something mushy on its underside. Taryn studied me and asked, "What?" as I pulled my hand away and saw a line of white gum that smelled like peppermint. Nasty.

I plucked a napkin from the dispenser. "That sounds like a pretty powerful Touch. And that other one. The one you're doing tonight. The power to make people do what you tell them to do. You're saying that in hundreds of years, your ancestors couldn't find someone who wanted that Touch?"

"First of all, if you looked at every Touch in this book, you'd see that they're all really powerful. And second, the ones left over are the hardest ones to perform. So my ancestors never recruited for them."

"Recruited?"

"Well, we don't actively recruit. When someone approaches me, if I touch them, I can tell what their need is. Or I can tell what Touch they've been given. If I have a Touch they might like, I'm supposed to take them aside and explain things to them. Grandma says she's never had anyone say 'no thanks,' even after she explained how much it cost or what the dangers are."

I smirked at the thought of my mom dropping everything and running to Babe's tent with all the money in her savings account. Nan had said she'd been a free spirit, always doing things without care to the consequences of her actions. That was nothing like what I knew of her. I sat there, not speaking, thinking of my mother piling that money on the table in the tent and demanding her Touch. I wondered what she did when she realized that her life had been changed irrevocably for the worse. I wondered if she'd lost her sense of adventure overnight, or if it had happened in baby steps. Maybe she had tried to stay the free spirit she once was, but the Touch had eventually beaten her down, taking all the things she loved and twisting them into something ugly and frightening. Then I said, "I really can't wait for tonight, then. Watching another unsuspecting person ruin his life. Good times."

Taryn looked me up and down. She furrowed her brow for a moment. "I know it might be a lot to ask, knowing your mother . . . If you really feel bad about it. . . ."

"I said I'll be there. I'm not backing out," I told her.

"Thank you. Maybe we should have signals. In case Grandma suspects something. Like, if I yawn, that means get out."

"Okay." I couldn't help sounding amused, which was probably why she thought I was making fun of her. She was really cute when she thought seriously about things. "And if you cough, that means all clear. I can come out."

She nodded. "Right. And we should have a meeting place. The front of the arcade, next to the crane game with the fuzzy dice. If I run my fingers through my hair, it means we should meet there."

I tried to think of what a secret agent would say, but nothing came to mind. "Got it."

She stood up. "I've got to get going. Grandma will be there any minute. You know how to get to the hiding spot? Through the arcade?"

"No problem."

"And . . ." She looked a little flustered. "You know, forget the cough. Don't come out, okay? No matter what happens. If Grandma finds out you're there, she'll . . . I don't know what. But it won't be good."

"Okay," I said, shrugging.

The whole thing seemed kind of pointless, me hiding there, unable to do anything to help her, but then I thought of what she'd said. What if she died tonight? I didn't see that happening. I knew when she would die. But we couldn't talk of things like that. Not now. Not when she was so on edge.

She was visibly shivering, her lower lip trembling, so when she leaned forward—to give me a hug? A kiss on the cheek? I'm still not sure—I turned the wrong way and ended up jabbing her cheek with my jaw. We both pulled back suddenly, and I could tell she was in just as much pain as I was by the way she rubbed her cheek and grimaced. Total idiot move. I wanted to bury my head in the sand. Instead I walked to the Kohr's stand and got an orangeade so I could have adequate refreshment for the "show."

Chapter 26

Ten minutes later, I'd thrown away my last dollar's worth of quarters on a classic video game called *Mr. Do!* and my orangeade was gone. The clock on the wall said 4:45. The arcade wasn't busy yet, but I knew it would be soon; it was Sunday. Right now, it was mostly families, a lot of kids trying their luck at *Frog Bog* and the fishing game. From where I stood, I could just see the wall I'd need to shimmy over to make it to the hiding spot. Part of me wanted to go there right away, but I'd forgotten to ask Taryn how long the Touch took, and another part of me didn't want to be sitting there for hours. As I stood there trying to decide, the orangeade hit me full force.

When I came back from the men's room, I saw a face I recognized. I stopped abruptly because I wasn't expecting to see anyone I knew. It took a while to place the face, but it was her, my old babysitter and Seventh Avenue badge checker. Jocelyn. She'd been there the day Emma died. It was Jocelyn who'd finally gotten through to me as I tried to revive the little girl. She'd put her hand on my shoulder and yanked me back from the lifeless body, saying, "Nick! Nick. Get ahold of yourself." She'd looked at me the way she'd done when she sat for me, and I'd found the knife drawer. Condescending, but mostly just horrified.

Now she was the one who looked small and vulnerable. It was right at that in-between time, the blurred line where family-friendly fun and party-all-night mixed. But despite the fact that she belonged to neither category, she melted into the scenery perfectly. She stood alone, but she wasn't dressed for a night out on the town. She had on a prim white sweater, the kind old ladies at church socials wear. She had her hands laced in front of her, as if praying. Jocelyn was probably in her late twenties, but she looked a lot older, probably because she was so serious and proper. Her hair was pulled back in a very severe way that made every line and flaw in her face visible. She was always frowning, but with her hair like that, the frown looked mean. She fidgeted, taking in all the games and attractions as if she'd never seen them before. I almost had to laugh, watching her standing there like she'd rather be anywhere else.

It was hard for someone to be more out of place than I was, but she managed. Why the hell she was here, of all places? Maybe she was meeting someone. Maybe she was going on a date.

I was trying to think of what kind of guy she'd date when I neared her. I wasn't expecting to stop and talk to her, but then she folded her arms across herself. She was shivering. Her face was pale and ghostlike. There was something wrong.

She glanced at her wristwatch, and in that moment,

something caught in my mind. It was the first night I'd met her. She'd taken some Hot Wheels out of her backpack and let me play with them. She had one that was aqua blue, with doors and a trunk that opened. It was the coolest thing I'd ever seen. She was telling me that I could keep it when my mother began moaning from upstairs. That night, when Nan came home, I'd cried, clutching that car in my hands, knowing I'd probably never see Jocelyn again. But she came back. She babysat for me a few more times, until she went to college.

I stopped short in front of her. Immediately, pangs of pain thudded in my head. I wasn't sure if I could bring myself to speak to her, if I could find the right words. I opened my mouth, still not certain what would come out. "Jocelyn? Are you okay?"

"Yeah." She'd been inspecting her fingernails and I startled her. When she recognized me, her face softened. "Hey."

"You looking for something or someone?" I ventured.

She just stood there for a second, perplexed. Then she smirked as if to say, "Wouldn't you like to know?"

"You just look a little out of your element," I explained, and as I did I saw it all in perfect clarity.

When we were done speaking, she would walk away from me, step out onto the boardwalk, and go next door. To the tent. I swallowed as I saw it, as if it had already happened.

Jocelyn was the one getting the Touch.

"I'm perfectly fine, thanks," she said, her voice a whisper. "I have an . . . I'm meeting someone."

She began to turn away, but I grabbed her hand before she

could. When she turned back, the shock and anger in her face made me flinch. She started to yank free when I said, "Why are you doing it?"

She stood there, her cheeks aflame and eyes intent. "What?"

I didn't need her to confirm it. I knew it like I knew my own birthday. "The Touch. It's you, isn't it?"

Her eyes softened, but she finally yanked her arm away from me. "Why should you care?"

"Because I . . ." I searched for the words. "Because I don't want you to do it. It could ruin your life."

"I already got the warnings and precautions talk," she said, her voice dull. "What do you know about it, anyway?"

I laughed under my breath. "More than you."

"Oh, really?"

"Why do you want people to do whatever you say?" I asked. "You really think it would be that great?"

Surprise dawned on her face. She opened her mouth to speak, but I stopped her.

"What if you told someone to go jump off a bridge?"

She bit her tongue. "Well, I wouldn't—"

"How do you know? What if the Touch made everyone do everything you said, no matter what? Even if it killed them?"

"Then I would just be careful to—"

"Have you ever said anything you didn't mean?"

She choked on her words. "Well, yes, but . . ." She sighed. "Please go away. This has nothing to do with you. You don't know what it's like. What my life is like." I waited for her to say more, to tell me what it was like, but she didn't. She just stood there, staring at the ground, her breathing short and erratic. "I can't. I can't go into this with you."

I backed away. Of course she couldn't. I was everything she detested; that much I could see in her eyes. "Do you remember when you used to come over to my house to babysit?"

She nodded. "So?"

"My mom. The moaning upstairs. Nan probably told you she was sick," I said. "She wasn't sick. She was Touched. Jocelyn, I'm Touched."

She drew in a breath, her fists clenched slightly. "You . . . you are?"

I nodded.

"What do you have?"

"I can see my future."

She slumped against the pinball machine, dropped her bag to the ground, and shook her head. "But then you should understand how important—"

"I understand that you can ruin your life. My Touch ruined mine. Sure, some things about it are good, but they're seriously overshadowed by the bad. Just . . . keep that in mind."

She looked out the door, toward the seagulls circling above the beach in the clear blue sky. "My whole life, everyone ignores me. Everyone walks all over me. I'm about to lose my job. It's like nobody even sees me." She buried her face in her hands. "I am so sick of being walked on, and I don't know what else to do."

I shrugged. I knew what she meant. Sometimes I was so sick of being a freak that I probably would get a Touch if it promised to make me normal. I said, "You were the best babysitter I ever had, you know. You were the only one who ever played with me. I was crushed when you went to college."

Her frown didn't soften, but her eyes brightened for an instant. She looked away. "I've got to go," she said. From the way she said it, I didn't think she'd pay any attention to me. Now the arcade was a little more crowded. I walked to the outer edge of the room, where the cinder-block wall stood, and, checking to make sure nobody was watching, quietly slid over it. I hit the ground unsteadily and had to grasp the velvet curtain to prevent myself from landing in the tent. I found the opening and crouched there, where I could hear Taryn's smooth, sweet voice and her grandmother's gruff one playing off each other. Just another way in which they were extreme opposites. They were busy gazing at the entrance and hadn't noticed my less-than-slick appearance.

"What time is it now?" her grandmother croaked.

"Ten after," Taryn said. From between the decorative tassels on the curtains, I could see her peeking outside the tent.

Ten after, I thought. I hadn't realized I was that late. But Jocelyn still wasn't there. If she'd gone straight from talking to me to the tent, she would have been. I tried to think of the future but couldn't place Jocelyn in the tent. Maybe I had convinced her. Yes!

The tent was dark, lit only by the cobwebbed crystal chandelier that was up so high it barely cast down any light. But I could see creases in Taryn's face. She looked in my direction, shrugged, and then sighed. "Well, what do we do if she doesn't show up?" she asked.

Her grandmother was sitting with her back toward me, and I could see the book opened on the table in front of her. "We go home, *sevgili*," she said.

"But I only have three days left," Taryn said.

"Yes. We will find another. I have some interest."

I found myself leaning forward, my forehead almost out the opening of the curtains, trying to figure out what they were talking about. Three days? Three days for what?

"But don't worry, *sevgili*. This one's a stupid girl. She will come. Stupid people are easily led to us," her grandmother croaked.

"But what if she isn't?" Taryn's voice was an octave higher, clearly worried. And here I thought she'd be happy if she didn't have to do a Touch tonight.

"Calm. Like I say, we have other interest."

Taryn walked to the table and leaned her knuckles on it. She said, "I don't understand how you can be that way. Calling the people stupid. They're people. And we might just ruin their lives."

"We don't ruin life. They ruin life."

"But we help them do it. Doesn't that bother you?"

Her grandmother shifted her weighty bottom in the seat, and the small chair creaked in protest. "Let me tell you something, *sevgili*. It bother me. Of course it bother me. Once, long time ago, I learn something about one of them. Something terrible. Too late. It made me very, very sad. I told God to take me then. I did not care if I live or die. I went many, many years before I open the book again. But then you came. And you were the one, the next in line. And so I start again. I hoped I could finish the book before God take me. For you. But not so. Not so."

Her grandmother's voice trailed off, and Taryn walked around the table, leaned down, and hugged her. Her grandmother didn't move, despite the extra weight on her. It occurred to me that hugging a cactus would probably be more natural. But then her grandmother trembled a little, and I realized they were both crying. Who knew the old lady had feelings? I felt stupid, witnessing that. First, maybe I'd misjudged Taryn's grandmother, and second, it was a private moment, not something I was meant to witness. I rose to my feet, turned, and scuttled up the wall and into the arcade.

I'd just gotten another dollar's worth of quarters to blow on *Mr. Do!* when Taryn came rushing up to me. "There you are! What happened?"

"I just—"

"She's over a half hour late," she said, chewing on her thumbnail.

"Why aren't you in there?"

"I excused myself to use the ladies' room."

"What is the deal with three days?" I asked.

"That's when I turn seventeen," she said, ripping the thumbnail off. "I have to perform my first Touch before then."

"You what?" I asked, my voice rising. "Or else what?"

She bit her lip. "Can we not talk about that?"

"Are you telling me that you needed to perform that Touch or else you'll die?" My voice was now so loud a kid at the video game next to us stopped killing zombies and stared at me.

"Shhh!" She threw her hand over my mouth. Her voice was just as loud as mine, which was probably why a bunch of other people started giving us looks, too. "I did tell you. I told you we had to perform these Touches or we'd . . ."

"Well, I know, but I thought you'd have longer than three days," I said.

"It's fine, though," she said. "All I need to do is—"

"She's not coming," I muttered.

She stared at me. "What?"

"Your five o'clock appointment." When her eyes narrowed I said, "I figured out who it was. I knew the person. I didn't want her to ruin her life. So I convinced her not to do it."

Her eyes filled with something, not anger, but desperation. Horror. "You . . . what? Why?"

"Because I thought I was doing you a favor! I thought you wanted to get out of it. That was before I knew you would drop dead in three days if you didn't go through with it. That makes a big difference." I squeezed the words out of my tightening throat.

She turned and walked away, hands on hips, and then came back. Her voice was softer, more in control. "Can we ixnay the eying-day talk?"

"Sorry," I muttered. "But hell! I can't believe I . . . What are we going to do now?"

"Shhh, don't freak. Grandma says she has some other interest," Taryn said, thinking aloud. But she shivered as she tightened the scarf around her shoulders. She was trying to convince herself.

I studied her. She looked perfect, and there wasn't a trace of sickness, fatigue, anything bad on her. It seemed impossible to believe that someone so full of life could succumb to that curse and die within seventy-two hours. Not an hour ago, she was acting so nonchalant about the whole thing, joking with me and laughing about it. "I'm so sorry, Taryn. Are you—I mean, how are you? Do you feel okay?"

She nodded. "Yeah. Sometimes I think it must be wrong. That it's all a bunch of bunk. Sometimes I think I can just go about my life, ignore it, and it will leave me alone. So I push it out of my head. Like if I can keep it out of my head, it will be okay."

"It will be," I said, and I put my arm around her. Her brow was still tense, knitted, so I said, "Remember, I can see the future? You are not dying anytime in the near future. You have nothing to worry about."

It was the only lie I ever told her. But wow, what a lie.

Chapter 27

I walked Taryn home on the boardwalk. It was a long walk, two miles, and a cold breeze was blowing in from the ocean, but it felt good to move, to have the wind blowing against my chest. It was a reminder that we were still here.

"Have your visions changed?" she asked me quietly.

"Maybe," I said to her, silently adding, Doubtfully. I didn't bother to tell her that I'd seen it again, in the pizza place. And that it scared me. I wasn't sure why the vision of us in Beauty was so persistent. Just making the promise never to get into her Jeep should have been enough to steer it off course. And these past few days, I'd often disregarded the script, so much so that the ache in my head was a dull, constant pain between my eyes. I'd hoped that by doing that, something would change. Still, whenever I let the visions come in now, it was always there, the final act of the sad and tumultuous play that was my life. I'd been starting to wonder if some things about life were like that: meant to be, unbreakable. Destiny. Like building a house of cards, it doesn't matter how you build it, or what you do to make it strong. Eventually, it always comes down. But I couldn't tell Taryn that. She had enough going on anyway. "It's hard to tell. The You Wills aren't as strong when I'm with you. And I haven't been paying attention to them as much because I was trying to . . . I don't know."

We walked a little while longer, until she stopped and said, "I want to walk on the beach. Don't you?"

I didn't. It was freezing, and after Emma I didn't know if I'd be okay with going out there. But I kicked off my shoes and followed her anyway. The sand was warm between my toes. She was right. It felt good. When we were halfway down the beach, she turned to me.

"Thank you for being there tonight," she said.

I laughed. "I ruined everything."

"No, you didn't," she said. "It meant a lot to me that you would be there. I knew it probably wouldn't be easy for you to see what your mother went through."

That didn't bother me. After all, she'd signed up for it. "Not so much. I can be there for the next one. And I won't mess it up. I promise."

"Yeah? Okay, cool."

She looked up at me, and we were standing pretty close to each other, so I thought it would be a good time to kiss her. I mean, beach, romantic sunset, et cetera. But I didn't know how to go in for the kill. I had a vision of me gnashing my teeth against hers and I couldn't tell if that was real or me being paranoid. So I just said, "Your grandmother . . . when she gave up the practice for a lot of years . . . do you think she did it because of my mom? Because she found out she'd given a Touch to a pregnant woman and infected an innocent kid?"

"Oh," Taryn said, thinking it over. "Yeah. Maybe. That makes sense. I think Grandma would hate that. She always talks about her subjects taking responsibility for their actions. But to give it to someone who didn't ask for it ..."

I laughed again and sucked in a mouthful of cool sea air. "Wow."

"What?"

"Nothing. I just realized how much I've ruined your life."

She stared at me, confused. "What do you mean?"

"Well, if your grandmother hadn't given it up for all those years, because of me, she would have most likely been able to dispense with all the Touches left in the book way before now. And didn't you say that once the book is done, your family curse is over? You wouldn't have had to ..."

Her eyes widened. "Oh."

She started walking another few steps, and all the while I let it sink in. Whatever attraction we felt for each other, it was dangerous. All this time, I was thinking that my attraction to her was endangering me. But first I left her to a lifetime of slavery under the Book of Touch. And then I went ahead and stopped her from performing the Touch she needed to perform in order to stay alive. Not to mention that we were going to die together. Even if we vowed to stay away from her Jeep, something else would probably get us. We were bad for each other. Bad. Sure, it felt good being with her, but that was the problem. In my life, bad always accompanied the good. Always.

Suddenly she grabbed my hand and said, "Let's go," pulling me in the opposite direction.

Her pace quickened, and I had to pick it up to follow. At first I thought maybe she saw it, too. The writing on the wall in capital letters that we were going to be the death of each other and needed to separate as quickly as possible. When we got to the boardwalk, I caught her looking over her shoulder. I followed her gaze to two forms in the gazebo. Two men, it looked like, standing on the wooden seats and smoking cigarettes. They were staring at us.

Maybe it was just because of the chill in the air, but the hairs on the back of my neck prickled. "Who are they?" I asked.

They were standing in our way. To get by on the boardwalk we would have had to walk right past them. And from the way Taryn stood there, frozen, it was like she was facing a rabid dog. The men stubbed out their smokes and started walking our way. The only thing I could tell was that they were wearing all black, and in movies the bad guys always wear black from head to toe. She tugged on my sleeve. "Let's go another way."

I was not really in the mood to get my ass whipped in front of her, so I followed her. "Who are they?" I repeated.

"No one," she replied, hustling down the ramp on Third Avenue.

I looked over my shoulder. They were coming closer. "More weak people with an unexplained attraction to you?"

She rolled her eyes. "Bryce is an old . . . family friend."

"Bryce?" I swallowed and looked back. It was dark, but the taller guy looked vaguely familiar, from photos I had seen at the Reese home, and from the cemetery. I hadn't been able to get that picture of him, standing over Emma's grave, out of my mind. He wasn't much bigger than I was, but grief did things to people, which was how he'd been able to knock me down at the cemetery. He hated me. And he had every right to. I picked up the pace until I was walking in front of Taryn. "He's a family *friend*?"

"He lives next door to my grandmother." She mumbled, "He's Emma's brother."

This was all getting worse and worse by the minute. "I know. I had a little run-in with him at Emma's funeral." I pointed to my eye, which was turning yellow in places.

"He did that to you? I thought you said—"

"He wanted to kill me. Because of Emma," I said. "He knows that I'm responsible."

"You're not responsible," she said. "He's a weak person, looking for someone to blame."

"Weak? He sure didn't feel that way when he was pressing my face into the grass."

"I bet he's drunk. I've heard he's spent every night since he got back to town at the Sawmill."

Even better. Likely he was getting drunk to numb the pain of Emma's death. Not only had I killed her, I'd created an alcoholic.

The two men slowed down and then disappeared somewhere among the darkness and the dunes. It was worse, not being able to see them. We were in Seaside Park, and nobody was nearby. This could be incredibly bad. I'm putting Taryn in danger, I thought. We shouldn't be here, together.

She said, "Maybe he's not following you. Maybe he's—"

"He told me he wanted me dead." I grabbed Taryn's shoulder a little rougher than I meant to. "Let's go."

She looked at me, eyes wide with surprise. All I wanted to do was bolt, away from this whole thing. Someplace safe. Home. My bedroom. Somewhere I couldn't feel anything, because everything always ended up hurting. But Taryn was just standing there, this confused expression on her face, as if she was trying to figure Bryce out. But there was nothing to figure out. Bryce Reese hated me.

"Let's go," I muttered, turning. I didn't want to see her expression. At that point, I didn't care if she followed. I didn't care about anything as I hurried down the street, toward home. Everything about me being there, in that moment, was wrong.

Taryn called after me, "Wait up! Wait up! You're not mad, Nick, are you?", but I only increased my speed. Finally she let out a small, strangled "Please!"

I had to stop. I turned. Waited for her to catch up. "What?"

She studied my face in the streetlight. "You are mad?"

I shook my head. I wasn't. I was tired. Tired of trying for things that the universe didn't want me to have. "I'll walk you home."

We walked the rest of the way in silence. I didn't even stop when we reached her house, and I didn't say goodbye, just left her alone in her front yard, where she probably stared after me until I was gone from sight. She was like that. Good. Too good for someone like me.

When I left her, I broke into a run. As I raced, breathless, toward home, I thought of my mom, staying in her room day after day, alone. Battering through the salty mist swirling in the streetlights, for a brief, flickering moment, I understood her. Some people have a knack for messing up everything and everyone they touch. Love. Happiness. Walking down the beach, feeling nothing but the wind on my face and the hand of someone I care about in mine. Those things would never be for us. Any momentary thought that they could be ours was just an illusion. That was the house of cards.

Chapter 28

I spent the next two days in bed. The You Wills fought to get me out, but I ignored them and thought of the low, dull headache they caused as punishment for my stupidity. When I slept, I dreamt of Emma, floating to the surface of a black sea, but when I was awake, I found myself thinking mostly about Taryn. I tried to convince myself that she was in more danger near me than without me. I wondered if she'd performed the Touch yet. When I wasn't thinking about Taryn, I felt guilty and disgusted with myself for the large portion of time I had spent thinking about her. I should have been thinking and caring about other things, things I *could* do something about. Nan with her broken arm. My last year of high school. Not turning into a recluse like my mother. Despite all that, the thing center stage in my brain was Taryn. I didn't want to care about her. But I did. Too much. And I hated it.

Strangely, even though I vowed to myself I would never talk to her again, that I would run in the other direction if I ever saw her, the visions of us in her Jeep didn't change. It was useless to tell myself it was over, because I didn't mean it. After all, school was coming up. I wouldn't be able to avoid her there.

And then it was the first day of school. I realized that it was also Taryn's birthday. She was seventeen. I had what I thought was a vision of buying her a cake and singing happy birthday to her on the beach, but then I realized it was just my imagination. We were not together. We could never be together.

But why did it seem, in my muddled mind filled with future and past and everything in between, like we were? It was as if every day without her was killing every happy vision of the future I'd ever had, over and over again, slicing through them until only shredded, faded remains.

I woke up late. Actually, I hadn't slept much, but I couldn't manage to get myself out of bed. I didn't want to think of facing the day. Of facing school.

I threw on the first T-shirt I could find, my favorite blue one with the words DON'T BOTHER ME on the front. Totally appropriate. Then I trudged down the stairs, where Nan had put my backpack and lunch. She was so prepared; even with the broken arm, she'd managed to go through the normal routine. Nan always made a big fuss over the first day of school, so I slipped out the door before she could ask me if I wanted breakfast.

I felt bad as soon as I left. I saw the smiley face in ketchup on my eggs, which she'd been doing since I was four to psych me up for "big days" like the first day of school. I hated school completely. The academic part was downright painful, since I could barely concentrate on anything with the script in my head. And as bad as that was, it was no match for my social life, or lack thereof. I pretty much kept to myself. I was the one who sat in the back of the classroom, alone. People didn't mess with Crazy Cross.

When the bus dropped me off and I walked toward the front doors, thinking of too much perfume, Bill Runyon's Land Rover, silver butterfly, I saw the piece-of-crap vehicle I had so many memories of dying in parked in the first spot in the nearest lot, taunting me. She'd peeled all the bumper stickers off; all that was left was their white, flaking remains. I wasn't really surprised to see Taryn's Jeep. Of course, without me to interfere, her life was going fine. She'd performed the Touch, and now all was right with the world.

I tried to convince myself it didn't matter. What she did was her own business. It had nothing to do with me.

The problem was, I couldn't not think of her. I had nothing else that was interesting enough to fill the void.

When you get to the twelfth grade, the first day of school is numbing. You don't even get that nervous feeling in your stomach; you just have that sense of exhaustion that overpowers you when you've run most of a ten-mile race and know the finish line is coming but can't see it anywhere. I got my schedule and locker combination and made it to homeroom, where I was told I needed to see the guidance counselor, Mrs. Gross, which was a misleading name because she was really pretty. The only thing was that she tried too hard to look young and like "one of us." She was wearing ripped jeans and a T-shirt, and had pulled one knee up to her chin as she studied some papers on her desk. I didn't buy it. I knew that somewhere in her closet were pearl earrings or a sweater set or mom jeans or whatever it was that old people wore.

"Oh, Nick!" she said, coming around to give me a hug. She was totally touchy-feely, too, and even more so with me, probably because she thought I was one of the mental ones who needed her. "It is so good to see you. Have a nice summer?"

I thought about Emma. "Wonderful," I muttered as she embraced me. She smelled like stale coffee and too much perfume.

It was weird to be summoned here on the first day of school. I'd spoken to Mrs. Gross a handful of times during my high school career, and mostly she asked me questions about where I wanted to be and what I saw myself doing in ten years. Hilarious. Sometimes I could tell her exactly where I'd be in ten years, but it always depended on the day. She was wary of me because once, on a particularly bad day, I made a really stupid slip in my foul mood and told her I saw myself dead. It was the truth; that was when I ended up in Vegas, married to a stripper and dealing drugs to make ends meet. But the obvious inference was that I was contemplating suicide. Mrs. Gross called in Nan and set up an appointment with a psychiatrist for me and I had to spend the next three months trying to convince them that no, whoops, I misspoke, I'm actually just fine. So for the past couple of times I'd told her I wanted to be a dentist. It's something I have no interest in doing, but it keeps her from calling the men with strait-jackets.

Anyway, even though it was weird to be summoned, I knew why she did it. She wanted to ask me why I hadn't used the "wealth of helpful free services" the school provided to put together my college applications. Truth was, applying to college was the furthest thing from my mind. But I guess an aspiring dentist like myself should have been knee-deep in applications by now. I just smiled when she said, "I'd be happy to look over your application materials."

"Thanks," I said.

Her face turned troubled and by then the You Wills had traveled far enough into the future to allow me to see it. And then I suddenly realized something.

I was a sucker.

She hadn't called me in here at all to talk college.

She wanted to . . . oh, hell.

"No. I'm fine," I said quickly, then cleared my throat when I realized she hadn't asked the question yet. "I mean, I have to go to class."

"I found out that you tried out for cross-country," she said brightly. "That's so wonderful. You have no idea how happy that made me, to see you finally trying to participate. I know I've told you time and time again how important extracurriculars are for a well-rounded college app. It upset me to find out that you didn't make the team, though. As you can imagine."

"Yeah, but that's okay. I don't want to—"

"No, it's not. You're a good runner. And so I spoke to Coach Garner about having you try out again."

I stared at her, feeling the horror slowly cracking through the mask of indifference on my face.

She gave me a look that reeked of sympathy. "Nick, we heard about what happened before tryouts. That unfortunate incident. Of course that would affect your performance."

I wanted to clap my hands over my ears. I felt all the blood in my body rushing to my face. "It didn't affect me. I was fine. And I lost, fair and square."

She shook her head as if to say, "Silly you." As if I should jump at the chance to receive her charity.

"Look, I am not trying out again," I said, wooden.

She smiled at me. "Now, Nick—"

"No, listen," I seethed.

I hadn't meant it to come out as a seethe, but I guess it did because I saw little droplets of spit shooting out of my mouth. She leaned back in her chair, surprised and probably a little grossed out. Guess kids didn't cut her off very often, because her eyes narrowed.

"I mean, thank you," I managed, backpedaling. "But no thank you. I mean it."

She just stared at me for what felt like a year.

"Am I done here?" I asked, motioning toward the door. As if I couldn't wait to be in physics. She waved me on and I escaped into the hallway, closing the door with such force that the frosted glass panel clattered in its frame.

Gritting my teeth, I stalked down the hallway, completely

oblivious to everything else going on around me. Not even seven in the morning, and I was already in a crappy mood. I was sure physics, my worst subject, wasn't going to help anything. I checked my schedule. Room 231.

I wish I had kept my head down as I found my way to the math wing. I wish I had been so well versed in the layout of the school that I didn't have to look up to see the room numbers. As it was, though, I'd never been to Room 231, and it was in the middle of a very busy section of the building, where two hallways intersected. If I had kept my head down, I wouldn't have seen Taryn walking down the other hallway, right toward me, holding hands with a guy wearing a black leather jacket, gloves, and a nose ring.

She looked up at him and gave him a smile, while I stared, too dumbstruck to look away. Not three days ago, that guy could have been me. And wasn't she supposed to be concerned about dying? She'd really been devoting her time to finding someone to Touch, but in a totally different way than I had thought. All this time, I'd been worrying about her, and she . . . she didn't give a crap about me.

At the last second before I made it to the classroom, her eyes brushed over me. She pulled away from the guy and whispered, "Nick!", and the redness was already starting to pool in her cheeks. I could hear her trying to say something to me, but I didn't care what it was. By then, I was so out of there. I went into the room and slammed the door in her face. The teacher, Mr. Baumgartner, started screaming at me immediately. Something about "This is not your personal office,

Mister. What is your name?", but I just shoved myself into a seat, the first seat I could find, and clenched my fists.

The door opened a second later, as the teacher was screaming, "Answer me!" Taryn walked in, her eyes wide. She was wearing cutoffs that made her legs look phenomenal, but the second I thought that I hated myself for thinking anything good about her. Her gaze shifted between me and the teacher, and she started to walk toward me, cautiously. Baumgartner's eyes flashed to her, like he was trying to figure out what part she played in all this, but he didn't say anything. I stood up, grabbed my schedule, and faked like I was coming toward her, then quickly skirted around another row of desks and out the door.

The crowds in the hallway were thinning. The bell was about to ring. Taryn's Nose Ring Dude was still hanging out there, waiting for her with a stupid expression on his face, and I scowled as I passed, wanting to do a whole lot worse. I mean, what the hell? He wasn't anything like her type. And he was just plain nasty-looking. There were a thousand things wrong with him, but I forced myself to remember that it didn't matter what she did with him. We were over. That was the way it needed to be. She needed to get on with her life so that she could have one. A nice, long one, probably filled with many more dudes who weren't me.

Baumgartner shrieked behind me, the noise echoing down the hall—"Stop right there! You! Listen to me! Mister!"—but I didn't care. People were gawking at me, stepping aside to let me pass like I had some infectious disease, but it didn't matter what they thought. In the future, the near future, I was dead. Nothing I did now mattered. Not teachers, or students, or cross-country, or even Taryn.

Only one obstacle dared to stay in my way. I heard him before I saw him. "What did you do now, Cross?" the voice said, sparkling with amusement.

Sphincter.

And I thought the morning couldn't get any worse.

He didn't have time to wipe the smile off his face. I blew into his broad shoulder with more force than I knew possible, knocking him back, so he stumbled a little before he recovered. I didn't see who he was with, only caught a glimpse of a red mane. The air was perfumed with competing scents, a stew of flowers and chemicals that clawed at my nostrils, making it even harder to breathe. Sphincter laughed and turned to the red sea of hair. "Crazy Cross," he said with the same affectionate tinge in his voice I'd come to know and hate.

I lost it.

I turned to him, my hands balling into fists. My first punch hit him squarely in the jaw, throwing him back against the locker. The second jab, from my other arm, drove him upward, so that his chin was thrust up, and the blood, which had begun to course down his face, pooled in the crease of his lips, which were pulled into a tight grimace. He tried to say something but spat crimson droplets into the air, like a fountain. I pressed my forearm against his throat. "Stop laughing. You're rotting from the inside," I snarled, in a voice foreign even to me. "You hear me?"

His eyes had widened for a second, but now they narrowed. His mouth parted, revealing a black window in his once perfect set of pearly whites.

"Nick, stop it!" someone called down the hall. Taryn. I turned to see her running toward me, two teachers and a security guard on her heels.

I released him. "Freak," he sputtered, clamping his hand over his bloody nose. "You broke my nose. My tooth."

"You're rotting. Go to the doctor. He'll tell you," I muttered as the security guard grabbed me from behind. The bell screamed overhead as I turned to follow.

Sphincter's arm candy, the other students in the hall, Taryn . . . Everyone was looking at me in the same way as the guard led me away. Like I was, just as Sphincter had said, Crazy Cross. It wasn't anything I wasn't used to. Strangely, it was a relief to stop pretending and finally own up to what I really was.

Chapter 29

"Suspended on the first day of school," Nan said under her breath as we pulled up the driveway. We were both sitting in the back of Bill Runyon's Land Rover, being chauffeured like celebrities. She'd had to call around to get someone to drive her, and Bill was the lucky winner. I could tell the second she came to pick me up that she was pissed, because she didn't bother to say hello to the ladies in the principal's office and her face looked like she'd sucked on lemons. Bill was cordial when I'd first gotten into the car, but eventually he fell under Nan's spell and just drove, though I caught him inspecting me a few times in the rearview mirror. After fifteen minutes of icy silence, I was kind of relieved when words finally erupted from her mouth.

I didn't answer. I was busy staring at my knuckles. They were red and ached. Maybe my hand was broken.

"For an entire week, no less," she said when Bill threw the car into park in front of the house. She pulled open the door and thanked Bill.

As I got out of the car, Bill whispered to me, "You know, kid. Take it easy. You're going to be the death of her."

"Thanks, Dad," I mumbled, slamming the door with unnatural force. I rolled my eyes and they caught on the sky. The clouds were perfectly round and white in the shockingly blue sky, like stepping stones to heaven. I pulled open the front door and trudged into the house. The floorboard at the doorway to my mom's room creaked. I knew she was standing there, waiting to give me crap. I climbed the stairs quickly, but she'd already begun her assault: "Suspension? Nick! You will mess up your life!"

"You already took care of that," I muttered, slamming the door behind me. It was about a thousand degrees in my room. I opened a window and stripped off my T-shirt and jeans, then lay in bed in my boxers, clenching and unclenching my fist, massaging my knuckles. Okay, maybe my hand wasn't broken. But that still didn't stop the rest of me from feeling like crap.

About ten minutes later, someone knocked on the door. "Go away," I muttered, figuring it was Nan bringing me crackers or a cool washcloth or whatever it was she felt I needed at this time. I tried to convince myself I didn't need anything from anyone, that all I wanted was to be left alone. But the thought of being alone felt like stumbling down a long dark hole with no idea what was at the bottom.

The door opened a crack. Leave it to Nan to never listen to my pleas for privacy. I looked up, about to yell at her, and instead of Nan's wizened face, I saw platinum blond curls. "Can I come in?" Taryn asked softly.

"What? No." I stumbled over my words, then realized I was practically naked and did a visual check for my jeans. All the way on the other side of the room. Great. Luckily my T-shirt was within arm's distance, mingling with some dirty socks and underwear on the floor. I grabbed the shirt and threw it over my head. "Why—why are you here? You should be in school."

She opened the door wider. Her hair looked as if she'd ridden all the way here in Sphincter's convertible, and who knew? Considering his weakness, maybe she had. But her eyes looked heavy and her skin had a sickly green tinge to it. She cleared her throat and it looked like she was swallowing marbles. "I cut out. I need to explain."

"You don't have to explain to me. You and I are . . . nothing," I said, almost choking on the word. "You should be in school."

"No, this is important."

"School is important. I shouldn't be."

"No," she said, closing the door tightly behind her. "You seem to know I have trouble saying no. But I do know how to say no when it matters. So I'm not going anywhere."

"Suit yourself," I said, shrugging in an "it's a free country" kind of way. But it wasn't possible to ignore her when we were the only two people in a nine-by-nine-foot room. I knew I should kick her out, but I couldn't. It wasn't possible.

"What did you get?"

"Suspension. One week."

She nodded. "Brutal. But not entirely unjustified. You nearly killed him! Considering how sick he is. Where did you get those Ali moves?"

Great. First she gets cozy with Nose Ring Dude, and then she pours sympathy on Sphincter. Not what I wanted to hear right now. "I did him a favor," I muttered. "Now he'll go to the doctor and find out what's wrong with him. Maybe it won't be too late."

"It's already too late. The tumors are spreading. They won't be able to stop it," she said softly. She dropped her bag and sat down on the edge of my bed. She must have noticed the dump trucks and airplanes on the sheets because she smiled a little but didn't say anything. Then she looked around, probably trying to find out what other things I had in my room that the normal four-year-old would go crazy over.

"I have glow-in-the-dark planet stickers on the ceiling," I offered. "But you can't see them since it's daytime."

"I have them, too!" she said brightly, then started to cough. It was a horrible, wracking cough, like that of someone with TB, and it went on long enough that I wondered if I should get her some water or smack her on the back. Then she wrapped her arms around herself and said, her voice weak, "Well, I had them at my old house, in Maine."

She stared up at the ceiling for a long time, and finally I said, "You were about to explain something? Something about why you were getting with that guy in the hallway? What was his name?"

She blushed. "His name's Kent. Kent Something. And we were not with each other!" she said, slapping me on the shoulder.

"Okay. Well, Kent Something looks charming. I can totally tell why you'd get with him."

"Stop being so smug. You know he's far from charming. And if you say I was getting with him one more time, I will smack you. It's all perfectly innocent."

I stared at her. "Don't tell me he's your brother. That excuse has been pretty much done to death."

"No. He is not my brother," she whispered. "And he's gross. Seriously."

"You were the one getting with him," I said, emphasizing the words she didn't want to hear. Just because.

"Clearly, you're an idiot," she mumbled, smacking me again on the shoulder, which was starting to hurt. "I needed skin-to-skin contact to see what was going on with him."

I narrowed my eyes. "You mean, he's . . . Touched?"

"No, but he wants to be. He'd been following me around ever since yesterday. He really has a need. It's so strong. And I was trying to figure out what it is, if maybe I have the Touch he'd want."

"Do you?"

She shrugged. "I didn't have a chance to process it. It happened so fast. I saw you and I felt so terrible." She sighed, but then ended up coughing the last bit of air. "I am really sorry if I made you feel bad in front of Bryce and his friend. Is that why you ran away?"

I shrugged. "It's not that. It's . . . you're right. I want to protect you. The vision—the bad one."

Her eyes widened. "It's still there? But we changed—"

"I know. I don't get it. Maybe it's going haywire because that's what my Touch does around you. Maybe I'm seeing things in my head that aren't real. I have no idea. But to be safe, I think we have to stay away from each other."

She threw up her hands, exasperated. "What? Why? Really, Nick, you're so infuriating. Every time we talk about this you keep saying you need to stay away from me. But you never do. I mean, what's the deal? Do you want to stay away from me?"

I shook my head immediately. "No way."

"But that's what you make me think. I don't want to stay away from you, either," she said, her voice barely a whisper. "I like you. You make me happy. When you aren't avoiding me or thinking I'm trying to get with other guys."

I rolled my eyes. "I don't do a really good job of that."

She nodded. "Yeah. You pretty much suck at that." Then she surprised me by leaning forward. She lifted up a small chain around her neck. "See what I got for my birthday?"

She was so close. I tried to concentrate on the piece of jewelry, a silver butterfly or a dragonfly or something, but the only thing registering in my head was that she smelled so good, apples again, and that she wouldn't be this close if she didn't want me as much as I wanted her. So I kissed her. "I meant to tell you . . . happy birthday," I whispered into her hair.

She looked a little dazed, probably as dazed as I felt, when she finally pulled away. She smiled.

"Better than Kent Something?" I asked.

"I never . . . ," she began, and then she sort of fainted. She leaned backward, closed her eyes, and then straightened up and shook her head. "Whoa. I feel sick."

I fanned her face. "Want some water or something?"

She shook her head, a small, embarrassed smile on her face. "No, I'm good."

"I have that kind of effect on women," I joked. But then I realized something. "The Touch. You haven't performed it yet?"

The corners of her mouth turned down. "No. Tonight. Hopefully. Grandma has the person all lined up. But it's . . . I'm so nervous."

I nodded. I got it.

"I mean, what if the person doesn't show up? What if they change their mind? That was why I was . . . with Kent . . . I thought maybe he could be my backup."

"Calm down," I said. "Don't worry. They'll show up. Do you know who it is?"

"No. But it's not just that," she said. "Grandma says this person wants a whole different Touch. So I had to learn a new spell. And it's a hard one. I didn't have a lot of time and I'm not really sure I know it. And I feel so weak. And—" She stopped and buried her face in her hands. "Nick. It's terrible. This whole thing is so terrible."

I took her in my arms and that's when she started to cry on my shoulder. So of course it went without saying that I would be there tonight. I had no doubt about that. "I'll be there for you, okay? I promise. Even if my family bars my doors because of the suspension. And I won't get in the way this time."

She sniffled. "Okay."

"And if this person doesn't show up, I'll kidnap some poor loser off the street and you can perform the Touch on them. Okay?"

She laughed. "But nobody should have this Touch," she said into my T-shirt. "It's the really bad one. Invisible Assassin. The one that scares me the most."

Chapter 30

The You Wills told me I'd meet with resistance while trying to leave the house, and as usual, they were right. "You
don't think you're going somewhere tonight," my mom remarked from her room as I appeared at the top of the stairs
in a clean T-shirt. It was like, not only could she see the future, but she had radar and Spidey sense, too. Or maybe she
could just sniff my shaving cream and deodorant and hear
the jingling sound of my house keys going into my pocket.
"You're grounded for as long as you're suspended."

"I need to—"

"Should have thought of that before you got yourself suspended," she snapped.

I stared at her, hard. Funny that she would pick now to play
mother, when she never did the other 1,439 minutes of the
day. "Fine. Guess I'll just go downstairs and watch TV."

"Fine," she answered, and I could hear the groaning of her
mattress as she settled into it to watch whatever action movie
she had picked out.

That was the good thing about having a mom who was

confined to her bedroom. Sneaking out was no problem. I didn't even feel bad about it; if she wanted to keep tabs on me, she could get up and come downstairs.

Nan was watching *Wheel of Fortune* with her broken arm supported on an old velour pillow. "You don't think you're going out?" she said, but her voice was a lot gentler than my mom's.

"I have to," I whispered. "It's important."

She studied my face. "All right. I'll cover for you. But only until ten. Even if you aren't going to school tomorrow, it's still a school night."

"Right," I said, taking care to make as little noise as possible when I opened and shut the screen door. I walked my bicycle down the driveway because I was afraid my mother would hear the sound of it kicking up gravel, but the second I was on the sidewalk I raced away. It was late; the sun was setting, and in the distance it looked like more storm clouds were bulging over the mainland. The air was humid but carried that icy chill that usually comes on early September evenings. I shuddered as I sailed up the ramp and onto the boardwalk.

Taryn was waiting for me outside the arcade, our prearranged spot. She looked even worse than before. Her face was the color of old snow, which was a huge contrast to the bloodred rims around each of her eyes. She tried to wave to me, but her hand only made it to hip level before she let it fall. She didn't smile.

"You ready?" I asked, which was a stupid question. I realized too late I probably shouldn't be reminding her of the task ahead. She was worried enough as it was.

She just nodded and looked down at the ground.

"You want something to eat before you go on?" I asked, remembering how she ate when she was nervous.

I started to fish through my pockets for money, but she wrinkled her nose and said, "I'm all set." It was a good thing, since all I had in my pocket was a crumpled dollar and a Trident wrapper. I hoped she was more prepared than I was.

The You Wills had me checking the clock in the arcade, so I did. "Ten minutes. Guess I'll get back there. I'll see you after, okay?"

She nodded looking dazed, small, and lonely.

"Hey," I said to her, taking her by the hand and just soaking in that feeling of peace she gave me. "It'll be okay."

She looked into my eyes. "I know. I believe you," she said, and she tilted her head up and gave me a small kiss, nothing like the one we'd shared earlier that day. Her lips were cold and so weak, I could barely feel their pressure on mine. "See you."

And she turned and walked to the tent, disappearing beneath its folds.

All I could think of was how stupid it was as I made my way over the arcade wall. That because of this family curse, she'd die tonight if she didn't Touch someone else. There was no question in my mind—she had it worse than I did. I might not have been able to live a normal day in my life because of my curse, but I didn't hold another person's fate in my hands.

I lowered myself into that dark void and smelled the incense and sea as I opened the curtain a crack. It looked like Taryn was alone. She glanced in my direction and sat down in the chair, then let out a small sigh. I thought about saying something to her, something to make her relax, when a rough voice came from the corner of the tent: "You are late. Open the book."

"Yes, Grandma," she said. I instinctively shifted backward. As Taryn did what she was told, her grandmother shuffled into sight. Though her back was to me, I could reach out and touch her. I could smell something like sour milk and mothballs as she moved near me, something that combined with the incense to make my eyes water. I rubbed them and swallowed. I realized this space was like a tomb, something that captured scents and never let them go. I pulled my T-shirt up in front of my mouth and crouched lower, wishing I'd brought a can of Coke with me. Wishing someone would pull back the entrance flap to the tent so that more of that cleansing sea air would come in.

Everything around me felt damp, sticky. It was darker than usual in there and I could hear thunder rumbling over the buzz and ringing of the arcade games. Suddenly the sound of a thousand hoofbeats started to pound above me. Rain. More than rain. Downpour. Taryn said something, but I couldn't hear it amidst the pounding on the roof. The flap opened, and rain and cold air swirled in.

The client was here. A shape stood in the doorway, shaking the rain off itself like a dog. It was too dark. I couldn't see more than a hulking black shape. "Freaking rain," a voice rumbled. It was a man. A young one. He moved forward. Taryn's grandmother nodded at him and he stepped under the lamp to sign the book.

I was so busy trying to figure out who it was, what kind of guy would want something like Invisible Assassin, that I almost didn't notice Taryn, sitting there, shaking. His face came into view under the chandelier just as I realized she was yawning. But there was nothing about her face that was tired—she was sitting bolt upright, her eyes wide with fear. She yawned again—what did a yawn mean?—and I finally took in the face that was standing over the table, the face that belonged to the man who was signing his life away.

Bryce Reese.

And the yawn.

Get out.

She wanted me to leave.

Her grandmother and Bryce were busy standing over the book, so I opened the curtain a little and shrugged at her. She looked carefully at the two of them, then nonchalantly turned to me, biting her lip. Her eyes glistened in the minimal orange light from the chandelier. Then she ran her hand through her hair. "Grandma, before we start, I have to use the bathroom."

That was another signal. She wanted me to meet her out by the crane game. I hoisted myself up and hurried over there. By that time the rain was pouring down in sheets. Taryn's hair hung in her face in wet ropes. She didn't wait for me to be standing next to her before she began to sob. "He's going to use it on you," she wailed. "The Invisible Assassin."

I swallowed. "Wait. What? What is the Invisible Assassin?"

"It's so horrible," she said. I tried to grab her hands, but they were wet and trembling so much I couldn't get hold of them. She tried to get more words out but instead another sob caught in her throat. Finally, her breathing calmed enough so she could speak again. "It allows him to target people, and he can just walk away. It will kill their family. And it will kill them. In the worst ways you can imagine."

"You mean . . . ," I started. I suddenly thought of my visions, or the lack of them. "Why would he use it on me?"

"You know why. Emma was always his world. And you saw him." She sighed, but the last bit of air came out as a cough. "And he kind of . . . He's not all there. He's crazy and he hates you."

"It kills my family, too?" I asked. I thought of Nan and Mom.

"All of them," she sobbed.

"But my mother never leaves the house."

"It doesn't matter. It will find her."

I studied her. Oh, she was still beautiful. She'd always be. Fifty years from now, if she lived that long, she'd still turn heads. But now, she was dying. Her hair was no longer golden and platinum but frizzy and strawlike, and her pretty features were all sunken in her colorless skin. Then I looked out toward the sea. Everything beyond the boardwalk was gray, the color of nothingness. "You'd better go back in there. He's going to wonder where you are."

She narrowed her eyes. "I can't. Nick. I can't do it to you. To your family."

I grabbed her wrist with a lot more force than I meant to. "You have to."

"No. I'll find someone else. I'll—"

"Who?" I demanded, dropping her wrist. "You'll be dead in three hours if you don't. Go. Do it. And don't worry about me and my family. I can take care of us."

"But you can't. How can you—"

I didn't know how I did it, because my heart was beating its way out of my chest, but I managed a smile. "It's okay. I can see the future, remember?"

She bit her lip. She started to leave but then ran toward me, pushing her lips against mine. When she pulled away, her eyes didn't meet mine. Maybe because she was ashamed, or maybe because they were so filled with tears she couldn't see straight. Her voice was barely a whisper when she spoke. "I love you, you know."

Before I had a chance to tell her that I loved her, too, she was gone.

Chapter 31

The gutters flooded and the puddles in the streets grew to rivers, so that I sloshed through ankle-deep water, the soles of my Vans squishing with every step. Though rain fell in waves, lightning lit the sky like daytime, and the thunder rumbled and boomed continuously overhead, I walked my bicycle home slowly, as if I had all the time in the world.

What could I do? People were going to die. And I had no way to fix it.

For some reason, I found myself thinking of Jocelyn. If I had just let her get the Touch she wanted, Taryn would be okay. Taryn wouldn't need to perform the Touch tonight, and we would all be safe. Instead, I'd messed everything up. Just like my mom had. Funny how one decision can mean so much.

But the thing was, I'd envisioned us dying in Taryn's Jeep before that. So maybe I'd always been meant to mess with Jocelyn's Touch. It was almost as if my screwing everything up was beyond my control, destined, written in the stars.

And maybe my dying was, too. Maybe all the iterations of

my life, all the people I was destined to be before this, were just preparing me for this one ending. It was only fitting that I'd find the perfect girl and the most tragic death in the same future.

The rain poured down on my face, obscuring my vision as I walked along the boardwalk ramp to Seventh Avenue. If only I could get that Touch, that Flight of Song. Then I could tell Bryce to call back the curse, and he would have to obey. But Taryn had said a person couldn't be Touched twice.

There really was no way out of this.

A car horn blared at me as I tried to cross the street, and I jumped back in time to be hit by a wave of cold water kicked up from one of the enormous puddles in the road. I thought of Nan, and how she used to dress me in my duck outfit— galoshes and matching raincoat—when I was a kid. How she always did so much for me.

She'd do anything to make sure I was okay. And look what I gave her in return. It wasn't fair to her. It wasn't right.

Suddenly, something came to me. She'd do anything to make sure I was okay. Anything. I was sure of that.

All at once, I knew what had to happen. It was our only chance. I climbed on my bicycle and pedaled furiously down Seventh. I tossed my bike on the gravel in the front yard and stormed inside, bolting the door behind me. "Nan!"

She was, of course, sleeping in her recliner. Some reality-show host was talking about the voting process on television. I started to go into the living room, but my mom called to me. "Nick! Come up here!"

I didn't want to. Her voice sounded strange. No doubt she was going to scold me for being out when I was grounded. But as I neared the foot of the staircase, I realized she wasn't angry. She was excited about something, no doubt something she'd seen in a vision. I tried ignoring her, but she kept speaking. "I was wrong! I was wrong!" she said, over and over again. I didn't want to know what it was, though. I could see fragments of the scene in the Jeep clearly now, almost as if the accident was due to happen soon, and that was all I needed to know.

"Ma, I'll be up in a sec," I said, and Nan started to stir at the sound of my voice.

She looked at me, still dazed. "What? What's going on?"

"Nan," I said, kneeling beside her. "Listen. We're in trouble. I need you to do something for me."

She kicked the recliner upright. "Of course. What?"

"Someone took out a Touch. And they're going to use it on us. I need you to take out another Touch to stop him. We can go there tonight, and I'll—"

She held out a hand. "Wait. Slow down."

"I can't," I said, the words falling on top of one another. "They're going to kill us."

She stared at me. "You need to start from the beginning."

I took a breath. "Bryce Reese. He's the brother of the girl who died. Right now he's at the boardwalk getting his own Touch. And his Touch is going to give him the ability to kill me and my family. Because he hates me. And so what I want you to do is—"

"He hates you? Why?"

"Long story. Basically, he wants me to get what I gave him. So what I need you to do is—"

"I am not dealing in that nonsense," she said. "It's all about people wanting to play God. Your mother thought she could play God, and she learned she was wrong. There's only one God, and I know I'm not him. You need to talk it out with this Reese person."

"No, Nan. It's not nonsense. Bryce Reese won't listen to reason. And we are going to die. You have to."

She stood up. "I don't have to do anything," she said softly, turning her back on me and walking into the kitchen. "And I won't."

I just stared at her.

"And it is nonsense," she whispered. "It ruined both of you. And I'll have no part in it. Not ever."

I opened my mouth to argue, but her tone was so cold, so final, I knew it would do no good. "Then we've got to go. We've got to get out of here. Hide, or something."

She snorted and jutted her chin upward, towards my mom's bedroom. "Good luck getting that one to go anywhere." She picked up a tray with a half-eaten sandwich on it, then placed it on the kitchen counter. "You hungry?"

I clenched my fists to keep from latching on to something hard and throwing it at her, then walked up into the stairwell. My mom was standing on the landing, in the doorway. "What?" I asked her.

She narrowed her eyes. "What were you saying to your grandmother?"

I shook my head. After all, Nan was right. If my mom wouldn't go anywhere for her son's own funeral, she wouldn't go if I told her she needed to get away, even if it meant her life. Not that running would make any difference.

"I was wrong," she said, her tone light. "It wasn't yours."

I stared at her for a minute, annoyed that everything she said always had to be so cryptic. "My what?"

"Your funeral."

I'd already started to head back downstairs, since I was so sure I didn't want to hear what she had to say. But I stopped in midstep. "What? Whose was it, then?"

The thing was, I didn't have to ask that. It didn't really matter. There would be more funerals. Many more. And eventually, mine would be one of them.

I said, "I'm going to die, too. Because I don't remember anything after—" My voice hitched when I was suddenly struck blind by two strong beams of light, streaming in through the sidelights at the front door. A car was here.

I didn't need to be able to see the future to know that Taryn had successfully performed her first Touch. And that something terrible had begun.

Chapter 32

As I peered out the window, the headlights flickered off. A You Will was just coming through when images began to play in my head, hot and rapid, making me dizzy.

Flashing lights and rain on glass. A horrible squealing tore through my eardrums.

I strained to see the automobile in the darkness, but the rain made patterns on the pane, distorting everything beyond. Something moved in the darkness and suddenly someone rapped on the door.

"Nick?" a voice called out. Taryn.

By then my heart was in my throat. I swallowed it and unbolted the door.

"Are you okay?" we said in unison. And then, to confirm how eerily alike we were, we both exhaled and said "I'm fine" at the same time.

I ushered her into the hallway. She had her scarf over her head like a peasant girl, but she was still drenched from head to toe. Water dripped off the end of her nose. But she was alive. Her skin was glowing again and her eyes were back to normal. I didn't have to ask her if the Touch had worked, but I did anyway. "Did everything go all right?"

She pulled the scarf off her head and her curls sprang out, vibrant once more. "I did it. But I can't say that anything is right. Just like I thought, Bryce used the Touch on Pedro and you the second he got it. You shouldn't be here. You need to hide or something."

I shook my head. "My family won't leave. And I can't leave them."

Her eyes widened. "You have to make them understand that—"

At that moment, Nan stepped into the hallway. "I do understand," she said.

Taryn looked from me to Nan, questioning.

Nan smiled like she was a hostess, greeting guests at a tea party. "Nick won't properly introduce us, but I'm his grandmother. And you are Taryn. It is nice to finally meet you, after all I've heard. Come in and have something to eat."

Normally I'd shrink away in embarrassment, but I was too busy trying to sort out the visions that were flashing in my head. Headlights. Screams. They seemed so close. Taryn reluctantly followed us to the kitchen, like it was the last thing on earth she wanted to do. She helped Nan set the table and pour the tea anyway. Ten minutes later we sat around the kitchen table, nursing steaming mugs. I guess none of us felt much like drinking. Taryn didn't even bother to remove her tea bag. She just stared at it. "I'm sorry that your family has become such a big part of my family's curse," she said softly. I couldn't tell if she was addressing me or Nan.

"It seems that our family had some responsibility for inserting ourselves into it," Nan answered. She looked Taryn over. Now that she was drying out, her hair was shiny and her cheeks were turning rosy. She looked even hotter than I remembered. It was pretty stupid considering everything else that was going on, but I still wanted her. "Nick has told me so much about you."

I kicked her under the table to get her to stop giving the poor girl the hairy eyeball. Then I said, "Um. So what do we do now?"

Taryn shrugged. "Well, I wanted you to run away."

"But would that do any good? Wouldn't it just find us?"

She nodded. "Wishful thinking. It doesn't stop until it does."

I took a big gulp of tea and remembered too late that it was still hot. It scalded all the way down my throat and I grimaced back the pain. "What is it anyway? This thing that's coming for us?"

She shuddered. "It's death. And it can take any one of a million forms."

"So like, TB? Being chopped up in a meat grinder?" Lightning flashed in the sky. "Electrocution? Anything?"

"No. It's the worst. It's whatever form you fear most."

I stared at her. "I've never thought about that. Do people seriously sit around and try to think of the worst way to die?"

"Well, dear," Nan said, "that's because you've always been

busy thinking of so many other things. But truthfully, I think that, deep down, most people know very well which type of death they would fear the most."

Taryn nodded. I stared at her, confused, but then I suddenly remembered what she said. "I always have this feeling I'm going to die in a horrific car crash."

Nan continued, "When I was five, I almost drowned in the ocean. I've been so afraid of drowning ever since."

"Shhh," I muttered, scanning the corners of the ceiling for—I don't know what. Shadows, ghosts, some guy with a sickle. "You don't want it to hear you. Whatever it is."

Taryn said, "You don't have to say it out loud. It already knows. Even if you don't think you know. It does." She shuddered again.

"Let's find something else to talk about," Nan said, slitting open a box of Entenmann's with a knife. "Crumb cake?"

We all stared at it like it was a brick of dog crap. We'd lost our appetites. And clearly Nan was off her rocker. Death was coming for us, and she wanted us to sit and enjoy crumb cake. She'd let us go through our most feared deaths instead of getting a Touch just because she hated "that nonsense" so much.

"Nan," I said, trying to keep my voice even, "can we talk in the other room?"

She shook her head and cut herself a large piece of cake. "I don't want my tea to get cold."

"Nan," I grumbled. "Fine. Don't you understand? This is why you have to do it. You have to."

Taryn stopped staring at her tea and looked at me. "Do what?"

I explained my idea of Nan getting the Flight of Song Touch, and Taryn's eyes widened.

"Right! Wait." She turned to Nan. "You don't want to?"

Nan pushed her plate away without taking a bite and began fingering the Miraculous Medal around her neck. I knew what she thought: Leave it in the hands of God. He will make everything right. I'd heard her feelings about the Heights all too often, too: nothing good could be found in the Devil's Playground. "That's right. The Touch is the source of my family's problem. It's not the solution. It's sinful."

"Oh, I guess," Taryn said softly, then gave me an "is she insane?" look. "Good thought, though."

Nan stood up. Her expression, for once, was grave. "Lovely chatting with you both. Now I must get ready for bed."

She started for the staircase, her shoulders slumped and her head down. Normally she would have cleared the table and loaded the dishwasher, but I could tell she was rattled. And who wouldn't be?

"Good night," I called after her, and then I couldn't resist getting one last dig in there. "You might want to forgo your bath. I'd stay away from water altogether, if I were you."

Nan didn't respond. Taryn swallowed and grimaced like there were knives in her throat. She'd shredded the paper napkin into a pile of confetti. "Maybe she will sleep on it and change her mind?" she offered.

I shrugged. "Maybe." I kept my voice light to hide the dread that had crept over me. There was still a long night ahead of us, and evil always seemed more possible in the darkness.

Chapter 33

Lightning lit the sky far away, but the thunder didn't come as an answer. As I walked Taryn outside, there was no noise at all—no crickets, no humming of the streetlights—as if the entire town was holding its breath for what was to come. The Park was between storms, so the clouds had parted like a curtain, revealing the silver-dollar moon and thousands of pinpoint stars. Now, everything seemed hushed, the way the Park liked. As I held Taryn's hand, even the You Wills were gone, leaving a silence that was almost too silent. It was unnatural. Foreboding.

"Can we talk somewhere else?" Taryn asked.

I nodded and followed her down the gravel driveway, but when we were walking together, still holding hands, she did very little talking. It seemed like she was afraid to say something. The air was so humid you could almost taste it. We ambled slowly to the corner in the darkness, then kept right on going to the playground on the Fifth Avenue bay.

Tiny pools of water glistened on the seats of the swings. Taryn's skirt was still damp from before, so she didn't bother to wipe the swing dry before she sat on it. I sat down on the swing next to hers.

"I've known a lot of guys," she said, digging her bare toes into the sand. "They all wanted something from me. But not you. You're different. You're like my angel."

I laughed. "Are you crazy? I am not your angel. I ruined your life in a thousand ways, remember?"

"Why are you so nice to me, then?" she said.

I snorted. "I'm not nice to you."

"You let me give Bryce that Touch. You risked your life—the lives of your family—for me. You didn't have to do that."

"Yes, I did," I said. "You would have died if I didn't."

"I could have found someone else, maybe," she said. "You felt guilty? Is that what it is?"

"No. Look. You're as important to me as my family. In my life, I've known hundreds—thousands of girls, maybe. I've married them, had kids with them, grown old with them, loved them. But you are . . . I can't explain it. Every time you even walk away from me, I feel like there's a hole in my chest. I think I would die if anything happened to you. Literally. The pain would kill me."

She didn't say anything for a while, just sat there watching the lights of the bridge dancing on the smooth ripples of the dark bay. Finally, she said, "Wow."

I wasn't sure if she meant "Wow, that's amazing" or "Wow, you freak," but when she turned to me, there were tears in her eyes. So I inched forward in my swing and kissed her again. She exhaled sweetly, the way girls do, and I put my hand through her hair, wanting more of her, wanting to pull her closer. But it snagged on something, and when I rubbed my thumb to my fingers it was gummy and thick, like she'd used too much hair gel. I pulled my hand out.

"What the . . ." I looked at my hand. Sniffed. Oh, hell.

"What is that smell?" She stared at my hands. "Is that . . . peanut butter?"

"Ugh. Kid who sat on this swing before must have been eating peanut butter," I said, inspecting the chains. I couldn't tell much in the dark, but now I could smell nothing but peanut butter. It made me want to retch. "Ugh."

"Calm down, it's okay," she said, laughing. She took her shawl off and gently wiped my hands.

"You don't understand. I hate peanut butter." I pouted like a kid, but then suddenly

Glass raining down, shadows swirling in the headlights

I straightened. She just kept swabbing at my hands, oblivious to the things rushing through my head. "There. Better?"

I nodded, shaking the thought away. "Yeah. I think we better get back. I need to check on my family."

We walked back, and I held her hand. With the hand that wasn't still sticky with peanut butter. Peanut butter. Crap. Why was everything good always mixed with bad? I didn't want to think about it anymore. I was burned out, thinking of the bad all the time. And in this moment, all I wanted to concentrate on was Taryn. How right she felt. Comfortable. It was chilly, and we were both still damp from the rain, so she leaned in close to me, her hair ticking my chin. I smelled the cinnamon apples. With her hand in mine, my mind calmed and all I could think of was how, if I could pick one moment in my life and freeze it forever, it would be this one. There was all this craziness threatening, but I don't think I'd ever been happier. I knew it wouldn't last. It couldn't. But for that second, everything was perfect.

It started to drizzle by the time we reached my block, and when we came to her car, she said, "There's something else I have to tell you," just as the skies opened up and it began to pour.

I tugged on her sleeve, trying to get her to go into my house, but she pulled me toward her Jeep. "Are you crazy? I'm not getting in there," I said.

She laughed. "Don't be nuts. We're not going anywhere. I won't even put the keys in the ignition." She dangled them in front of me, then dropped them in my hand. "Here, take them."

I held them in my palm, staring at them like they were diseased. Okay. We wouldn't leave the driveway. That we could do. Besides, her Jeep was closer, and maybe the thing she had to tell me was something private, that she (and I) didn't want my family to hear. So I went with her. We piled into the passenger-side door as the clouds threw rain down upon us. But the second I slammed the car door, I had the weirdest and most uncomfortable feeling of déjà vu, like I'd just made the biggest and gravest mistake of my life. Suddenly the back of my neck prickled with the sensation I got whenever something big was coming. The cabin was humid and dark and dark and smelled of peanut butter. Water poured on the roof like a marching army and splashed on the windshield in long clear sheets. The dream catcher dangling from her rearview mirror swayed gently from side to side.

And we were going to die.

But no no no, I thought. In my vision I'm driving. I'm at the steering wheel. I'm—

But I realized too late that the trivial things didn't matter. That what mattered was the horrible, irreparable end result.

"Taryn," I said. "This isn't right. This is—"

"Shhh," she said, grabbing my hand. "Listen. It's okay."

"No, you don't get it." I reached for the door handle. But I couldn't find it.

"Nick, no worries," she said, holding her arms over the steering wheel as if to say, "Look, Ma, no hands!" but I grabbed the one closest to me and held it. It was so warm and my hand was dead in contrast. I lunged for the lock. I clawed at the door handle, trying to figure out how to get it open. I pulled on the door, pushed buttons, but nothing happened. All I could feel was something tightening around my neck, my pulse thudding in my ears, the stench of peanut butter making it impossible to breathe, and the cabin closing in on itself, on me. Finally she said, "Nick. Just relax, we're not going anywhere."

"No. No. NO! Tar, watch ou—" I shouted, but by then it was too late. She was facing me, away from the headlights as they came on us at warp speed. It was a truck, and a big one, judging from the eardrum-bursting squeal of the air brakes.

The entire cabin lit up for one brilliant second before the impact. Her face contorted into a terrified mask and her lips curved into an almost smile, yet her body was rigid, all points and right angles as it was propelled toward me. I grabbed hold of her at one of those awkward, wrong places, trying to pull her to me, to protect her, but my hands tangled in locks of her sticky wet hair. There was the shriek of shattering glass and the sting of it spraying on my skin. We began to career into a mind-scattering tailspin where earth and sky and everything in between seemed like the pieces of a giant jigsaw puzzle thrown into the air. When everything settled, I knew only one image would be left, the same image I'd already lived a hundred times: holding her blood-soaked head in my lap and screaming, screaming, screaming as the glass rained down upon us.

Chapter 34

I guess everything after the glass shattering around us was too much. The last thing I could remember was screaming endlessly as I held her head in my lap, feeling her hair, slick and gummy with blood.

The rest of Taryn's death was too much to get through my brain.

She was the one destined to die in the Jeep, in the horrible accident she'd feared most. I wasn't supposed to die then. Soon, but not then. After her death, though, I didn't care. I wanted it.

The rest of that week was like gazing at snapshots from an old camera. Disjointed and distant. Me at the funeral. Me lying in bed. Me banging my head against the wall, delirious, wishing I would go next. I didn't, couldn't think about Nan or my mom, or the danger they were in. The hole in my chest opened to a chasm. It ached so bad sometimes I scratched and clawed at it, trying to get whatever poison was in there out. I green-elephanted constantly. I don't think I ate, but maybe I did. I know I didn't sleep. I don't remember doing any of the things the living are supposed to do. No wonder I couldn't see any of that in my visions. It all seemed so surreal, so vague. Like watching someone else's life.

The next thing I remembered with perfect clarity was sitting on the lumpy sofa in front of Pat Sajak, staring at the dull brown shag carpet, feeling Nan's heavy eyes on me. She asked me a question, probably something stupid, like whether I wanted more iced tea, but I didn't hear her, didn't answer, just watched the giant wheel tick to a stop on the big black Bankrupt.

"We're all going to die," I muttered.

She pursed her lips, then said, "Oh, honey bunny, you don't—"

"I do!" I growled at her in an almost animal voice I didn't know I had. "The Touch is already working. It's going to kill my family. Everyone. It knew. Taryn was my family. In the future. I would have married her, grown old with her. It got her first. You'll be next. Or Mom. It won't stop until we're all dead."

She sat teetering on the very edge of the recliner, looking small, like she was ready to fall off. "It's sinful. And two wrongs don't make—"

I jumped to my feet. "Don't talk in clichés! You know it. It's the only way we can stop it." I knelt beside her. By that time a picture of Taryn, looking alive and beautiful, appeared in my head and I began to sob. "Please. I don't want you to die because of me, too."

She took my hand. Hers was trembling. "What is it called again?"

I raised my head to look in her eyes. She'd sucked in her bottom lip, something she only did when she was thinking hard. Hope flooded me. "Flight of Song," I said. "She'll be there today at five. We can go together."

She shook her head. "I think your mother is coming down with something. She's not right. Someone has to stay with her."

"What?"

"She was coughing blood. She didn't want you to see, but—"

I swallowed. Oh, no. "Nan. She's dying, don't you see?"

She nodded. "Yes. I see. What do I have to do?"

She had her arm propped up on the velour pillow. I motioned to it. "Can you drive?"

"I will. It's not far. Now, tell me. What is it I have to do?"

"All you have to do is go in and tell her you want it. I have extra money from lifeguarding upstairs. Give it all to her. Tell her it can't wait. Make sure she does it right away. Bryce Reese spends most of his nights at the Sawmill. Once you get the Touch, you need to go there and tell him to withdraw the curse on my family. He'll have to listen. Flight of Song makes people do exactly what you say."

She nodded. "All right," she said. "Tonight."

I went upstairs as Nan got ready to go out. I could smell the perfume she always wore and knew she was probably changing out of her cooking-grease-stained clothes so that she could head to the boardwalk. I knew she would do it; once she said she'd go ahead with something, she never went back. I just hoped it would work. In theory, it should have worked. For them, not for me. It was too late for me. I felt as good as dead. As if death would feel better.

"Nick?" a voice called to me in the darkness of the hallway.

"Yeah, Mom," I said, turning into her room. I'd planned on going in there anyway. I hadn't been inside her room in a while. She was propped against the headboard, paler and smaller than her usual pale and small. I'd never known a time when she looked right, but now something was especially wrong. "You okay? Can I get you anything?"

She shook her head and placed a hand on mine. "I know what has been happening," she said, her voice weak.

"Well, you can see the future." I started the joke I'd told her a hundred times, wondering how much she knew. I'd kept a lot from her. "So that doesn't make you Einstein."

She smiled a small, sad smile. "The funeral I saw . . . that girl? She was your girlfriend. I'm sorry we couldn't . . . do something."

I shrugged. It was once in a long line of times that this gift or curse or whatever it was had let me down in an epic way. But it really didn't matter. Eventually, we'd all go. And maybe it was better that way. The world would probably be a better place without the two of us.

"And I know that we are going to die," she said.

"We all die," I said quickly, and then realized that she was saying she knew about the Touch. She knew we were going to die soon. "Did you have a vision?"

She shook her head and picked up the water glass next to her bed. "Did you know that if you put this to the floor, you can hear everything downstairs? I was listening when you, Nan, and your girlfriend were talking about it."

I just stood there, startled. Mom usually lived in her own little world up here. She didn't want to know anything that was going on outside, but it always invaded her space, anyway.

"What was her name? She seemed very nice."

My tongue lolled in my mouth, almost like it didn't want to form the word. "Taryn. And she was."

She sighed. "I ruined that for you. Oh, my dear, how many things have I ruined for you?" she said, burying her face in her hands. "I don't blame you for hating me."

"I don't hate you," I said.

"Yes, you do."

I started to argue again, to say no, no I didn't, when in fact I did, just a little, but it didn't matter because she was still my mom, and as much as I hated her, I loved her more. But suddenly she threw her shoulders forward and began to cough so violently it seemed her whole body would break apart. It reminded me so much of Taryn that I cringed and took a step back. Then I patted her back and helped her bring the straw in her water glass to her lips. She swallowed with a loud gulp and rubbed her temples. "The cycling is bad today."

I hadn't noticed. Every part of me ached with a brilliant, crushing pain. Especially my chest.

"You were always better at handling the pain. What was that thing you used to say?"

"Green elephant," I said as she began coughing again. She brought a tissue to her mouth, and the bright crimson was a shock against the doughy white of her skin and everything else around her. I motioned to my neck. "Because of that necklace you used to wear."

She coughed more, then reached behind her neck and pulled out a white string. It had blended with her shirt so, that I'd never seen it before. As she lifted the string she freed the green elephant from underneath her shirt. The black cord was gone and the white string she put in its place was longer, allowing the necklace to hide lower on her chest, which is why I hadn't seen it. I stared at it. It was larger than I remembered.

The trunk was gone, broken off. "I thought you . . . ," I began. And here I'd convinced myself a mother who couldn't bring herself to make me breakfast, go to school concerts, or take me to the beach couldn't care about me. "The trunk is gone. That's bad luck."

She smiled. "Nick. I have enough good-luck charms around. Little good they do me." She fingered the green elephant before dropping it back to her chest. "This was never a symbol of luck to me."

I put my hands in the pockets of my shorts and studied the dresser mirror, decorated with dozens of fortune-cookie papers. I wondered if any of them had come true. When I turned back, I noticed her face had gotten darker. "What's wrong?"

"I was just thinking. What is yours?" she asked.

"My what?"

"What death do you fear the most?" she asked.

"Mom," I protested. She'd always loved the morbid. "I wouldn't tell you if I knew. But I really have no idea."

She gave me an "I'm your mom and I know better" look. "Like your grandmother said, everyone has one."

"Oh, really?" I thought for a second. "Well, it's whatever would be most painful, I guess. The wood chipper would kind of suck. And being drawn and quartered doesn't sound very fun, either." My stomach started to churn. I really hoped that by saying it I wasn't sealing my fate with the wood chipper. "I don't want to talk about—"

"It's not what would hurt the most. It's what you're most afraid of. Those are two different things," she said, reaching over and placing a lock of my hair back over my forehead. "And I'm your mother. Even though I've spent most of my time up here, I know what you are most afraid of, Nick."

"Come on. How can you know, when I don't even—"

"Nick," she said softly.

I stared at her, and at that moment I knew. I thought of the crowds watching me at tryouts, of how they parted to avoid me. I thought of Sphincter, calling me Crazy Cross in front of everyone in the busy hallway at school. The way they'd stared at me, eyes narrowed, faces wrinkled in disgust, as if I was an infection, a disease, the absolute embodiment of everything they didn't want to be. I'd convinced myself it didn't matter, that I didn't care. I'd convinced myself I was used to it, but can anyone get used to treatment like that? Each time, there was a chink in my armor, a dent in my wall.

It was only a matter of time before everything came crumbling down.

"I don't want to die in a way where everyone would think I was a freak," I choked out.

She nodded, and a tear trickled down her cheek. "Another one of your quirks I'm responsible for, I'm afraid."

I didn't want to think what kind of death that meant I was in for. I didn't want to know. Maybe it would be a public death. Maybe something pathetic, like a suicide. I thought of what I'd said to Nan. My life is already over. Suicide had never entered my mind before, but now, I wanted death more than anything. I wanted to be with Taryn. Now, it seemed like a definite option. In school the next day, people would whisper and raise eyebrows and some would say, "Well, what did you expect? Cross was a freak." I would cement my status as Crazy Cross, in capital letters, until the world decided to forget about me, which wouldn't take very long. Well, they would forget about me, but not the way I died. Years from now, at reunions, they'd say, "Remember that kid from our class who died? The freak? What was his name?" And everyone would know the sad, morbid details of the event, but nobody would recall anything else about me.

"Well," I finally said, swallowing the lump in my throat. "What's yours, then?"

A slow smile spread on her face. "What do you think?"

I shrugged.

She said, "Do you ever wonder about how things might have been? Without the Touch?"

I nodded. I'd thought about that often. I wondered what kind of mother she'd have been. Would she be more like Nan? I wondered what kind of person I'd be. Would I like myself? Would I be normal? Or would I find other things to obsess about? But it was useless. "What's done is done. I know you never wanted this."

"You were my perfect baby. Even before you were born. I wanted so many things for you." At that moment I knew what she wanted to do. She picked a lock of hair out of my eye and swept it back. She started to say it, but I didn't have to hear it to know.

"I know you're sorry, Mom. And I forgive you."

She squeezed my hand harder, and I saw everything in my head. I moved against the headboard and she didn't say a word, just laid her head on my shoulder. We sat there for a long time, until she settled down into the covers and fell asleep. Afterward, as the minutes and hours ticked by, I sat in the vinyl chair across from her, watching her chest rise and fall. When the sea breeze picked up, I wrapped an afghan over her and thought about the irony of it all.

But I stayed. I stayed there as if glued to that uncomfortable vinyl chair. I stayed until my legs fell asleep and the sound of cars whizzing by on Central Avenue faded to the sad song of the crickets. Because I knew.

Hers was the reason she'd gotten the Touch in the first place. The scariest thing to her was losing her fiancé, or being left to raise a child on her own. That was what she'd always been most afraid of.

She didn't want to be alone, and she didn't want to die that way, either.

That night, I thought of death. I had visions of me being strung out in front of the world, of people laughing and screaming "freak!" as they paraded by my mutilated body. I saw children crying at the hideous sight of me. I saw people who once acted friendly to me recoiling in horror as they passed. No, they weren't visions of the future—they couldn't be. I knew that. But the knowledge didn't stop me from tossing back and forth on my old, creaky mattress, as if trying to shake the thoughts out of bed with me.

Sometime in the middle of the night, I became aware I was back in my own room. It could have been night or early morning, but I felt as if days had passed. I saw the headlights on the wall. I heard the staircase creaking under her footsteps. The door opened and I felt the mattress dip. "It's done," my grandmother whispered, placing her hand on my forehead. It was cold. She smelled like butterscotch.

She didn't say any more after that. She simply left and closed the door. For the first time in months, I lapsed into a deep and dreamless sleep.

Chapter 35

What's the first thing you notice when you wake up? Sounds, right? Sensations? Well, for me, always, the first thing was a You Will, telling me what I'd feel when I first came into complete consciousness, what I'd see when my eyes finally flickered open.

But there was nothing. My mind was silent as a graveyard. The only explanation I could think of for that was because I was in a graveyard, or destined for one. I was dead.

But then I managed to push open my eyes. I was lying on my side, so the first thing I saw was my bedsheet. I ran my hand over it. It was smooth, not threadbare and pilled. I tossed and turned a couple of times, then pulled the pillow over my face. The pillowcase felt different, too. Sleek. New.

I was just lapsing back into sleep when I got the feeling that someone was in the room with me. Something creaked, and soft footfalls made their way toward the edge of the bed. Someone was standing over me. "Nan, go away," I muttered, trying to swat her out of the room, but then suddenly everything, once a million miles from my consciousness, came flooding back to me. Taryn. Peanut butter. The Touch. The accident. Mom. Freak.

I skyrocketed upright, ready to defend myself. I lunged forward, flailing my arms awkwardly, and toppled out of bed. Right on two feet. Two very tiny feet.

"Ha ha! Did I scare you, Nicky?" an impish voice said. "Huh, Nicky? You surprised? You jumped a mile high!"

It was a kid. Just a kid, maybe like six or seven. He was bouncing up and down, giving me whiplash. What the hell? Was this what death looked like? A little kid with red hair and freckles and a Spider-Man T-shirt? "Who are you?"

He didn't answer, just did this Muhammad Ali dance in front of me, and I thought about how weird it all was and that's when I realized something else. I was thinking. Not seeing the future. Not cycling. Not suppressing visions. All that was gone. Taryn was dead, and yet . . . I could think. Maybe my brain was having trouble waking up. I thwacked the side of my head to get it going again, but nothing. My mind was silent.

The kid jumped on me, tackling me so that I fell backward. I braced myself for the impact on the rickety old night table, but instead I descended against a plush white carpet. What the hell? When did Nan have that installed? Where was my night table with the toy truck lamp? I jumped back onto the bed, trying to escape the hands of the little booger who seemed to think I was his live punching bag. "Nicky! Nicky! Nicky!" he shouted, careering onto the bed. I began to lift my hands to defend myself when I noticed that the dump trucks and planes were gone from my sheets. They were plain white. Nice, clean, plain white. The kid's fist smashed into my cheek, making my teeth rattle in my mouth. For a tiny thing, he had power.

The kid lunged at me again, but this time I managed to get the scrawny little devil into a headlock. I looked around. "Ow! Nicky!" he shouted, but I didn't let go because I was momentarily stunned. It was my bedroom, but not. Somebody had to have been playing a cruel trick on me. Everything was modern, dark blue. There was a desk in the corner with a brand-new MacBook on it, and above that, a shelf with at least a dozen trophies. Running trophies, from the looks of them. It looked like a furniture store showroom, made up like someone could live there, but way too clean and perfect for any actual, living teen.

I rubbed my head and the back of my neck with my free hand. No weird lacerations or bumps or anything of the kind that would have me hallucinating. Because that had to be what this was. A hallucination. A really vivid one. After a minute I realized the imp was just kind of lying like a dead fish in my hands. I quickly let him go. He massaged his neck. "Ow, Nicky," he said, pouting.

"Sorry," I said, running a cautious eye over the rest of the room. Ninety percent of it was foreign. The only things that I recognized were my Phillies cap, dangling from the mirror, and my backpack. "Who are you?"

He narrowed his eyes at me and then plodded out of the

room. A second later I heard him shuffling down the stairs, calling, "Ma! Nicky's on something."

Not only was there a weird kid living in my house, but he thought his mom lived there, too. Great. I sat up and ran my toes through the cushy white carpeting that was not there when I went to bed. Then I got up, went to the drawers and rifled through them. All the T-shirts were folded into neat little squares. But they must have belonged to someone else because none of them looked familiar. I couldn't find my favorite DON'T BOTHER ME T-shirt anywhere. It was definitely not on the floor, because there was nothing on the floor. For once, I could see every inch of it, that show-room carpeting in all its glory. It had vacuum tracks running through it. What the hell had Nan been up to? Didn't she have a broken arm? Did she hire a maid? A maid with a little kid?

I looked up. And where the hell did those trophies come from? I inspected the little gold plaque on the base of each of them. First place. Mile. Nicholas Cross. When had I done that? They had the years engraved in them. Last year. The year before. Freshman year.

It was like a broken record, constantly playing the same three words over and over again in my head, but each time, the words got louder. Now they were practically screaming in my ears. What. The. Hell.

I grabbed the first tee I could find, some lame *Steamboat Willie* shirt that I swear I never owned before, and a pair of jeans. When I pulled the shirt over my head, I caught a glimpse of myself in the mirror. I ran a hand through my hair. I hadn't gotten a haircut since the beginning of summer, so it had been getting shaggy. Nan had given me crap about cutting it before school started, but I didn't. Now, it was cut short, almost a buzz cut, except the top was long. I stared at it. Wow, I looked lame. It was so bad I thought it very plausible I could have given it to myself last night, while I was sleeping.

In the hallway I stopped outside my mom's room. Her door was closed and I listened there for a minute but heard nothing. I didn't stay long because I had other things on my mind. I thought of Nan, going off to get the Touch the night before. She told me it was done. She'd gotten Flight of Song and told Bryce to leave us alone. And that had worked, right? I was alive. In fact, I was better than alive, I realized as I descended into the living room.

I was cured.

And not only that, the living room was better, too. There was a new, leather sofa and a big-screen television. Nan's old recliner was still there, but everything else was posh and expensive-looking. I could hear that kid giggling and smell eggs frying in the kitchen, so I went in, expecting to see Nan at the stove.

Instead, there was a party going on. I don't think I'd ever seen that many people in my house at once. My mouth gaped. Some lady—the new maid?—stood in front of the stove, scraping a pan and holding a gurgling infant on her hip. The Spider-Man imp and another kid chased each other around a nice kitchen table. Some older guy sat in the midst of it all, reading the newspaper and sipping coffee.

Okay. So the maid came to clean and brought her entire family? Where was Nan? She definitely wouldn't be putting up with this if she were here. I cleared my throat, and the lady turned around. Before I could say something to put her in her place, she said, "Oh, Nicky! Sit down. You're late. You've got to get off to school soon."

But I wasn't listening. I was staring at her. Her hair was short. Her eyes weren't dark-circled. And then there was the necklace, on a fraying cord. The green elephant, with its trunk up. It was her.

It was my mom.

I swallowed. Again and again.

She tried to hand me a plate of eggs, but I couldn't think clearly enough to take it, so she jabbed me in the chest with it. "Why are you just standing there? Eat. What's wrong with your hands?"

Hands? I looked down. They were shaking. I almost couldn't stand. I almost couldn't breathe anymore. Finally I took the eggs and said, "Mom?"

She wiped a little drool from the baby's mouth. "Yeah? What?" She studied me. I studied her back. Trying to see what was there from before. What was new. What about her I still remembered. "Why are you staring?"

"Because you're . . . beautiful," I finally said.

"Aw, honey," she said, giving me a kiss on the cheek. Then her face hardened. She inspected me closely, as I did the same to her. "I think your brother's right. Are you on something?"

"My . . . brother?" I spat out.

She pointed at the food. "Sit. Eat."

I sat down, but eating was the furthest thing from my mind. Instead, I watched the kids run around the table. There were new, sparkling white appliances everywhere. Nan's tomatoes were gone. In fact, if Nan's *Heaven's a little closer in a house by the sea* mural wasn't hanging under the cabinets, I would have definitely thought I was in the wrong house. I tried to shovel a forkful of eggs into my mouth to make New Mom happy, but then I stopped halfway when my eyes caught on the guy across the table, reading the paper. If these kids were my brothers, then was he . . . ? He munched an English muffin like this was any ordinary day, like he'd eaten with me a million times before, and said, "Hey, Nicky. Fun night last night?"

I stared at him, completely disregarding the question. Maybe it was the way he fidgeted his long legs under the table the way I did, or that he had very familiar dark hair that kind of went every which way, or that he had the same eyebrows that arched in a point in the center. He was a stranger; I was positive I'd never seen him before, but something about him was like déjà vu. I opened my mouth and the only word that I could find came out, strangled and weak: "Dad?"

He took a sip of his coffee. "Uh-huh?" Then he studied me like Mom had—like there was something wrong with me. Like everything about them was completely normal. "Is everything okay, kid?"

The eggs tumbled off my fork. I dropped it on the plate, and the clatter was so loud that the kids stopped giggling, the baby stopped gurgling, and everyone stared at me.

I couldn't bring myself to answer. I looked around. At the kids. My siblings. At my dad again. At my mom, bouncing that baby on her hip. My family. Why couldn't I remember them?

Just then the baby giggled and my mom smiled. She *smiled*. It was an expression I'd never seen on her. An expression I never thought I would see. And wow, her face just lit up. She had a smile that could take over the world. It was amazing.

And so I nodded. "Everything's okay," I said, scooping the eggs back onto my fork. "Yeah."

Mom was instructing the man who was my dad about her having to take Izzy and the twins for their flu shots. "So you'll have to open the shop, okay?"

"Yes, dear," he answered. "Poopsie. Love of my life."

"And don't you forget it," she teased, swatting him with her dish towel, the way Nan used to do to me. New Mom checked the clock and pointed at me. "You're going to be late! Get moving!"

I didn't know how to explain it to New Mom. It was easier to break it to the other version of my mom, the broken one, the one who was used to bad news. "I can't. I was suspended."

Her eyes widened. "What? What did you do?"

I shook my head. "Maybe I wasn't," I said, knowing how

stupid I looked. I realized that version of the past seemed like a dream. That everything before last night seemed like something I made up. Even Taryn seemed so far away, like one of those perfect dreams that made you wish you never had to wake up.

New Mom came over to me and felt my forehead. "That is the last time I let you stay out past eleven on a school night. You look wiped out. And you have the meet this weekend."

A horn beeped outside. I just stood there, wondering how I could be expected at a meet when I clearly remembered falling and bleeding everywhere. I looked down. There was nothing on my knees, not even the slightest hint of a scab.

My mother—this alien that had invaded my mother's body—pushed me toward the door. "Your ride?"

I moved to the door, wondering what else to expect. Part of me didn't want to make a fool of myself, and yet at the same time I desperately wanted to figure this out. Nan. Nan would have the answers. "Wait. I have to talk to Nan."

"Nan?" She looked as if she'd never heard the name.

"Yeah. My grandmother?" I prompted.

She stared at me, this horrified expression on her face. "Tommy's right. Are you doing drugs?"

Tommy and the nameless brother—Timmy, I guessed—laughed and chortled, "Nicky's on drugs! Nicky's on drugs!"

"No, I—" A feeling of dread washed over me. Something had happened to Nan. "What's wrong with her?"

My father spoke up. "Well, my mother lives in Texas. She's

an eccentric lady. You've never spoken to her before. Why this sudden interest?"

"No . . . *your* mother," I said to my mom.

"Nicky, you're scaring me." I just stared at her, willing the information out of her. Finally, she sighed. "You never knew her. She's been dead since before you were born."

Chapter 36

The sun beat down on me the second I stepped outside; just one of many things that seemed to be beating down on me. I squinted at the battered Ford in the driveway. Then a head poked out from the other side. It was a guy with shaggier hair than mine, wearing sunglasses. He didn't look at all familiar. "You coming or what? I've been waiting out here forever."

"Sorry," I said, still trying to make out his face. Then I realized I was dragging along, so I quickly opened the passenger-side door and slid inside, gagging at the stench of cigarette smoke.

I stared at the guy again. He was wearing an old T-shirt and jeans and flip-flops. He took a drag on his cigarette and pulled the car into reverse. "Man, I hate getting up at crack of ass every morning. I can't do it anymore. I'll be happy when this year is over and we can do what we want."

I nodded a little. I had nothing to add to the conversation because (a) I was still stunned over Nan, and (b) I had no freaking idea who this was.

"And we have to get up at five for the meet on Saturday.

Five! On a Saturday. What. The. Hell, man," he went on, taking another drag on his cigarette.

So he was a runner, too. Even if he was puffing on that cigarette like it was the source of his power. After a minute he looked over at me. I was vaguely aware I was staring at him in a way guys are not supposed to stare at their friends, so I looked away and coughed.

"What the hell is wrong with you?" he asked. "You look like you have to take a crap."

That was the ultimate question. I wished someone would answer for me. "I . . . had a bad night's sleep, I guess," I answered. "Everything's all messed up."

"Yeah, after last night . . . ," he began. I guess he was thinking I'd complete the sentence. How come everyone remembered last night except me?

And Nan . . . what happened to her? She was supposed to go and get Flight of Song. She'd come home and told me it was done. She should not have been dead. Not only dead, but *dead for seventeen years.*

We got to school as the first warning bell was ringing and hightailed it into the music wing, which was closest to the senior parking lot and the bus drop-off. Except it wasn't called the music wing. It was called the Edith Laubach Memorial Wing. "Who is Edith Laubach?" I mumbled as we went in the double doors. There were colorful murals painted on all the cinder-block walls, murals I swear were not there the day before. Murals of rainbows and people holding hands and hearts and flowers and crap like that.

Friend Guy shrugged. "What is up with you, man? You come through these doors every day for three years and *now* you ask who Edith Laubach is? Some crazy chick who did herself in a dozen years ago is all I know."

Two other guys gave Friend Guy a one-finger salute and he told them to screw off. They said the same to me. I knew them, but I was never friends with them. They started talking to me like we were. "Yo, what did you and Spitz do last night?" a guy, who'd once painted the word "freak" on my locker in his girlfriend's red nail polish, said to me.

Spitz. I look back at the guy who drove me to school. Hell, of course. It was Evan Spitzer. My once-best friend. Who for some reason, like the past nine years never happened, is acting like my *always* best friend.

That's it.

It was like it never happened. Like my mom and I never even got the Touch.

And if we never got the Touch, maybe everything in my past never happened. Maybe it was all a dream. Maybe Taryn was still . . .

Still what? Taryn's grandmother said she'd given up performing Touches after she realized she'd given one to my mom, a pregnant lady, and passed it on to an innocent child. If we hadn't gotten the Touch, her grandmother wouldn't have given up performing Touches for all those years, and maybe she would have completed all the Touches in the book by now. And then Taryn would have been free. If she didn't have to come down to New Jersey to take over performing

Touches for her ailing grandmother, then maybe she was still living happily up in Maine. Maybe she was still alive. Alive . . . and completely unaware that Nick Cross existed.

Great.

Still, that was better than she was last night. Loads better.

I started wondering whether I could go up to Maine and find her. As a complete stranger, I probably wouldn't be able to insert myself into her life, but I could at least check to make sure she was okay. I'd have to drive, something that after that night with Taryn I'd never wanted to do again. But that rainy night in her Jeep felt like nothing more than part of a dream, or a scene from a bad movie. I could barely feel the shower of glass on my face now. Had it even happened? Fingers snapped in my face. "Whoa. We've got a zoner," one of the dudes said.

Sphincter, or Spitzer, or whatever he was these days, said, "Yeah, I think he got bitten by a zombie." They walked down the hall and I followed, feeling like a stranger in a strange land. Was physics my first class? Hell, I didn't even know my locker combination.

Spitzer said something about how he was going to quit track, and all the guys nodded except me. All I could think of was The Sergeant, stalking back and forth at tryouts and pumping his fist in the air when his son made the new school record. I said, "Your dad's really going to love that."

He stopped midstride and stared me up and down, frowning. "Then I guess I should be glad he's been in the ground for nine years."

What? His dad wasn't dead. If his dad had been in the ground for nine years, who was that at tryouts last week, giving Sphincter the thumbs-up and the New School Record shoulder rub? I felt the back of my neck burning as they all stared at me. His dad was The Sergeant, the guy who kept his son in line. He went to all the track meets and brought his own stopwatch and gave Sphincter and everyone crap for just about everything from the condition of the track to the shade of blue the sky was. I mean, I wasn't part of Spitzer's life for very long after the Disney Trip Debacle, but I had heard enough to know that . . .

The trip. The trip I'd tried to prevent. The one I'd successfully delayed by taking the air out of the Spitzers' tires the night before. Or had I? "There was an . . . accident on 95?" I muttered. "In Richmond?"

Spitzer glanced at the group and waved them on, then turned to me and pushed me up against the locker. Not hard, but he got in my face. "What the hell is up with you, man?" he hissed. "Do you want me to relive it? You know damn well what happened. Or did you forget coming to the hospital to visit me every day for three months when I was in la-la land?"

I swallowed, realizing I was about three minutes away from making him Sphincter the Non-Friend again. "No. Sorry, man."

After that I walked aimlessly and silently down the hall alone, feeling like a zombie. Of course, if Sphincter's Army sergeant of a dad had died long before, he wouldn't feel pressured to be on the track team. He wouldn't have to clip his hair and stop smoking and whatever it was his father valued. And he probably wouldn't have felt the need to get the Touch of physical perfection that would grow tumors in his body that would kill him by the end of the year.

I was so deep in thought that when I felt someone brush up behind me and tickle the back of my neck, I turned, thinking, What now? At this point, anything seemed possible.

I was right. I almost broke down right there. My knees felt loose and wobbly, like twigs.

Because standing in front of me, smiling with angelic innocence, different yet wonderfully, miraculously, marvelously the same, was Taryn.

Chapter 37

"Hey, you," she said, giving me a kiss on the cheek.

I just stared at her, stiff. I couldn't move. She was alive. Alive, and not only that, she knew me? Could it be that even though so much had changed, our relationship hadn't?

"Why are you staring at me like I have two heads?" she asked. She wiped her mouth. "Is my lip gloss on my chin?"

"No, you're . . . you're fine. You're here," I said. And I reached out to touch her, slowly, like testing a fence to see if it's electrified. Yes, real. The skin of her wrist was warm and smooth.

She studied me. "You don't look so good."

I might not have looked so good, but I felt great. "I love you," I said, taking her by the shoulders. My eyes got all wet and bleary, and I rubbed the tears away to look at her again. I never wanted to stop looking at her.

Her eyes widened. She touched my cheek. "I love you, too. Hey, are you okay? You're worrying me."

I just grabbed her and pulled her to me, so close that I could feel her heartbeat and she giggled in my ear. "Yeah. I'm perfect." We stayed that way for a long time, until the final bell rang overhead.

"We're late!" she said, pulling away from me. "Baumgartner is going to maim us."

Baumgartner. The physics teacher. I followed behind her. "You're . . . you're in my class?"

She raised an eyebrow at me. "Duh. What, did you already forget whose notes you copied yesterday? Your ass would fail if it wasn't for me!"

When we got to class, Baumgartner did the furthest thing from maiming us. The stodgy old guy beamed at Taryn like she was his own child. So she's the teacher's pet, I observed as she waved at him. I wondered if she still wanted to be a veterinarian. I took the seat next to her at the lab station and as she opened her notebook, a huge red *A+ Great Work!* caught my eye. She was the star student. And it made sense. All that stuff about her falling in with the wrong crowd in Maine never happened. She was no longer a year behind. She was a year ahead.

She patted my hand and whispered, "Don't worry. It was just the first quiz. You have plenty of time to erase that F."

I looked at her, at those beautiful eyes, that beautiful everything that I never thought I'd see again. Like I cared that I got an F and in this life I was an intellectual amoeba. There were so many other things out there.

I spent most—well, pretty much all—of the rest of the period, sitting back on the stool, staring at my girlfriend. She was wearing this cute blue schoolgirl miniskirt that showed off her smooth, pale runner's legs. Every so often she looked back at me and gave me a smile, especially when Baumgartner asked me a question. I slowly became aware everyone was staring at me. He'd asked me a question, after all.

Crap. He'd asked me a question.

"Um," I said. I would have done the signature thing and flipped through the pages of my physics book to pretend I was trying to find the answer. That is, if I had remembered my physics book. If I had remembered anything at all. I didn't really even know what the question was.

Baumgartner tapped on the side of his desk. Taryn pretended to cough and cover her lips from him, then secretly mouthed the word to me.

"Velocity," I mumbled.

"Ah. It takes a village," Baumgartner said, as if he thought he was the funniest dude on the planet, giving Taryn a wink. "By the way, Cross, what happened to your textbooks?"

I shrugged. "I forgot them." At least, I thought I had. In the world I remembered, I got suspended before I could pick up any books on the first day of school. After the accident, things were a blur. Did I have books in that neat, plush room I woke up in this morning? The place was so spotless, you'd think I would have noticed a stack of books there. But the last book I could recall getting my hands on, much less opening, was . . .

Of course.

I didn't want to incur Baumgartner's wrath, so I waited for the bell to ring, making it pretty much the longest class period of my life. I think I successfully bored a hole into the linoleum with all the fidgeting I was doing with my foot. Before Taryn could pack up her stack of books, I said, "Where's the book?"

She slid the physics book across to me. "You want to borrow it? Okay."

"No. The book. The Book of Touch. I need to see it."

"What is the Book of Touch?" she asked.

Right. The world was upside down. Of course this wasn't going to be easy. "You know. Your grandmother's book. The book she used up at her tent, on the boardwalk."

She'd been packing her stuff up, but suddenly she just stopped, grabbed the rest of her books in her arms, slung her backpack over her shoulder, and walked away from me. "I don't know what you're talking about," she muttered.

"You have to. Your grandmother. She has the book, right?"

She stopped and stared at me. "Nick, what's going on? You're acting really . . . intense. Are you okay?"

"I'm fine. I just need to . . . understand things. I need to see that book."

She hitched her shoulders, exasperated. "What book? I have no clue what you're talking about!"

I sighed. "Your grandmother. She tells fortunes at the Heights, right?"

"No," she said as I followed her out into the hall, "she's dead. She died earlier this year. That's why we moved here. We inherited her house. You know all this. Why are you acting so weird?"

"Oh. I'm sorry," I said.

She rolled her eyes. "You know I barely knew her. She was a

grouchy old lady. But yes, she did tell fortunes at the Heights or something. Before she died."

I nodded. "And did she use a book?"

She exhaled slowly and flitted her eyes away. "I told you, I have no clue about the book. You're freaking me out and I have to get to pre-calc." She started to walk down the hall, and I just followed her. Then she turned, planted her hand on my chest, and gave me another kiss on the cheek. "You have to go to gym. Remember?"

I shrugged. I didn't.

She had to pry her hand out of mine. She looked kind of weirded out when she said, "Don't worry. I'll see you for third. English. Room 116." It was actually kind of a comfortable feeling. I'd spent all my life weirding people out, even if now I was doing it for another reason entirely.

"Okay," I said, but it didn't make things easier. I stood there in the hallway, watching her walk away until the crowds swallowed her up and she was gone. I didn't want to let her go again, not even for a forty-five-minute period.

Chapter 38

The rest of school was just as weird. People didn't swerve to avoid me. Girls smiled at me. I ate lunch with the guys I'd hung out with earlier, and it was clear that I fit in. Or at least, I had, once before. They kept talking about things I'd done, or at least, they all seemed to *think* I'd done them. "Hey, Cross, remember in seventh grade when you went into the girls' locker room and Spanner caught you and you said you were just looking for deodorant?" and "Hey, Cross, what store was it on South Street that you got those fake hamster pellets last year?" I just nodded or grinned or said "I don't know" more times than I could count.

When the guy I spent too many brain cells trying to remember not to call by a certain part of the posterior anatomy and not to bring up his dad's death, since he was my best friend and all, dropped me off at home, I walked into the backyard and got a little sad to see that Nan's garden had been replaced by one of those sad, lopsided metal swing sets. As I stared at the spot by the garage, I walked face-first into the pole to a basketball net. After the resulting *thrunk*

I cupped my hands over my face and checked for bleeding, wondering who in the family played basketball. I certainly never did. Organized sports were far from my thing.

"Hey, kid. Want to shoot a few?" a voice called. It was my father. He was lying back on a lounge chair that also wasn't there the day before, wearing sunglasses and clicking on his phone. "I've got about ten before I have to pick the twins up at preschool."

The answer was obvious. I wouldn't know how to dribble if you held a gun to my head. But surprisingly, I had this urge to wrap my hands around the ball, to shoot. And I was even more surprised when I opened my mouth and "Sure" popped out instead of "No way in hell."

We started to play. To my astonishment, when I dribbled the ball, it didn't fly out of my hands. I didn't fall to the driveway in a heap. And when I raised the ball to shoot it, it felt strangely comfortable. I made the first basket. And the second. In fact, I made them all. I was even able to do some pretty quick moves to get around my dad and yeah, so what, he's an old dude, but I almost felt like I knew what I was doing. When I sunk another basket, I asked, "Am I on the basketball team?"

My father just laughed like I was an idiot. Understandable.

Okay. So if I'd played basketball before and I was this awesome athlete, shouldn't I have remembered that?

After a few minutes, my dad started to double over, breathing heavy. I kept dribbling as he sat down and slurped a bottle of water. It was weird the things that I knew now.

Before I never knew really what I'd be like in twenty years. But my dad was pretty okay-looking. He had all his hair. He wasn't a hunchback. All of these things boded well for me. "Dad," I said, still feeling really weird even speaking that word, "how did Nan die?"

He rubbed the back of his neck. "Nan. You mean, your mother's mother? Why all this interest in a lady you never met?"

I shrugged, nonchalant. "We're doing a genealogy project in school and it made me wonder. You met her, right?"

He nodded. "I did. She was very nice. But I didn't know her well. I only met her twice before . . ." His voice trailed off. I could tell it was something he didn't feel right discussing with me.

"Before what?" I prompted.

He said, "She'd been acting strangely that night. I was supposed to meet your mother for a late meal, but I got a call that something was wrong. By the time I got there, she was gone. Heart trouble, we were told." He shrugged. "Simple as that."

"B-but . . . ," I stuttered, "there's got to be more than that. Were they talking about something? Is there a reason she had the heart attack?"

He thought for a minute. "Well, now that I think about it, there was something about missing money. Your mom's entire summer's savings disappeared that night. We were going to use that money for a wedding, but we ended up getting married at town hall." He sighed. "As far as your grandmother, it could have been that she overexerted herself, helping your mom look for the money. They tore the house apart trying to find it. The place was a mess when I got there."

I rubbed my eyes. It didn't make any sense. The money disappeared because it went to Taryn's grandmother so that Mom could get the Touch. Or did it? In this alternate version of reality, Mom didn't have the Touch. Then what happened to the money? It made my head ache to think about it.

"Come on," he said, wrapping his arm around my neck in a choke hold. "Let's go get the little monsters."

I smiled. Alternate reality or whatever, it did have its benefits.

Chapter 39

My dad had a sweet brand-new Ford Explorer, I realized when he opened up the door to the three-car garage. There was also an older, but still awesome, Jeep Wrangler in the slot next to it. Maybe I should have been freaked out after what had happened in the last Jeep I'd been in, but I was surprised at how much it had faded from my memory over the past few hours, almost like it had never happened. Had it happened? And this was my Jeep. My totally sweet ride. In a ride like that, I might actually learn to like driving.

I didn't get the chance to drool over it because at that moment, I turned around and saw Taryn standing in the garage entrance. She had a messenger bag slung over her shoulder and was fiddling with the pull on her hooded jacket, looking nervous. "Hi," she said, giving me a half-wave.

"I'll go pick up the twins on my own," Dad said, climbing into the SUV. "Nice seeing you, Taryn."

She stared at me as if she expected me to say something. I'd probably forgotten something big. Maybe we were supposed to hang out. Maybe she'd expected me over at her house. I felt like I needed to apologize, so I did.

"What are you sorry for?" she asked.

I shrugged. "It just felt like the right thing to say."

"Can we go inside?" she asked when my dad had pulled out of the driveway and disappeared.

I nodded and led her inside. I offered her lemonade because that was what Nan always did on the rare occasions when we had a visitor, but then I realized I didn't know if we had any lemonade. I was glad when Taryn declined. She reached up to swipe a short corkscrew from her face and I saw a picture painted on the back of her hand, a blond-haired, lopsidedly smiling girl. I grabbed it. "Cute. I didn't know you were an artist."

She wrinkled her nose at me, teasing. "I just came from babysitting Emma. She says hi."

Emma. I swallowed. "You mean . . . Emma? Emma Reese?"

She nodded. I instinctively doubled over as if I'd just ran a marathon, trying desperately to suck air into my lungs. Emma Reese. Emma. The little girl.

Taryn moved beside me, put a hand on my back. "Hey, it's okay. Having flashbacks to that day on the beach?"

Her words echoed in my head. "On . . . the . . . beach?" I managed to cough out.

"Yeah. When you pulled her out."

Every part of me tingled, as if readying to spring to life for the first time. I thought about those cold blue lips, about how I'd tried, over and over, to bring her back to life. Somehow, I'd done it. Somehow everything I remembered—Emma's death, Taryn's death, all of it—was nothing but a dream. "I guess . . . I guess I keep thinking of what could have happened."

"It could have been bad, yeah. But everything's okay," she said, squeezing my shoulder. "Now come on. I have something to show you."

It was weird to see how comfortable she was in my house. She went right to the staircase, climbed the stairs, and entered my bedroom, where she threw her bag on my bed. "How did you know about it?" she asked.

"Know about what?"

She reached into her bag and pulled out the book. It looked, like everything, different and yet the same. The cover was a deeper brown, the edges not as battered, the pages a cleaner white. The lock was missing. It looked as if someone had ripped the lock off, trying to get inside to read the pages. It seemed more ordinary than before, more like any other book. "This is it, right? The book you were talking about?"

I nodded. "Where did you find it?"

"My parents have a bunch of my grandmother's things in a bedroom upstairs. They've been putting off going through it because it's a lot of junk. I found it in a box, with a bunch of other books. It looks like a witchcraft book, but a lot of the pages are mostly blank, like something was written there before but erased." She stared at the book, a disgusted look on her face. "So how did you know about it?"

I sat down next to her. "You'll think I'm crazy if I tell you."

She narrowed her eyes. "I already think that."

I studied her. How could I tell her? I couldn't expect anyone to believe a story that warped. But this was Taryn. The Taryn that, once upon a time, I knew I'd be with forever. Things were different, sure . . . but in some ways, like the way she looked at me, very much the same. "Okay," I said.

So I told her. I told her about the book, and what it used to be able to do. What it had done to me. She listened, her face stone. She didn't make any comments, didn't react to anything, even the most unbelievable things. She didn't even gasp when I told her that only three days ago, I'd held her as she died. When I finished, there were tears in her eyes.

"Oh," she said. She looked like she was trying to think of something to say, but nothing was coming out.

"Crazy, right?"

She shook her head. "Well, yeah. But it's not that I don't believe you. I can't not believe you. It's obvious you believe every word of it."

"The thing is, I'm the only one who still remembers the old version of the past. And I don't remember what happened in this version of the past. Not a thing." I exhaled slowly.

"Why?"

"Got me."

"And so much has changed. How can it be that we were together then, and we're together now?"

"Well, that I can answer."

She raised her eyebrows. "And?"

I shrugged. "Because some things just have to happen. Like, the sun has to rise and set. Time has to go by. We have to get older. And I guess we are one of those things. It's destiny. Unchangeable."

She smiled. "Corny. But I like it."

She swallowed and then opened the book. She frowned at the first page. After a few minutes, I realized why. If she hadn't had to follow in her grandmother's footsteps, she wouldn't have needed to learn the language of the text.

"It's in Hungarian," I said. "You can't read that, can you?"

She grimaced. "A little. When I was a kid Grandpa and I were pen pals." She flipped the pages. "You said your grandmother was supposed to get Flight of Song that night? What was her name?"

"Evangeline Cross."

She stopped at one of the pages. "Here it is. And the signature looks like *Marilyn*. Marilyn Haas. Who is that?"

"No clue. Okay. So she didn't get it. What did she get, then? Anything?" I asked, standing over her as she flipped the pages. "There. There's her name. What's that one?"

Taryn read it. "Um. I can't . . . It has something to do with time." She was quiet for a moment. "The taker of this Touch . . . may return to one moment in time and change anything she wants." She looked up at me. "That's it. She—"

I stood up. "Architect of Time. Of course. She went back to the day my mom got the Touch. And she . . ." I thought back to my father's words. Nan and Mom were upset. They'd spent the day looking for my mother's money. And then Nan . . . "She hid the money. That was why she had the heart attack. She hid the money that my mom would have used to get the Touch."

Taryn pointed to some scrawling beside the name. "Look at the date."

I inspected it. It was signed yeserday. "It makes sense. That's when she took the Touch out."

"But that has to be a misprint. This book was under a pile of junk yesterday. When I found it today, it was covered with ten years of dust."

I shrugged. It made no sense. And yet . . .

"Wait." She flipped the pages again. "What was the name of the Touch your mom got?"

"Eagle Eye, or something like that."

When she found the page, I recognized the name. It took a moment to realize from where, but it came to me. The music wing. The Edith Laubach Memorial Wing. The poor girl who'd ended her own life because she'd had to live with a terrible, life-destroying curse.

Taryn just gasped. "Poor girl. Now we know why she killed herself." She looked at me, her face grave. "It was that bad?"

I nodded. Though it wasn't my curse anymore, I could still feel the pain from it. The overwhelming grief of Taryn's death, the fear of knowing what might lie in the future. It was like scars running deep under the surface, and who knew how many years it would take to erase them?

"Where would your grandmother have hidden the money?" Taryn asked softly.

I looked out the window. "In her garden. It's under the swing set now," I said. I was more certain of that than anything. And then I laughed, Nan's words still ringing in my ears. "The root of all evil."

"Should we try to dig it up?"

I shook my head. I felt strangely light. Light in a way I'd

never felt before in my life. It was then I noticed something dangling in the mirror above my dresser. Something small but glistening brightly in the small sliver of light shining through the window. As I neared it, I knew it instantly. Nan's Miraculous Medal. She'd once told me it was a symbol of faith. I slipped the chain over my neck. Then I looked at Taryn, who watched me without question. "This was Nan's," I said as she inspected it. "Thanks for finding the book."

She wrapped her arms around me, stood on her toes, and kissed me. "Thanks for telling me everything."

In the days that followed, I thought about tracking down Edith Laubach's family, to provide them with answers they might have been searching for. But I never did. I wasn't sure it would serve any purpose. Taryn and I did leave flowers under the plaque in the hallway, though, on the very date she'd died.

We did the same at Nan's gravesite. I tried hard not to talk about the old past, the past that really hadn't happened, but every once in a while I would quietly bring up something about Nan to Taryn. It was like not talking about her was denying the existence of the wonderful, amazing human being who sacrificed everything to save my mom and me.

I still miss her, every day. I miss everything about her, from the way she used to paint smiley faces with ketchup on my eggs to the way her bones used to creak and her engagement ring clinked against the railing as she climbed the stairs. Sometimes I think this Touch was the best thing that ever happened to me, because it allowed me to spend seventeen years with her.

But then I remember the hell it put me through. Sometimes I have nightmares. I will wake up and feel a You Will popping through, but then I will force my eyes open and realize that I'm okay, that it's just my imagination. Anything swirling in my head now, creating chaos, is just my imagination.

It took some time, but after a while, I learned enough to settle into this drastically different life. I learned that my mom has a beautiful smile. I learned not to assume that a person staring at me meant I was a freak. I learned to stop pushing Taryn away, to feel comfortable and relaxed when she put her arms around me. I learned to adore Izzy, Tommy, Elliot, and my dad as if I'd known them every day of my life. I learned to get along without Nan, because I knew that was what she wanted most for me. I learned that the negative doesn't always accompany the positive, and that some things can be all good. I learned.

I learned to love the gift of every single day I've been given.

Now the thing I love most is when Taryn calls me up and asks me what we're going to do this weekend, saying I have no clue.

Turns out, I love surprises.

cooler of lemonade, and the spot where I'd plant my back-side. A lot of times when it rained, it was underwater. But now it wasn't. It was a perfect time for fishing.

He wiggled his toes in the mud, looked around, patted the ground beside him. "Room enough for two."

Just barely. I eyed the spot suspiciously. That was where I usually put my cooler. His backside was where mine usually went. I couldn't tell how old he was; most everyone on my street was so much older than me, they might as well have been from another planet. He was a younger older, though. Maybe only a decade or so older. That made him the most interesting thing I'd seen all day. So I deigned to sit beside him on my mound in the river. "You talk funny," I said.

He laughed. "Way I see it, you're the one talking funny, kid."

I gave him a big "hmph" and cast my line. He watched my every move, silently, like a cat, until his string began to bob. He pulled a big fat silver beauty out of the water and grabbed it in his hands as its tail swished back and forth, painting dots of midnight blue on his faded denim. Then he smiled and let it go.

"What did you do that for?" I asked.

"Don't eat fish," he answered.

"Then why catch them?"

He shrugged. "Somethin' to pass the time."

I shook my head. "There're a lot funner ways to pass the time, if you don't eat fish."

He chuckled. "Well, kid, if you must know, I'm waitin' on someone."

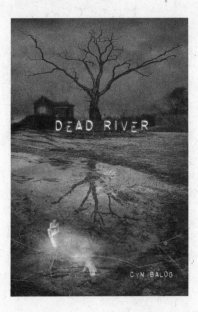

Kiandra and her friends are spending prom weekend at a cabin on the Dead. The Dead River.

She thought it was going to be just the four of them.

She was wrong.

Nothing is what it seems in this creepy paranormal thriller by Cyn Balog.

PROLOGUE

"Who are you?" I asked, my voice flat. Seven-year-olds are all about blunt. No "Hi, how do you do, nice weather we're having." After all, he was fishing in my spot.

"No one worth knowin'," he said in a gooey Southern twang, turning back to his fishing pole. "Fish're bitin' like mosquitoes on a hog."

I took a step closer. His fishing pole wasn't a nice one like mine. Just a stick with string tied to it. His jeans were holey and dirty, too. He didn't have a shirt; from the color of his skin he was probably one of those boys who went shirtless from May to September. Freckles like tiny coffee beans mingled with the deep russet hue on his shoulders and nose.

I kicked a stone with my big toe. "You're in my spot," I said as the stone skittered off the bright red paint of my dingh nicking it.

My spot was the best on the whole Delaware. It was an island twenty yards off the bank on the Jersey side. T island was big enough for only a couple of shade trees

"Oh yeah? Who?"

"A missus. She'll be along in a shake."

"A what?" When he didn't answer, I asked, "Your girl-friend?"

"Nah." His fishing line bobbed again. He pulled in another one, silver and beautiful. The fish dangled from the fraying, sad excuse for a line as he inspected it closely, smiling with pride. I looked at my own rod, glittering red in the sun, a present from my mother for my birthday. The sinker floated on the water, still.

"Well, she's not taking my spot," I muttered as he tossed the fish back. "You're just catching the same fish over and over again. What bait you using?"

"Just some worms and bugs I dug up." He looked at my pole. "You ain't gonna catch nothin' with that gleamin' piece of horse manure. The fish'll spot that thing a mile away."

"I do just fine," I said, even though I hadn't caught anything with it yet. My fishing spot had always been good to me, but not lately. I'd been thinking that maybe it was a cursed pole, since I'd gotten a paper cut on the wrapping when I opened it. "I may be a girl, but I know plenty about fishing."

He shrugged again. "You underestimate them fish," he said with a snicker. "Fish're suspicious creatures, kid."

Know-it-all. And that was stupid. Fish, suspicious? Fish are dumb. About as dumb as he sounded.

His line bobbed again. I wanted to punch him. Instead, I just wrinkled my nose at him. Then I got my pole, stuffed it in my dinghy, and grabbed my oars. "You could give whatever you catch to my family. We eat fish. Which is what you're supposed to do with them."

"Maybe so, maybe so. You going, girl?"

"Yeah. You're in my spot." I sighed heavily, hoping he wouldn't decide he liked my spot enough to frequent it. Then I pointed at my house on the bank. "I live in that white house over there. Where do you live?"

He didn't seem interested, didn't even bother looking toward where my finger pointed. "Other side of the river."

"In Pennsylvania?"

He nodded at the tree-lined bank as if it had just been introduced to him. "That where that is?" Then he smiled. In all my days on this earth I would never forget that smile. The hot summer sun paled in comparison. "Yeah. Pennsylvania."

"Wait. How'd you get here, without a boat?"

He laughed. "Swam."

"No way. The current?"

"I'm a powerful good swimmer, kid. Current's no match for a powerful good swimmer like me."

I raised my eyebrows. My parents would never let me out in the middle of the river like that. The island was as far as I was allowed to venture, because even when it was rough, the water was barely up to my waist. "Oh. Well. You ever catch any fish you want to give me, I'm right over there," I said slowly, pointing the way to my house again. But he didn't bother to turn. He just stared at the ripples in the water. His line began to bob again. I couldn't stand it.

"Sorry," he said, shaking his head. "Can't."

I fought back the urge to shove him as he pulled another big beauty in. "Why not? Are you some kind of fish-loving wacko or something?"

"'Cause I don't go over there." He looked at me, the corners of his mouth hanging low. That was another thing I'd always remember. That look. Not frightening. Sad. More than sad. Regretful. "Not unless I have to."

Turned out I didn't have to worry about him taking up permanent residence on my fishing spot. I suppose he found who he was waiting for and moved on, just like the river, never settling in one place for too long.

CHAPTER ONE

Row row row your boat
and please please please take me
gently down the stream
to where I can't be hurt. We'll go
merrily merrily merrily merrily
and I won't fight
for life is but a dream
and death I think is the awakening.

Have you ever heard of suicide by river? You just wade out deeper and deeper, and before long the current carries you away. And by then there is nothing you can do about it.

A lot of people wonder what goes through a person's mind during the moments they're pulled away. Do they regret those steps into the churning waves? Do their lungs burn as they gulp for air and get nothing but earthy, thick liquid instead?

I don't wonder, though. Because wondering means I'd have

to start thinking of *her*. And I won't spend a second thinking of someone who didn't think of me.

"You're zoning," a voice calls me back. Justin. One of his arms is draped over the steering wheel, and for the first time I realize his other arm is around me. He drums his thick fingers on my shoulder.

I give him a smile. "No, I'm not."

"Then what was the last thing I said?"

"The river is going to be outrageous," I answer.

That's only a guess, but a safe one, since all winter he's been talking about this trip and how the river is going to be outrageous. He keeps fidgeting the foot that's not on the gas pedal. Justin likes outdoorsy things, like climbing mountains and sleeping under the stars in subzero temperatures. He's been going to dam releases on the Dead since he was eleven. He's wearing a red-and-black-check lumberjack shirt, for God's sake. How did we ever get together? I much prefer sleeping in a warm bed. Hot cocoa. Icy water *not* dripping off the end of my nose. I'm, like Jack says in *Titanic*, more of an "indoor girl." Nothing wrong with that.

Though I should probably *not* be thinking about freezing waves and peril in the water right now.

"You write a good poem?" he asks me as I close the cover of the little leather-bound book I carry everywhere.

I wrinkle my nose. I'm never sure anything I write is good. I'm the editor of the yearbook and literary magazine only because nobody else wanted those jobs. Wayview High is big into hockey, and that's about it. My school puts out only one issue of its literary magazine, *The Comet,* a year, mostly because we get no submissions, and so half of the poems in this year's issue were from me. I'd even written a few haiku *about* hockey, hoping it would get someone's, anyone's, interest. Little good it did. I'm not sure anyone read them, other than my English teacher. Oh, and Justin. At least he said he did. But looking down at my most recent effort, I'm not sure if I want anyone to see it. "Please take me gently down the stream to where I can't be hurt"? Somehow I can't escape the thought of icy cold water and death, even in my writing.

"Are you scared?" Justin asks me.

"No," I say quickly, resolute. "Of course not." At least, I try to sound resolute, but it's hard, especially since the thought that's now center stage in my brain is that of a thousand human icicles bobbing in a black, endless sea.

"Of course you are, Ki. This is the Dead River we're talking about," Hugo Holbrook says from the back of the truck. I dig my fingers into the vinyl armrest. Of all the people my cousin Angela could have invited on this trip, I can't believe it's Hugo I'll be sleeping in a cramped cabin with for four nights. It's bad enough that I have to spend hours after school in the closet-sized yearbook office with him when we're on deadline. How does she find him even remotely attractive? He has nostrils like black holes and eyes so close together that the space between them is a rickety footbridge.

And I'm convinced that his laugh is why earplugs were invented. *Wahah wahah wahah.* "Look at her. She's shaking."

"It's freaking cold," I mutter, grimacing at Angela, Miss He's-Kind-of-Cute-and-Really-Likes-Me, in the rearview mirror. She's the same cousin who nursed a frighteningly ugly and smelly three-legged lizard back to health in her bedroom when we were eight, after my aunt and uncle ran it over with their Cadillac SUV. Most people wouldn't have touched it with the back of a shovel, but Angela let it sleep on her pillow.

But Angela doesn't notice my scowl. Her eyes are focused on the river. It's black and churning because they released the dam yesterday, something they do about ten times a year so that the rapids will be intense for rafting. Not exactly as inviting as, say, a dance floor. And lucky me, I'll be in the middle of it tomorrow.

We pass a wooden sign in a stark field: WHAT A MAN SOWS THAT SHALL HE ALSO REAP—GALATIANS 6:7. I shudder and avert my eyes. I'd actually convinced myself that I wanted this. That this would be fun. The sparkling white frost in the bottom of a roadside ditch makes me think about the ice-blue satin gown I saw in Macy's. Then Angela says, "Turn here."

She points down a narrow dirt road descending into the thick forest.

"You're not going down there," I say, incredulous, as Justin barrels in. It's clear, of course, that he is, that we all are, but

I think the visions of white water are dancing through his head, crowding out all the sane thoughts.

"Why not?"

"Hello? Mud season?" Among other things. It looks so dark and final down that road. As in *People have gone in, but they've never come out.*

"That's what four-wheel drive is for," he says, shifting into gear. The engine revs and we push forward. He pats the dashboard. "That a boy, Monster." Justin always wanted a dog, so since his parents forbade it, he named his truck Monster.

"It's cool, Ki." Angela smiles and pounds her fists on her thighs. "Come on, Monster. You can do it!"

I shiver again, thinking that if my aunt and uncle, Angela's parents, didn't own a cabin in Caratunk, we never would have considered coming here. But Justin, Angela, and I have been planning this forever. Well, mostly Justin and Angela. They've talked about it constantly. It was Justin's idea. Instead of going to the prom, we would skip school and drive up to the cabin for a long weekend during the release. The two of them were so into it, and so anti-prom, that I didn't want to be the brat to tell them I thought dressing up for one evening might be fun. Of course, since I thought my dad would freak out if I even mentioned the word "river" to him, I told Justin we'd have to lie. I didn't explain the details to Justin, just that my father thought rafting was dangerous. So we decided to tell my dad that we were going camping at Baxter State Park. Justin hates deceiving anyone, so for him to lie to my father so convincingly, I knew this was where his heart was.

Back when the idea was hatched, I'd convinced myself I didn't care about the prom. My friends had a way of rolling their eyes and making snide jokes about the event every time it was mentioned, so I went along with it. Angela is a flip-flops and T-shirt girl, so she was dying for an excuse to dodge tripping in three-inch heels. Plus, she's been on the Dead a hundred times. I'd always seen myself in ice-blue satin, descending a long, winding staircase with a tuxedoed prince, but I couldn't tell them that. They would have laughed their heads off at me.

You reap what you sow, I think, leaning my forehead against the cool window, letting my breath condense on it in a circle so I can draw a smiley face. Then I wipe it out as Monster sticks again and Angela shrieks, "Just gun it! Gun it, boy!" like a total hick.

I *so* sowed this.

It's too late now. I should have said something to Justin. Something like "I'll go rafting with you if you go to the prom with me." After all, the heart of com*prom*ise is *prom*. But this weekend is all him. And it's too late to change that. I'll just need to suck it up, pretend I'm enjoying myself, and make him take me shopping next weekend. This weekend can be his, as long as the next one is mine.

Justin grins, digs his foot into the accelerator, and we lurch forward. More shrieking. Laughter. This morning's cinnamon raisin bagel gurgles in the back of my throat. I'm not even in the water yet and I can already feel the current carrying me away.

A minute later the cabin comes into view, and my spirits brighten considerably.

"Whoa, Angela. You said 'cabin'?" Justin asks, staring up at it.

"Yeah. Cozy, huh?"

My mouth drops open. Justin, Hugo, and I live in trailers on the west end of Wayview, Maine. It should be called Noview, though, because everywhere you look, there's nothing but tall pines. It was Dad's way of insulating me from anything that could possibly remind me of the river where my mother died. There's not a brook, a pond, or even a puddle anywhere in sight. Angela's house, or *mansion*, as most would say, is on the east end of the forest. Angela's dad, my uncle, is a retired CEO and owns a lot of real estate. This vacation "cabin," which they bought last year but have maybe used a total of twice, is probably bigger than all three of our trailers put together. I look over at Justin, and for once, his expression matches mine.

Then he sighs. I am sure he was looking forward to "roughing it." I'm feeling better already. I can keep my distance from Hugo. Maybe we'll even have running water. A steamy shower would be so . . .

She catches me smiling. "It's nice, huh? But my parents turned off the water for the winter, so . . ."

Of course. They only use the cabin in the warmer months. The pipes would have frozen and burst during the long

Maine winter if they hadn't turned off the water. I swallow the bad taste in my throat. "It's cool."

We pile out and Justin begins pulling things from the bed of his truck. Groceries, a backpack of my clothes, my travel chess set, the liter of Absolut Justin took from his dad's over-stocked and underused liquor cabinet to celebrate our con-quering of the Dead. Hugo starts snapping pictures of all the trees, as if we don't have enough of them back home. From here, the river sounds like the gentle hum of an electric toothbrush. The sky is the somber color of castle walls, and the leaves turn out, welcoming rain. Shapeless heaps of dingy snow fight for survival in the new spring grass. Angela grabs a handful of snow and molds it into a ball.

"Don't you dare," I whisper, shivering as I back away.

But it's obvious she has other plans. She launches it over to Justin. It breaks into pieces squarely at the back of his neck, making him jump. He turns to us, amused, but before I can point her out, I realize Angela is already pointing at me, an innocent expression on her face. "Dude, I know it's you," he says to Angela.

He throws my pillow at her. It lands in the mud. "Justin!" I shout, annoyed, but I stop when I realize everyone else is laughing. Sometimes it bothers me how well the two of them get along. After all, they are best friends, and have known each other since way before I came into the picture. Justin once told me that Angela is like the sister he never had, and physically she's not at all like the long line of fair, willowy blondes he's been associated with, of which I'm the latest. She's not fat, but she's solid, with wild, curly black hair and dark skin that turns almost chocolate in the sun. Angela was afraid that she would feel like a third wheel on this trip, which is why she invited Hugo, but she and Justin have so much in common, sometimes *I* feel like the odd person out.

I've heard the story a thousand times. They met on a skiing trip at Sugarloaf when they were both trying to learn the bunny slope. Their parents became friends and then they found out that they both lived in Wayview, so they kept in touch, going on vacations together sometimes in the winter and summer. Angela went to a private school in Massachusetts, but when I came up, my father insisted I go to the public school, mostly because we didn't have the money. Justin was in my class, but I didn't know him well. When we reached high school, Angela successfully convinced her parents to transfer her to public school by failing out of every class she took. Her parents thought that with my father teaching at Wayview High, maybe she'd be inclined to goof off less. Freshman year, she introduced me to Justin, but I didn't think anything of it other than that he was really cute. He was dating some other blonde in our class, but we always seemed to get thrown together when Angela had parties. It wasn't until junior year, when I had to do an article on the swim team for yearbook, that we fell for each other. He was the captain, and he came by the yearbook office one day after school to identify all the people in the group photo. He was leaning over me, really close, and then he just moved in and kissed me. We made out for an hour, right in the yearbook office. I remember constantly saying, "But Angela . . . ," and him whispering, "Angela has nothing to do with this."

I snatch the pillow up and dust it off. It's not that bad. I feel stupid for overreacting. Hugo confirms the fact by snapping a picture of me and captioning it "Girl About to Explode." He grins. "Not like there probably aren't four thousand pillows in this place."

I push the camera out of my face. I'm about to explain that my pillow is hypoallergenic and my allergies are always worst in the spring and it's the only pillow I've found that's comfortable enough, but he's right. I do need to loosen up. Funny, I've spent so much energy trying to convince my dad that he'd be okay if he took the shackles off my wrists that I never even thought about whether *I* would be okay once I finally got loose. This is my first trip away from my dad, away from home. And that is thrilling . . . but terrifying.

I stifle a sneeze, then cross my arms over my chest, pinching my skin and mentally reciting my motto: *You will be chill. Ice cubes will be jealous of you.*

I'm about to pick up my backpack from Justin's feet but stop when I see something in the woods. The curve of an elbow, pale white against the lush green, still and stark among the new leaves as they sway in the wind. But the next second, it's gone. I suck in a breath, exhale slowly. The last thing I need to be doing is seeing things. Again.

The thing is, nobody here knows about my mother. Not even Angela. Hell, *I* don't really even know. The mystery Nia Levesque became a part of is five hundred miles away, and I'd like it to stay there. Nobody here knows my history. And I'm going to keep it that way.

Excerpt from *Dead River* by Cyn Balog. Copyright © 2013 by Cyn Balog.
Published in the United States by Delacorte Press, an imprint of Random House Children's Books, a division of Random House, Inc., New York.